Turn the Stones
By: Barbara Phipps
ISBN: 978-0-908325-15-3

CW01460579

Bluewood Publishing Ltd
Christchurch, 8441, New Zealand
www.bluewoodpublishing.com

Turn The Stones

by

Barbara Phipps

For news of, or to purchase this or other
books, please visit:

www.bluewoodpublishing.com

Also by Barbara Phipps:

In this Series:
The Threlfalls
Dancing Upstairs

Other Titles:
Never Ask Why

CHAPTER ONE

June 1969

Jeanette clapped her hands three times and a cloud of flour billowed before her. On beautiful days like this it seemed as if La Vieille Ferme had been built around the old range cooker. Placing a square of white muslin over a bowl of dough, she set it to rise and wiped her hands on her apron. Morning birdsong penetrated the ill-fitting windows of the old farmhouse. Leafy shade moved its patterns across the tiled floor. Jeanette tilted her head to one side, listening for any sound from upstairs.

Susan, her daughter's friend since the very first day at school in Leeds, would always be welcome here. Only yesterday had she called it a home from home, the irony being that Susan didn't have a home, not any longer. On her previous visit she had been as poor as a church mouse.

Jeanette smiled. She liked the sayings of the English. Her husband and daughter spoke the language perfectly, unlike her own heavily-accented attempts. No matter how she tried, her tongue couldn't pronounce the 'th' sound, or the aitch at the beginning of a word—an impossibility.

A clunking noise from the pipes told her Susan was up, and in the shower.

* * * *

The aroma of fresh coffee pulled Susan from her bed. Throwing her arms into her dressing gown, an overwhelming feeling of nausea engulfed her. With her mouth under the tap, she gulped at the lukewarm water and gargled, rinsing away the metallic taste.

Her reflection in the mirror above the washbasin stared at her. Should she write to Roy? Or wait until she went back to Leeds and tell him face to face? Maybe a phone call? Her French wasn't good enough to speak to the operator, though, so she would have to ask Monsieur Fournier to set it up. She unfastened the latch on the little window and pushed open the shutters. Flecks of green paint fell from ancient louvres and the sunshine danced in.

The comforting flow from the old fashioned shower head soothed her body and relieved the tension in her shoulders with its massaging spray. Everything about the farmhouse was old fashioned. Its timelessness gave a sense of security. She couldn't imagine anything bad happening here.

Warm water ran over closed eyes, helping her to think more clearly—to set things right in her mind.

After petit dejeuner she would write to Roy and then walk to La Bureau de Poste. He would phone when he received the letter. Either Chaz or one of her parents would answer and want to know why he had phoned, but that was okay. It seemed right that he should know before anyone else. Susan turned off the shower and wrapped a towel around her hair.

Madame Fournier had asked her to call her Jeanette but it didn't feel right and she couldn't suddenly start calling her Auntie Jeanette. The Irish aunties were her blood relatives but she had known them for less than a year. They felt more like friends, whereas Madame Fournier was a friend who felt like an auntie.

Tying her dressing gown tightly around her, she went downstairs.

"Ah, Susan. I 'ave made some fresh coffee for you." Madame Fournier poured the strong black liquid into a china cup. "Come. Sit down. Ze first bread is ready and I 'ave more rising."

"Can I just have some water and a little bread with no butter, please?" Susan took a seat at the table.

Madame Fournier stood before her, and lifted her chin with a forefinger. "Does your baby make you feel a little sick already, ma fifille?"

Susan's eyes widened. "How…?"

"But I am right—yes?"

"Yes."

"And you are 'appy?"

"Oh yes, definitely." Her eyes sparkled.

"And what does ze fazer say? Is Roy 'appy too?" Jeanette passed her a roll of bread, and a glass of water with ice and a slice of fresh lemon.

Susan smiled. Madame Fournier couldn't give her a simple glass of water. Every morsel of food and every drink became something special in her hands.

"He doesn't know. Nobody knows. Only me—and you. But I'm sure he'll be happy. He loves me, and his dad has made no secret about wanting grandchildren."

"And what about his mozer—you call her Diana, I t'ink?"

"I remember her joking with Henry that she wanted a wedding before any grandchildren came along, but she won't mind." Susan took a tiny bite of bread and sipped the iced water.

Jeanette peeled an apple, dipping each piece in lemon juice before adding it to the bowl of chopped banana and strawberries. She pushed it across the table. "So you 'ave not told Charmaine?"

"No. It's not that I want to keep secrets from her. I thought I'd write to Roy today. He should be the first to know." She stabbed a strawberry with a fork.

Jeanette nodded slowly. "Yes. Zat is a good idea. But you must eat for your baby, Susan. 'Ave a little more bread wiz some jam."

Madame Fournier's jam was difficult to resist and the queasiness was passing. "Do you think Chaz and Jérôme will have children?"

"I 'ope so. She will make a good mozer. My Charmaine is very fond of 'er pupils in ze school. But she will want to marry first, I t'ink."

"I never really thought about whether I like children or not. I suppose I do—and I suppose we will be married."

"I am sure Roy will marry you in a flash. You are a pretty girl, Susan."

* * * *

3

La Vieille Ferme,
Vallée de la Route
Aix
Provence.
Monday 1st June 1970
Dear Roy,
I have some news for you.

Susan stared out into the rolling countryside, considering how she might word her news. 'I am pregnant' sounded harsh, and unloving—a statement of fact. In the film *Doctor Zhivago*, Lara had said *'I am carrying Yuri's child.'* That sounded too dramatic.

A hen scratched in the flower bed, her head jerking this way and that, clawing the earth in pursuit of unsuspecting insects.

Susan picked up her pen, sighed, put it down again, and then took it up and wrote,

I am having a baby. Madame Fournier has guessed but no-one else knows. I wanted you to know first.

All my love,

Susan. X

P.S. I hope your mum and dad are well. All fine here but I feel a bit sick sometimes. XX

She folded the blue air mail paper, damping the gummed edges with her tongue. It would have to do. If she wrote any more the P.S. would be longer than the letter.

Mr Roy Jessop
2 Lark's Hill Drive,
Barwick in Elmet,
Near Leeds,
Yorkshire,
Angleterre.

If she dressed quickly she could be in the village before La Bureau de Poste closed for the afternoon, and Roy would receive the letter on Thursday or Friday.

Ripening grapes hid beneath the vine leaves in the vast acres of Provence, sucking moisture from the crumbling earth.

Corn grew straight and strong in the still, hot air. Row upon row of lavender bushes paraded their blue-green foliage, thriving defiantly in the poor soil. By the time the heavy scent of flowers filled the air she would be back in Yorkshire. She had always been a city girl. Ireland was too…too…green. Provence was better.

She kicked a stone, raising a dust, daydreaming as she walked. She would never remove her wedding ring. Never. Chaz would be bridesmaid of course, and Jimmy would give her away—or Monsieur Fournier—or Patrick.

Jérôme made Chaz so happy. He never spoke of her wonky ankles, taking her arm as if it were the most natural thing in the world. They were both lucky, she and Chaz. Roy had been so kind and understanding about her past.

Raising her eyes from the ground, she realised she wasn't far from the school, and quickened her pace. If she hurried she could have a lift back to La Vieille Ferme with Chaz.

* * * *

Roy felt his mother's eyes boring into his back as he picked up the airmail letter. He smiled to himself and went upstairs.

"Dinner in fifteen minutes. Is your father on his way?" she shouted from the hall.

"As far as I know. I've been out of the office all day."

He closed his bedroom door and sat on the edge of his bed, anticipating a long and newsy letter. He read it once, and again, and then again, turning it over in the vain hope of more news. Anything. The flimsy paper quivered in his hand.

His father's Jaguar crunched across the gravel. Roy's heart thumped out of his chest, his breath quickening. Sitting perfectly still, the sound of his mother's footsteps on the stairs forced him into action, and he stuffed the letter in his jacket pocket.

"Is everything all right, Roy?"

"Yes. Yes, of course." He could tell she wanted to know what was in the letter, but he most definitely didn't want to talk about it. "Mind if I skip dinner? I'm not really hungry." Without giving her chance to reply, he brushed past her in the doorway and leapt down the stairs.

The maelstrom in his head blanked all thoughts of where he was going. He threw the sports car around increasingly tight corners, struggling to keep control on a particularly notorious bend. The rear of the Spitfire slid towards a dry stone wall. The knot in his stomach leapt to his throat just as the car gripped the surface and roared away. He gave a long outward breath, loosened his tight hold on the steering wheel, and took his foot from the accelerator until he had slowed to fifty miles an hour. Fast enough to be interesting, but not life threatening.

A signpost informed him he was four miles from Ilkley. Dropping a gear, he continued through the town and pulled into the car park of The Cow and Calf. His thoughts travelled back to the day he'd walked into the Threlfalls and fallen in love with Susan Fletcher.

He switched off the engine and took his keys from the ignition. A glow of light flickered through mullioned windows, beckoning him inside.

The log fire warmed his back as the first sip of cool beer chilled his stomach. It felt good. The rest of the pint slipped down in one long draught, followed by the warmth of single malt. As the residual froth slid down the sides of the beer glass, he ordered the same again.

"Whoever she is, mate, she isn't worth it. Take it from one who knows."

With a wry smile Roy put the change in his pocket and took the drinks to a table in a quiet corner. With the two glasses before him on cardboard mats and his back to the wall, he could see most of the room. Couples chatted together. A group of middle-aged men stood at the bar, laughing and smoking. Roy drank just under half of his beer and then leaned back into the upholstery.

The world continued to turn as if nothing had happened. He took Susan's letter from his pocket, straightening it out in front of him. She hadn't even said whether or not she was pleased. Come to think of it, she hadn't even said the baby was his. He shifted in his seat. Of course the baby was his. She had written, 'All my love'.

He swayed a little as he carried two empty glasses to the bar.

"So, is it good news, or bad?" the landlord asked.

Gripping the edge of the bar, Roy stared at the shiny surface. "Good—I think. I'm going to be a father." The words distanced themselves as they left his lips.

"Congratulations, mate. Me and the missus—we've two boys. Grand it is—being a dad."

Roy looked up. "Thank you. Yes—thank you. That's it. I'm going to be a dad. Have a drink yourself."

"Cheers. Don't mind if I do."

Roy sat on a barstool. He needed to talk to someone and the landlord was his only option.

* * * *

Friday passed without a phone call and Susan's doubt grew with every hour. She walked along the road towards the school, her morning sickness no more than a little queasiness. Chaz would be working until lunchtime. Saturday morning school was an anathema to Susan, and for that reason alone she was glad not to have lived here as a child.

She had arranged to meet her friend at the close of school for, as Chaz put it, 'some serious dress shopping'.

She closed the car door and Chaz drove off towards Aix. Susan had wanted to stay at La Vieille Ferme in case Roy rang, but without a plausible excuse had agreed to join her friend.

Chaz chatted as she drove. "Jérôme is taking me out to dinner next Saturday and I need a new dress. We can go to 'La Femme'. It's one of my favourite shops, but I want your help. You'll love the clothes there. I'm sure you'll find something for yourself."

"Oh, I don't know. I have enough clothes." Susan looked out of the window, unable to face her friend.

"But you love clothes, Susan. You lost loads of stuff in the fire."

"I know. I know. I've sort of lost interest, though. I mean, I'm happy to help you find something. I'm just not bothered for me, that's all."

"What? Susan Fletcher not interested in clothes? That's like saying the Pope isn't interested in religion."

Susan laughed her little tinkling bell laugh, and Chaz giggled.

"Seriously, Susan. What's wrong?"

Susan paused for a split second. "Nothing. Nothing at all."

"So what's on your mind, then? You haven't fallen out with Roy, have you? There's something you're not telling me." Chaz reversed her little Citroen into a parking space, switched off the engine, and turned to look at her friend.

"Oh, Chaz. Leave it, will you?"

"So there *is* something."

Almost a minute passed.

"I'm having a baby. I wanted to tell Roy before I told you. I wrote to him. He should have received the letter on Thursday and I thought he'd phone. But he hasn't."

Chaz opened the car door and pulled herself upright, her fingers grasped around the frame.

"Come on, Susan. We're going to celebrate with cakes and coffee in true Fournier style, even if the cakes aren't made by my mother."

Susan smiled and linked arms with her friend as they walked towards the shops. Stopping at the first café they came to, they took their seats at one of the tables set out on the pavement.

Susan fixed her eyes on the red and white gingham tablecloth, smoothing the fabric with her hands as Chaz ordered the coffee and cakes.

"Your mum knows."

"What! You told Mum and not me? Wait until I tell Jérôme. He thinks we're telepathic. This will come as an even greater shock to him than to me."

"I didn't tell her. She guessed, and I couldn't deny it."

"So, is this why you're not interested in clothes?"

"Maybe. I don't know. I'm all muddled. I just want Roy to ring and say he's happy about it." She leaned back as coffee and cakes were placed between them.

Chaz didn't reply until the waiter was out of earshot. "Which he will."

"Easily said, but I don't know for certain."

"Don't be daft. As soon as we're finished here we're going to the maternity shop, and the baby clothes shop, and then we'll go to La Femme to buy a dress each. You won't always be pregnant and you can wear it now for a while."

* * * *

Unrelenting sunbeams forced their way through a gap in the curtains. Roy raised a hand to his head, and swung his legs to sit on the edge of the bed, completely disorientated and, to his relief, fully clothed. Rubbing his face with both hands, he stood up. Faltering steps took him to the window. As he held the curtain to one side, narrowed eyes recognised his car, and the rocks of the Cow and Calf.

He went to the bathroom and peed for a long time, then splashed his face with cold water. Memories of the night before seeped into his brain. Beer—whisky—the landlord—Susan. Susan! He had to phone her. The Fourniers' number was in his diary—which was at home. He looked at his watch. Half past eleven.

He leapt down the stairs two at a time and pressed the bell on the bar. The ringing sounded far too loud. He put his hand over the brass dome to hush it.

"Ah, there you are. Sleep okay? Coffee?"

"Yes, I did, thanks. But no, no to the coffee. Thanks." He stuttered. "I must be off. Yes. Thanks. Was it you who…?"

"Took you upstairs?" He nodded as he spoke. "Didn't think you should drive, see."

"Yes. Of course. You were right. Thanks again. Erm…"

"Just give us a quid, mate. You spent enough at the bar to feed me and the family for a week."

Roy fumbled in his pocket and handed over a pound

note. The landlord swapped it for his keys. Roy nodded and the landlord picked up a larger bunch of keys to let him out into bright, bracing sunlight.

Not wanting to miss the opportunity to blast away the hangover, he folded away the soft top and set off with a roar down the hill into Ilkley. He slowed on the approach to the town centre, trying to remember if he had any appointments that day. The fresh morning air forced itself into his lungs, blowing hair into his eyes and biting his skin.

All he could think of was Susan and his need to speak with her.

The tyres of the Spitfire crunched on the gravel of 2 Lark's Hill Drive. His mother's watchful figure moved from the bay window of the lounge.

Roy pursed his lips.

The front door opened and she rushed towards him, arms outstretched. "Roy, I've…"

"You've been worried. I know. Sorry." He rushed past her and ran upstairs, two at a time. "I'll have a shower and a shave, and then I'm going away for a few days. Can't stop."

Cold water and minty toothpaste refreshed his mouth. The water pressure dipped for a few seconds, telling him his mother had turned on the tap in the kitchen. She would be filling the kettle.

The electric shaver she had given him for Christmas buzzed over his face. The decision to travel to France had come into his head unexpectedly, just as he'd entered the house. He had planned to telephone Susan, but now he had to see her, to know how she truly felt about the baby—and about him.

He showered quickly. The towel couldn't dry him fast enough. Wrapping it around his waist, he dashed to his room, razor and toothbrush in hand, ready to pack.

His mother's agitated voice travelled upstairs. She had phoned his father, and he couldn't help but hear snatches of her side of the conversation.

"Says he's going away for a few days. I don't know where to. I think he's out of the shower, so I'd better go."

He grabbed a sports bag from the top of his wardrobe and threw in a few clothes. Passport. God, yes, and driving licence. He'd need that to hire a car in France. Susan had flown to Marseille. That must be the nearest airport to Aix. He checked his wallet for the recently-acquired credit card. He had applied for it with no intention of using it, and now it would be a life saver.

He dressed quickly and ran his fingers through his wet hair. It would have to do. Taking the stairs two at a time, he swung around the newel post and into the kitchen.

"Sorry to dash off, Mum."

"What's happened? Is it Susan?"

"Please don't question me. Ask Dad to tell Miss Tanner to cancel my appointments."

"Have some breakfast, Roy."

"Sorry, Mum." He kissed her cheek.

"Bon Voyage."

He looked down into her eyes and nodded.

* * * *

Leaning against the door, Diana pressed her fingers against her lips. The click of the lock denoted a finality—a change that could not be reversed. Flopping down into her armchair, she gazed at the gate, willing him to return.

With a determined effort to do something, she went to the kitchen and poured herself a cup of tea. There was no point in wasting a whole potful. The refrigerator motor turned off with a shudder and silence shouted from the walls. She turned on the radio in an attempt to fill the void, but the disc jockey's banter was far too enthusiastic. Another click of the button and the shouting silence bounced off the walls once more.

Heavy feet carried her upstairs. Roy's clothes were strewn over the bathroom floor, and a damp towel lay across his bed. Diana picked them up as if she were an automaton and put them in the laundry basket on the landing. From the bedroom window she saw a small boy playing in a pedal car and the sandpit that was now no more than a dip in the lawn. A long empty rabbit hutch leaned against the fence, its door hanging by one hinge. Heaving a great sigh, she turned back into the room. Opening the drawer in his bedside table, she just knew his passport wouldn't be there, and that something intangible had changed forever.

Henry burst through the door as she came downstairs, his neck reddened.

"I was about to phone you again. Are you all right?"

"What's all this about, Diana? Has he gone already? He has several appointments next week."

"He wants you to ask Miss Tanner to cancel them. He's taken his passport, so there's no prize for guessing where he's going."

He followed her to the kitchen. She emptied the contents of the teapot down the sink and put the kettle on to boil again.

"I've no time for tea. I'll have to go back to the office. I'd hoped to be here before he left. What do you think's happened?"

"I don't know. It must be something she wrote. Maybe she's finished with him. He looked terrible, like he'd slept in his clothes."

"That's good news, isn't it?"

"What?"

"Well, if he came home after a night out and had lost his trousers, that might mean…"

"Oh, Henry. How can you think such a thing? He loves Susan."

"Yes, yes, of course. But you're assuming it's bad news, and he might have—you know."

"No. I don't. But I do know what you mean and I don't think any such thing. In any other circumstances I might find that funny, Henry Jessop." In spite of herself, and her anxiety, Diana smiled.

Henry put his arm around her, and she rested her head against his chest.

"Come on, love. He's not a child. He's gone to see his girlfriend in France, and maybe they've had a bit of a tiff. Now, how about that cuppa?"

"I thought you didn't have time."

"I'll make time. I'll phone Miss Tanner and tell her I'll be back as soon as I can, and ask her to sort out Roy's diary. She's perfectly capable of holding the fort for an hour or so."

* * * *

Roy parked in the long term car park at Yeadon airport, cursing the time it took to put the soft top back on. Walking briskly to the terminal building, he headed for the British Airways desk. He shifted his weight from one foot to the other as he waited in the queue.

Stepping forward, a professional—if unconvincing—smile, liveried in patriotic red white and blue, greeted him.

"When's the next flight to Marseille?"

A collar badge gave her name as Susan. Another Susan, but she was nowhere near as lovely as his Susan, for all her smart uniform. "There isn't a direct flight to Marseille, sir. You will have to change planes at Heathrow, or in Paris."

A surge of irritation grabbed his throat. He knew that. Chaz had changed planes at Heathrow. "So what's the best option? I need to be in Marseille as soon as possible."

"Do you need a return ticket?"

"No. I mean, I'll be coming back, but I don't know when."

"It's cheaper to book a return now."

Roy spoke through clenched teeth. "I'll take a single and book the return when I know what I'm doing."

She took a book from the shelf behind her desk, its weight needing both hands to lift what looked like an oversized telephone directory. Her left forefinger ran up and down the columns of numbers and destinations, while her right hand made notes. Roy's hands gripped into fists as the minutes ticked by. He could be missing a plane right now, for all he knew.

"Well, sir, you have some choices. There's a seat on flight BA314 leaving here for Heathrow in two hours but there are no seats on a connecting flight today. You would have to stay overnight in London. If you fly to Gatwick tonight there's a seat on a connecting flight tomorrow morning, arriving at Marseille at 13:35. Or you could take a flight BA481 to Paris. That leaves at 21:30 tonight and the connection would take you to Marseille for 10:45 tomorrow."

"So you're saying if I go via Paris I'll be there quicker, even though I would take off later."

"Yes, sir."

"I'll take it. And I'm sorry. I didn't mean to be rude. You've been very helpful." Her smile quavered into something more natural as he handed over his passport and credit card. Roy looked at his watch. Twelve o'clock. Nine and a half hours before take-off. He didn't want to go home and face his mother. Her face flashed into his head with her 'Bon Voyage'. He would just have to sit it out. British Airways Susan handed him his ticket, and he headed for passport control.

* * * *

Susan and Chaz returned from Aix tired but happy.

Shopping bags were piled on the sofas, with their contents scattered around the room.

"Look, Papa," Chaz said, holding up a pack of white and lemon baby-grows. "For Susan's baby."

He paused before taking his cue from Susan's smile. "Congratulations, Susan. I'm happy for you, and for Roy. You must both be delighted."

Susan kissed him on both cheeks. "Thank you."

"Roy doesn't know about the baby yet, Dad."

A rib of beef with roast garlic vegetables was served with the usual sense of occasion, and the chatter of celebration.

"You may 'ave a little wine only, Susan. Your baby will not like wine yet and you must eat plenty of good food." Anton carved the meat from the head of the table with his wife at the opposite end, and Susan and Chaz to each side.

"I don't really fancy any wine. It tastes funny."

"'Zat is good. Your baby knows best. Anton, will you

14

please bring a glass of my elderflower cordial for Susan?"

Anton went to the pantry, returning moments later with a jug.

"My baby will be the best fed baby in the world if I stay here, and I shall be like a bloated whale." Susan smiled.

"And the best loved," Chaz said between mouthfuls. "I love your baby to bits already. Have you thought of any names?"

"No. We have plenty of time to think about that. If we marry, the name will have to go with 'Jessop', if we don't, it will have to go with 'Fletcher'.

Everyone paused and stared at her.

Madame Fournier broke the silence. "What do you mean—'if'? Of course Roy will marry you. You cannot 'ave a baby and not be married."

Susan's eyes filled with tears.

Chaz rushed around the table as fast as she could, put her arms around her, and knelt at her side. "Roy loves you, Susan. He won't desert you. You don't even know for sure your letter arrived."

Susan trembled. "I'm sorry. I know. It's just that we haven't known each other very long and I'm afraid he'll think I've trapped him or something."

"Can I put forward a plan?" Anton took a sip of wine and set down his glass, twisting its stem. Jeanette, Chaz and Susan looked towards him, all awaiting his words of wisdom. "If Roy hasn't telephoned by tomorrow night, you phone him, Susan. He will probably be at home Sunday evening. People usually are."

Susan sighed. "You're right. I will. I know I'm worrying out of all proportion. But I can't help it."

"I 'ope your worry 'as not affected your appetite, ma petite."

Anton laughed, Chaz giggled and a smile slowly crept across Susan's face.

"What eez it? What eez so funny?"

"You are, my dear." Anton said. "Everything is fine as long as we have our appetite. Yes?"

"Mais oui, bien sûr." Jeanette smiled.

Susan had already picked up her knife and fork.

* * * *

Roy headed north out of Marseille, glad to be on the last leg of his tedious and uneventful journey. After a few gear changes, when his left hand instinctively sought the gear stick, he was surprised how easily he adapted to driving on the right hand side of the road. Morning shadows shortened as the sun rose into its cloudless sky.

His life was at a tipping point filled with uncertainty and he didn't even know whether or not he was happy. During the past twenty-four hours he had tried to rationalise his thoughts and feelings. The only conclusion he had been able to come to was that if Susan was happy to marry him, he would gladly marry her.

He indicated right and turned off the main road, travelling towards Aix. Following the signs to the town centre, he was soon driving into the square. He pulled up alongside an elderly couple to ask directions. "Excusez moi? Qui est la voie à La Vieille Ferme?"

The old man smiled and pointed towards the opposite side of the square. "Ainsi, à un kilometre, tournez à droit. C'est tout."

"Merci beaucoup, monsieur." Roy wound the window up. In just one kilometre all his questions would be answered.

* * * *

Hens scattered and squawked as the car came to a halt. Chaz peered out of the lounge window to see what had ruffled the silly birds' feathers. Hobbling to the front door, she shouted, "Mum, Dad, come quickly. Roy's here." She hugged him. "Oh, we're so pleased to see you. You can't know how happy this makes us."

"Charmaine, you must let Roy come in." Her mother tugged at her arm. They went inside, with Chaz clinging to Roy as if he might disappear into thin air.

"I am Jeanette, Charmaine's mozzer. I suppose you know 'er as Chaz?"

"I'm sorry, Roy. I'm forgetting you've never actually met my parents. This is my mother, Jeanette, and my father, Anton."

"We are pleased to meet you, perhaps more pleased than you know." Anton and Roy shook hands.

"I will make some coffee and we will 'ave biscuits. I made some almond slices zis morning. I t'ink I must 'ave known you were coming."

"Nonsense, Mum, you bake every day," Chaz giggled.

"Come, Anton, you can 'elp. We will leave Charmaine to speak wiz Roy."

"Is something wrong, Chaz? Where's Susan? You do know she's....?"

"Having a baby, yes. She couldn't keep it from us."

"And is she happy about it? I mean, does she want the baby. Her letter didn't say."

"Oh, Roy. You can't begin to imagine how much she loves her baby already."

"I think maybe I can, Chaz. It's my baby too, you know, and I…"

Chaz hugged him so tightly he could barely breathe. When she eventually released him she giggled so much she had to sit down.

"Where is she, Chaz?"

"Gone for a walk in the fields. She says she does her best thinking there." Chaz paused.

"There's something wrong, isn't there?" Anxiety dulled his tone.

Long seconds elapsed. "She thought you would phone."

"Which way did she go?"

CHAPTER TWO

Jimmy looked forward to weekends with Jill at 16 Vine Street. Years before there had been a doorway from his bedroom through to number fourteen where Granny Florrie used to live. Not his real Granny, but the only Granny he had ever known, and he remembered her with great affection. When she'd died the doorway had been bricked up, and her house sold.

"It just doesn't make sense." Jimmy passed a pile of papers to Jill. "We both work in York, your Mum and Dad live in York. I have no ties to Leeds anymore."

Rain pattered on the kitchen window, its steady rhythm adding to the cosy atmosphere.

Jill leafed through the property details from Norton's Estate Agents of York. "I don't know, Jimmy. I like it here. It's your decision of course but—I suppose it's my mum and dad really."

Jimmy placed two mugs of coffee on the table and, sitting opposite her, put his hand gently over hers. "What do you mean?" He frowned. "What difference would it make to them?"

"Oh, plenty. Especially my mum." With her eyes fixed on his hand, she continued, "I don't think my dad would be *too* bothered, but Mum would hit the roof and give him a hard time." She sighed deeply. "I just have the feeling they tolerate me spending every weekend with you here in an out-of-sight-out-of-mind sort of way. Does that make any sense to you?"

"I never thought of it like that. Are you sure?"

"Mum's a snob, Jimmy."

"What if we were engaged?"

She withdrew her hand and, gathering up the papers, threw them at him.

"What?" He ducked. "What did I say?" He had never seen her so angry. One minute they had been looking at houses for sale, and the next moment she was throwing them all over the place.

She pushed her chair back and stared down at him, making him feel at even more of a loss. "Correct me if I'm wrong, Jimmy Hanson, but you just proposed to me by way of suggesting it might please my parents." Jimmy cowed beneath the unexpected onslaught. Her face reddened as she struggled to control her anger. "Have you any idea how that sounds? How that makes me feel?"

Stepping towards her, he tried to put an arm around her. She shrugged him off.

"I'm sorry, Jill. You must know I didn't mean it to sound like that."

"People don't marry to solve a problem, Jimmy, and that's what you seem to be proposing." Speaking through gritted teeth, a thin veil of calm exaggerated her resentment. Folding her arms, she turned from him.

"It's just that all this travelling to York and back every day, and you just staying at weekends, I thought you'd like the idea of living in a house we chose together. This is nineteen sixty-nine, not sixteen eighty-nine. "

"I think you should stop there, Jimmy."

He tried to recall where the conversation had gone wrong. She still looked lovely, with her red hair tumbling around her shoulders, even when she was so cross. He moved in front of her, placing his hands upon her shoulders. She was looking directly at him now and he tried to decide whether her eyes were green or hazel. His own eyes were blue, inherited from his father. He forced the thought from his head.

"I love you, Jill Cawthorne."

He watched as she blinked repeatedly. *Why doesn't she say something?* He wished his mum could have met her. Mum would have told him off for being so crass. He didn't think of her as often as he used to and, shocking as the thought was, he wondered if that was a good thing, or if he should feel guilty about it. Maybe he felt guilty for not feeling guilty. His mind spun around at a hundred miles an hour, and all the while he was aware of the stupid, blank expression on his face.

"And I love you, Jimmy Hanson."

"Come here." He pulled her towards him.

"You're right, really, about moving to York."

* * * *

"Look at it this way, Diana. No news is good news."

"Oh, Henry, how can you say that? It's nonsense. He should phone and tell us he's all right. That's not too much for a mother to ask, is it?"

Diana had been to church and, as usual, had brought a tray of coffee and biscuits into the lounge.

Henry dunked his biscuit, and saw her flinch. He knew the habit irritated her and was waiting for the usual mini lecture of *'what's the point in keeping biscuits nice and dry in a tin just to make them soggy in a cup of hot coffee?'* He almost felt cheated when, after ten seconds, she was still staring at him, as if waiting for him to say something.

"Diana, be reasonable. He's been gone for just over twenty-four hours. Most men of his age—and he is a man, not a little boy—don't even live at home."

"What's that got to do with it?"

He held up his left hand, his palm towards her. "Let me finish, please." He sipped his coffee and replaced his cup in its saucer with exaggerated precision, turning the handle to ninety degrees from the edge of the table. "If he had his own place you wouldn't even know he'd gone away."

"We'd know something was wrong when he didn't turn up for work. Of course we'd know."

Henry sat back in his chair with an exasperated sigh. "He's twenty-eight, Diana."

"I know that, Henry." She raised her voice. "I was there when he was born—remember?"

"All I'm trying to say is that if there is a problem, like an accident or something, we would have heard. Bad news travels faster than good."

"It never crossed my mind that he might have had an accident."

"What is it, then?" Henry was totally bemused.

"Susan. If she's ditched him he'll be heartbroken."

Henry wanted to say, 'Is that all?' but thought better of it. After thirty-three years of marriage he pretty much knew when to keep his mouth shut.

"He has to live his own life, Diana. You can't live it for him. Would you like another coffee?"

Diana gawped at him with an astonished look on her face. As far as he could remember he had never offered to make a coffee before, but he needed an excuse to leave the room, and avoid the pointless conversation she seemed determined to perpetuate.

"Yes, please, Henry. That would be very nice."

Carrying her cup and saucer into the kitchen, he suddenly became aware he hadn't a clue where she kept the damned stuff. He put the kettle on. By the time it boiled he would have located the jar. He opened and closed one cupboard after another, as quietly as he could, without result.

In truth he was just as worried about Roy, and didn't understand why he felt the need to pretend otherwise. If Susan Fletcher had ditched him, as Diana had put it, they would be back to square one on the grandchildren front. Worse than that, he knew Roy was besotted with the girl and it would take time for him to forget her.

The kettle switched itself off, and still no coffee could be found.

Diana's voice startled him. "Second wall cupboard to the left of the sink."

"But I already looked in there."

"It's behind the tea caddy." She returned to the lounge.

To his annoyance the coffee was exactly where she'd said it would be.

* * * *

A walnut tree lay alongside the path that bordered the copse. Its trunk twisted this way and that in a pattern dictated by nature and the wind that had ripped its roots from the ground. Susan climbed to her favourite place, leaning against a branch that had once reached for the sky, and now made a comfortable support. From here the hazy rooftops of Aix could be seen against a backdrop of trees. Susan tried to put into words exactly why she loved Provence so much. Until just over a year before, vegetables had come from a market stall and milk out of a bottle.

If Roy didn't want her, maybe she could stay here in Aix and buy a little house, or just rent one. There would be no reason to go back to Leeds. No reason whatsoever if Roy was out of the picture. That wasn't what she wanted, of course. What she wanted was for Roy to love her, and their baby, and for them to be married. But a little house in Aix sounded like a good back-up plan.

Sunlight filtered through the leaves, flashing playfully on her face and closing her eyes. Her breathing shallowed and her senses drifted, leaving only birdsong, between wakefulness and sleep. A dream-driven smile flickered across her face. Her mother was holding a baby, loving her with the gentleness of her eyes. The love became tangible. A gift for her to pass to her baby. Roy's lips brushed her cheek and she was in her flat on the top floor of the Threlfalls, nestling in her new feather duvet. A rook squawked above, muting the songbirds as he shouted, "Fire! Fire!" Her eyes flew open and she was in Roy's arms, clinging to him for all she was worth. The sharp focus of the dream blurred and melted away.

"Hey, lady, let me breathe." He took a handkerchief from his pocket and dabbed her face. "Why the tears, Susan?"

"I thought you didn't—I thought you wouldn't—oh, Roy, I'm so happy."

"I take it you're glad to see me, then?"

She nodded vigorously.

"I needed to see you, not just phone or write a letter. You didn't make it plain if you wanted the baby." He pulled a small blue box from his pocket and pressed it into her hand. "I did a spot of shopping in Paris airport."

She gasped. Two rings nestled in white velvet, a plain gold band, and a ring set with a deep blue sapphire, surrounded by diamonds.

"To match your eyes, Susan." He took the engagement ring and slid it on her finger. As he let go, the stones slipped towards her palm, and she laughed her tinkling laugh.

"It's perfect. Perfectly beautiful," she said, twisting the ring to hold the stones upright.

"Looks like we need to make a trip to the jewellers to have it made smaller."

She placed the ring in the box and he put it in his pocket. He held out his arms and she jumped down. Hand in hand they walked towards La Vieille Ferme.

"What did your parents say when you told them about the baby?" she asked.

"I haven't told them."

"Why not?" Now she knew he was happy about the baby, and they were to marry, Susan had presumed he would have told his mother. "I thought they wanted grandchildren."

"Oh, they do. Especially Dad. I don't know, really. I was just so surprised, though I don't know why. I mean, we never used anything, did we? And until I knew for sure that you were happy about it I didn't want to say anything. I had to be sure, you see. Have you seen a doctor?"

"No, I thought I'd wait until I returned to Leeds. Doctor Ramsey has always been our family doctor, although he might be retired by now. I don't see any point seeing anyone here. It's not as if there's anything wrong with me. I'm not ill."

"But you are sure?" Roy held open the gate to the garden of La Vieille Ferme.

"Oh, yes. Quite sure."

He smiled. "It's a funny thing but, even though this wasn't exactly planned, I'd be really disappointed now if you weren't pregnant."

Jeanette's voice raised an octave when Roy suggested he find accommodation in Aix. "But of course you must stay 'ere, Roy. Where would you go? I insist. You must be wiz your bride." They were finishing another delicious feast, effortlessly produced by Jeanette. Chaz's boyfriend, Jérôme, had joined them and been introduced to Roy.

"I didn't want to presume."

"Nonsense. You Engleesh drive me mad. You must stay as long as you wish. Visit Aix toge'zer, wander around our wonderful galleries and shops." Jeanette waved her arms theatrically.

Chaz, Jérôme and Anton laughed at her feigned anger. They were joined by Susan and Roy and, finally, by Jeanette herself.

"What did your parents say, Roy?" Chaz asked. "Were they pleased?"

"Susan asked me the same thing and, actually, I haven't told them."

"What? Mon Dieu! Why not?" Jeanette almost screamed.

A look flashed between Roy and Susan.

"Oh, I get it," Chaz said.

"Get what?" Jeanette frowned. "What do I not get? Do you know what she is talking about, Anton?"

Anton shrugged.

"You know Susan was scared that Roy might not want the baby?" No-one answered, so Chaz continued, "Well, it's my guess that Roy thought Susan might not want the baby. I'm right, aren't I?"

Jeanette shook her head in disbelief. "You pair of silly sausages—if I may use an English idiom. You will 'ave lots of babies. Now, let me look at zat beautiful ring again. Lift it out of ze box, Roy. And while we females are all going gooey-eyed at your exquisite taste, you must go wiz Anton to the study and he will 'elp you make ze phone call to your dear parents. Jérôme, you may stay wiz us or go wiz ze men."

"Come with us," Anton beckoned. "I can't leave you here with this coven."

Jérôme smiled gratefully and followed Anton from the kitchen. It took a few minutes to make the connection to England. When the clicks and buzzes turned into a ring, Anton handed the receiver to Roy and signalled to Jérôme that they should leave the room.

* * * *

Anton walked side by side with Jérôme in the kitchen garden. "We're very happy—Jeanette and I—that you are dating our daughter."

Jérôme didn't know how to reply. The Fourniers had made him very welcome in their home but he was a naturally quiet person and felt awkward.

"We are protective towards her, perhaps more so than most parents. We don't want her to be hurt."

"I won't hurt her, Monsieur Fournier. I'm very fond of Chaz."

"Anton, please. Don't worry, Jérôme, I'm not putting any pressure on you. I'm just trying to say, rather clumsily, that we would be happy for you to be a permanent part of her life."

"I would like that, too. But its early days for Chaz and me. We're happy as we are. But for Susan and Roy things are rather different."

"With a baby on the way, yes, of course it is."

"Not just that. Chaz and I are very different to Susan and Roy. If I asked her to marry me now, I think she'd turn me down."

Anton laughed. "Then I'll say no more. You clearly know my daughter well. Maybe even better than I."

Hurrying footsteps on the gravel path turned their heads.

"How did it go, Roy?"

* * * *

Diana's secateurs dead-headed the roses with precision, occupying her hands but failing to occupy her mind, as she collected the faded blooms in a wicker basket.

Henry annoyed her beyond belief with the way he refused to worry about Roy. How could he be so calm when they had no idea where Roy was, how he was, or even *if* he was? Her temper wouldn't admit that Henry was right and they would know if he was in any real trouble, like an accident or something. But Henry hadn't been there when Roy had dashed into the house, and so hadn't seen how upset he had been.

Perhaps upset wasn't quite the right word. Distressed maybe, or overwrought.

The only possible explanation for all this was that Susan had ditched him. How could she hurt him so? The little minx had led him on, using all of them since the Threlfalls had burned down. There was more to that story, she was sure of it. From what she had gleaned, Susan's only remaining relatives were in Southern Ireland. She and Henry had willingly taken her into their home, even permitting her to sleep with Roy under their roof. No-one could say they weren't modern parents. To be fair to the girl, she had thanked them. Susan had manners. She conceded that much. And then she'd just disappeared off to France on a whim, leaving Roy behind, and worrying the poor boy half to death.

She took her basketful of dead heads to the compost bin, throwing them in with unnecessary force, before returning to the flower beds and continuing with her snip, snip, snip.

Henry's voice snapped into her thoughts. "Diana, phone. It's Roy."

She dropped her basket and secateurs and ran inside, pushing her way past Henry.

"Roy, are you all right?" The dialling tone buzzed. "Roy! Are you there?" she shouted. "HENRY!"

She turned and gave a start. She hadn't realised he was standing so close to her.

"Oh, there you are. He's gone. What did he say? Where is he? Is he all right? Is he with Susan Fletcher? When's he coming home? He's not bringing her back here, is he?"

Henry gently took the receiver from her trembling hand and placed it in its cradle.

"Come and sit down, Diana." He took her arm, guiding her to her armchair.

"What is it, Henry? Is it bad news?"

Henry shook his head. "No, Diana. It's the best news ever." He paused before pointing to the muddy footmarks on the carpet. "You see those?"

"Yes, yes. Of course. I'll clean it up in a minute. What did Roy say? Henry, stop fussing about a bit of mud."

"I'm not fussing about a bit of mud. I leave all that sort of thing to you. What I'm trying to say is that you might have to put up with that sort of thing before too long, because we're going to be grandparents."

He seemed to savour the seconds of silence, his cheeks blown out in a huge grin. Diana's face paled with shock before flushing from her neck. He laughed.

"Are you sure, Henry?" her voice whispered.

"That's what Roy just told me. I asked him to hang on so he could tell you himself but he must've been cut off. He's in Provence, of course, with Susan. Just like I said he would be."

"When's the baby due?"

"He didn't say."

"Is Susan all right?"

"I suppose so. I didn't ask."

"When are they coming home?"

"I don't know."

"Oh, Henry. Why didn't you ask?"

"I went to find you."

"Oh, Henry. That poor girl, all alone in a foreign country and you didn't even ask how she was."

"But she isn't all alone." Henry shuffled forward in his chair to hold both her hands in his. He looked straight into her eyes. "She's with her friends, and Roy. I thought you'd be happy. You can stop nattering about the lad. He's safe. He's with Susan and she hasn't chucked him. They're engaged. They're going to marry as soon as possible. Can't you be happy for them?"

Tears of relief ran down her face, their saltiness moistening the corners of her mouth. Taking a handkerchief from her cuff, she nodded in acknowledgement, permitting a smile of relief to pass her lips.

CHAPTER THREE

December 1969

Susan dusted the framed photograph and placed it back on the television, smiling at the captured memories. She and Roy were in the centre. Confetti speckled her wide-brimmed hat.

Diana had taken charge of the organisation, fussing about invitations, and cars, flowers and clothes. Roy had told her the wedding wasn't as important as the marriage and that they wanted something simple.

To her surprise, Henry had intervened. Susan couldn't be sure of his precise words but it went along the lines of,

'What you two lovebirds need to understand is that my wife is trying to help. She is painfully aware that you, Susan, do not have a mother or a father to organise your wedding. I do not mean to hurt you by my words, but Diana sees it as her happy duty to make sure your big day is all you wish it to be. As a churchgoer, she naturally thought a church wedding with all the trimmings would be what you would want.'

After that it had been easy for Susan to convince Diana that she really and truly wanted to be married at the registry office as her parents had been. Diana had even gone with her to Lavells to choose her outfit. She had fallen in love with the pale cream frilly blouse as soon as she'd seen it. The beige trousers and blue linen coat perfectly disguised her lack of waist line. Her hat matched the exact shade of blue.

The photograph showed Diana standing next to Roy, with Henry at her side. Jimmy had been his best man. Diana had suggested Roy should ask one of his old friends from university but Roy had said he wanted Jimmy because they both knew him. Being her next of kin, her cousin Patrick had given her away. He stood next to her, with Chaz next to him as her bridesmaid, then Jimmy and Jill, with her long-time friend Maggie at the end. Jeanette and Anton had come from Provence especially for the wedding, and stood next to Henry. Beside him was Alf, the retired policeman she had known all her life, with his wife, Hettie. After the short ceremony they had all had lunch at the Queen's Hotel, and Henry had announced he was making Roy a partner in the family firm, Jessop's Auction Rooms.

The honeymoon had been two nights at the Grand Hotel in Scarborough, which had been long enough. She would have preferred to be at Orchard Cottage, her first real home, but Diana and Henry had paid for the hotel as a wedding present, and so they'd had to go.

A sharp pain in her side brought her back to the present. Her hand flew to a point just below her ribs, and she rubbed it gently with circular movements. The sensation came frequently, and in exactly the same place. Susan had thought her baby's foot was kicking her, but when she'd had a scan, the radiographer had said it was a knee and she had laughed, but she wasn't laughing now. If her baby arrived on the due date of January the fifteenth she had another four weeks to wait, or it might be just two, or five, or six.

She and Roy wanted a big family. Both being only children, they felt they had missed out on the sibling thing. Right now she wasn't so sure how many times she wanted to go through with it, and she hadn't given birth yet.

A bauble fell from the Christmas tree. She turned and stared at it for a few seconds, and then left it where it had landed. Bending down to pick it up would take too much effort.

The short December day faded and dusk brightened the Christmas tree lights. Susan drew the curtains and lay down on the sofa. As she stared up at the beamed ceiling with the duster still in her hand, the baby wriggled and kicked. She arched her back and then relaxed into the feather cushions. The kicking stopped and she drifted into a light sleep, daydreaming through the recent past.

She and Roy had looked at dozens of houses. The new estate houses were light and modern but squashed together. The Victorian town houses had felt unwelcoming with their high ceilings and long hallways. Neither of them liked the idea of living in a flat, with the possibility of noisy neighbours trampling above. They had looked around a top floor flat which had a fantastic view, but no lift.

In the end Henry had found the cottage for them. He knew all the estate agents in Leeds and had asked them to let him know if anything suitable came on the market. He told Roy he had a pretty good idea of what they wanted, having taken note of what they had rejected, which was more than she could have said of herself at the time. Smiling sleepily, she recalled the grin on his face when he had shown them the information about Orchard Cottage. She'd had some reservations. *'In need of some modernisation'* was the cause of her concern.

After looking at so many properties she had been beginning to despair. When she and Roy had first looked around the cottage she had been surprised by his enthusiasm. The description had been an understatement. An air of neglect hung about the place. Apple trees struggled to show their presence above the brambles. In the distance, optimistic roses gave evidence that the wilderness had once been a garden.

With four bedrooms, Orchard Cottage was much larger than she had expected. The bathroom was in a terrible state with brown water marks staining a cast iron bath. The lounge had once been two smaller rooms. The dining room was about the same size. In the kitchen a nineteen-fifties style fireplace occupied the space where there should have been a range cooker like the one at La Vieille Ferme.

She had been four months pregnant at the time and beginning to think they would still be living with Henry and Diana when the baby was born.

They had wandered from room to room, up the creaking stairs, around the bedrooms and down again. To her surprise she had felt an affinity with the place. The décor was dreadful, the previous owners efforts at do-it-yourself showing more enthusiasm than skill. Stucco plasterwork begged to be ripped from uneven walls. And yet, somehow, Orchard Cottage was different, and it had been right under their noses the whole time.

She had begun to see the renovation work in a positive

light and, as Roy had pointed out, there had been no need for structural alteration. The dreadful state of the kitchen and bathroom had meant she could choose a brand-new fitted kitchen and a modern bathroom suite that were entirely to her taste.

It had taken just five weeks for Miss Jones of Holroyd and Jones to sort out the conveyance, and Sam Braithwaite had set to work the following day. He'd taken out the fireplace and torn down the plasterboard ceiling to expose beautiful oak beams. She'd known he wouldn't let her down. Sam had transformed the old ballroom at the Threlfalls into a disco in four weeks. He had worked a miracle at Orchard Cottage, consulting Susan and Roy over every detail. The whole place had been rewired, with central heating installed in three months.

The dining room furniture had been bought at Jessop's Auction Rooms. Roy would only buy furniture that he thought would increase in value. They had agreed they both had to like whatever he bought, and there had been a few disagreements—the most memorable being their discussion over a four-poster bed. Roy had argued she couldn't know for sure that someone had died in it, but in the end had given in because, as she had said, 'The odds are I'm right'.

To her surprise and delight the modern bedrooms, bathrooms, and kitchen worked well with the more traditional décor and furniture of the lounge and dining room.

Rolling onto her side, she pressed her hand on the edge of the sofa and stood up. She stretched her arms above her head and twisted her hands at the wrist before lowering them again. Her breasts were huge, and painful.

Roy would be home soon. She should be cooking their evening meal, but she went upstairs instead, pulling herself up on the rail to her favourite room. The nursery. In the soft moonlight she could just make out the back garden and her car in the drive. To her relief she had passed her driving test at the first attempt, and bought the estate car to accommodate a carrycot.

She closed the lemon and white curtains. Sitting in the

nursing chair, she leaned her head back, pointing her toes forward until she was almost horizontal.

The chest of drawers was already filled with baby clothes, talcum powder, baby lotions, and the best quality nappies. Supported on a frame, a baby bath stood in one corner. A carry cot on detachable wheels stood next to it. If it hadn't been for the fire at the Threlfalls she could have used the big coach-built pram. Mum would have liked that. She had thought to buy one, but Roy had pointed out that she wouldn't be able to fit a big pram in her car.

A shudder rippled through her. She had everything she needed, but what she really wanted right now was her mum.

* * * *

Jill sighed with relief and took two painkillers. The dull backache was three weeks late. Within an hour, as if a bad fairy had waved her wand over her, tell-tale dark rings would shadow her eyes, and horrid red spots blister her chin. Except, this time she was a good fairy, and a bit of pain, the dark rings and a few spots were a small price to pay. Jill hated her periods. She felt terrible for five days every month. But that was nothing compared to the fear of pregnancy. Her parents would kill her. Not literally, of course, but her father would be disappointed and mother would be incandescent with rage. Jill could hear her wailing, '*Oh Jill, how could you? After all we've done for you*'.

Their hopes and expectations weighed heavily on her shoulders. It came with the territory of being an only child. There were times, like right now, when she envied Susan Fletcher and her freedom. Susan had no parents. The thought shamed her.

Jimmy hadn't noticed her period was late or at least he hadn't said anything. She looked in the bathroom mirror. He would notice now. The question she couldn't answer was whether or not she wanted children at all. Jimmy did—and didn't. He'd said he would love to have three or four, and she had laughed at him, thinking he'd been joking. His hands had shaken when he'd told her his grandfather was also his father. He had already told her his mother had died, and of the strange circumstances of her death. She had held his shaking hands as he'd spoken of his fear that his children may have genetic defects. The word *'defects'* had stayed in the forefront of her mind for weeks, slowly turning into the fear that he could be right. The conversation had taken place shortly after their one and only row, when he had clumsily offered to marry her to please her parents.

Jill heard the front door open and close. Jimmy was home. He had been to see his old friends, Alf and Hettie Lawrence, who lived in Headingly. They were like family to him and he would have all their news. He would have told them about their thinking of moving to York and they would have been pleased for them, even though it would mean they wouldn't see him so often. Alf and Hettie were that sort of people.

She looked at her watch. He was back sooner than she had expected. Maybe they had been out. He was whistling, so must be happy. He would take one look at her and insist she sit down while he made her a cup of tea, and then spoil her and insist on cooking dinner and washing up.

She was halfway downstairs when he started to come up.

"Oh, there you are," he said. "I was beginning to think you'd gone out." He returned to the kitchen.

She thought he looked sort of jittery—on edge. "What is it? Is something wrong?"

"No. Nothing at all."

"Are Alf and Hettie all right?"

"Yes. Yes, I think so."

"What do you mean, you think so?"

"Come here, Jill." He stepped forward and put an arm around her. His free hand delved into his jacket pocket. "I have a confession to make." Her forehead creased with curiosity as she looked into his smiling face. "I didn't go to Headingly. I'm afraid that was a lie. I've been in town, doing a bit of shopping. Well, not exactly shopping—more just collecting." Before she could speak he opened a little box with his free hand. A row of three sparkling diamonds took her breath away. Her hand flew to her throat, taking any words with it.

He released his hold from her shoulder, took the ring from the box, and knelt before her on one knee. "Will you marry me, Jill?"

Laughter and tears mingled as she nodded. "Yes, I'll marry you, Jimmy."

He stood up and put the ring on her finger.

"A perfect fit." Jill wiped her tears of joy from her face with the back of her hand. "Like Cinderella and the glass slipper."

"Ah, well, yes. I have another confession to make there. Your mum lent me a ring from your jewellery box at home and I took it to the——"

"You mean my mum knows about this?"

"Oh yes. And your dad. I went to York to your parents' house and asked your father for your hand in marriage."

"When?"

"About two weeks ago. I slipped out of work."

"Anyone else?"

"What?"

"Does anyone else know?"

"No. Of course not."

Jill flopped down in the chair next to the fireplace.

"Now, I think it's time I made you a cup of tea. It's my guess you aren't feeling too good. I know you've been worried."

He had his back to her and didn't see her expression. Sometimes it felt as if she didn't know the first thing about this man she had just agreed to marry. It all made for mixed emotions. Part of her wanted to phone her mum and dad, and part of her wanted a quiet night in with Jimmy. By the time he handed her a cup of tea the quiet night in with Jimmy had won. If she spoke to her mother she would be going on and on about fixing a wedding date. For now she was happy just to look at her ring. She twisted it on her finger, making the glittering sparkles catch the light, turning them into rainbows on the wall above the fireplace.

* * * *

Jill didn't want a church wedding but was willing to go along with one to please her parents. Their large detached house was within walking distance of York Minster. The leaves of the silver birch trees sprinkled the pavement with dark coins of shadow as they fluttered in the breeze, creating a dappled shade, and taking the glare from the sunshine. Standing on the front step, beneath the porch, with its twists of wisteria binding its frame, Jill took a deep breath. Mum fussed so. She wished with all her heart that she had a load of brothers and sisters so the fussing could be shared out.

As she put her key in the lock she glanced at her watch, wondering how long it would be before her mum mentioned a wedding date. "Hello-o. It's me."

Her mother emerged from the kitchen as Jill dropped her weekend bag to the floor.

"Darling girl. You're here at last. Is Jimmy with you? Let me see your ring." Anthea Cawthorne lifted her daughter's hand. "Oh, Jill, it's divine. Come and show your father. He's in the kitchen. We were just saying you'd be here soon."

Jill followed the trail of perfume as her mother turned from her. Elegant as ever, her mother wore an expensive black skirt and a flesh-coloured silk blouse. Stiletto heels click-clacked on the tiled floor. Her hair and make-up were impeccable. "No Jimmy with you, then? Is it Jimmy or James these days? Jimmy makes him sound like a little boy. Have you thought of a date for the wedding?"

Jill looked at her watch. Less than twenty-five seconds.

"Hello, Dad. Jimmy's gone straight home. Says he'll see you soon."

"Hello, love." The kitchen table was partly covered by a broadsheet newspaper, shoe polish and brushes. He put down his wife's shoe.

"Not there, Maurice. Put it on the newspaper."

He gave a look of resignation and obediently moved the

offending shoe. "Let me see your ring," he said softly.

"Are you sure you haven't seen it already?" Jill smiled.

"Of course we haven't. Jimmy asked me, you know, for your hand. I thought it very nice of him."

"I suggested he took one of your rings, to be sure of the size. I remember when your father and I were engaged, and my ring was far too small. I hated parting with it."

"I was rather shocked to hear of your conspiracy." Jill heard her mother's sharp breath and knew her words had been taken as a criticism. "In the nicest possible way, Mum." Her mother's mouth twitched into a smile. "There are a few practicalities to sort out before we set a date."

"Oh yes, such as?"

"We want to buy a house in York."

"Why does that delay your wedding?"

Jill thought for a moment before replying. "It doesn't have to. But we've talked about it and that's what we want to do. So it's all sorted out."

"Well, I think it's ridiculous."

"Anthea, dear." Maurice spoke firmly. "They've made their decision."

"You would side with her," Anthea snapped.

"It isn't a case of taking sides, dear. We want a happy wedding day. And it's Jill and Jimmy's day, not yours or mine."

"But—"

"But nothing."

"Oh, Mum. Please, just be happy for me. There's no rush." Jill saw her mother's eyes glisten, not knowing whether they were tears of joy or anger.

"Well. If you say so. If your father agrees, then there's no more to be said." Her mother dabbed the corners of her eyes with a handkerchief.

"What's all this about, Dad? Mum?"

"Come and sit down, love." Maurice lifted the shoes from the table to the floor and screwed up the newspaper. Pulling a chair next to his, Jill did as she was asked. "Since you started staying over at Jimmy's house your Mum's been terrified you'd slip up, you know? She's wanted to see you married to a decent chap since the day you were born."

"But Jimmy is decent. What is it, Mum? Don't you think he's good enough?"

The slight pause before replying, the blinking of eyes and licking of lips told Jill she was right.

"It's not that, dear. Your father and I both like Jimmy. I would like to know about his background, that's all."

"What do you mean his background? What do you know?"

"Nothing. That's just it. What can I tell my friends about him?"

"You can tell them there's nothing to know." Jill struggled to control the anger welling up inside her. "He has no relatives. His parents are dead. No brothers, no sisters, no aunts or uncles or cousins. No grandparents. Nobody at all. Now that has to be better than a scandal, doesn't it? I wanted to have a happy conversation with you. I wanted to talk about our move to York and maybe—just to please you, Mum—I would have talked about bridesmaids and all that, but not now." She ran from the room.

"Jill, please."

High heels restricted her mother's speed, making it easy for Jill to grab her bag and be out of the front door before she could do or say anything to stop her.

CHAPTER FOUR

Doctor Hirst always wore tweed trousers and walking boots as if they were his uniform, like a confirmation of his position as a country GP. Susan decided he felt obliged to dress like that to create some sort of respect amongst the oldies of Barwick-in-Elmet. They certainly made him look older than twenty-eight. Diana had told her he had been there a couple of years, ever since their old family doctor had retired.

The district nurse was very nice. She insisted that Susan call her Valerie, and was forever saying how much she looked forward to meeting Baby Jessop.

Everything was organised. Roy would stay in the office to be contactable by phone. January was a quiet time of year at Jessop's Auction Rooms. If she went into labour he would come straight home and take her to the hospital. Brenda Tanner would have no difficultly in re-arranging whatever appointments he might have.

Henry pottered about between the Scarborough Arms and the office, with the occasional property valuation taking him further afield.

The fifteenth of January came and went. Each day seemed like two weeks. If her labour didn't start that day, Sunday, the birth would be induced.

Roy had cooked their breakfast and cleared away the dishes. He was out in the garden shovelling the overnight fall of snow from the drive. Chaz had phoned the day before, and Jimmy the day before that. She had told them she was fine but bored and tired. The days passed by lying on the sofa, drifting in and out of sleep, and wondering how it could be possible to do nothing and feel so tired. Heavy eyelids closed.

Music drifted through from the kitchen radio, its beat becoming her footsteps as she dreamt she was walking down Briggate, pushing the pram that had been hers as a baby. The summer sun warmed her back. She was thirsty, so very thirsty. The gates at the back of the Threlfalls were locked with a giant padlock hanging on the rusty chain. Someone was moving barrels around in the yard but, no matter how hard she beat her fist on the gate, nobody came. She pushed the pram to the front of the pub, but the high mahogany doors were locked and the once shining brass handles dull. Dust-laden cobwebs, strong as steel, bound them together. Her baby cried and Susan lifted her from the pram. The baby became her childhood doll, Angel Face, a gift from her father on her sixth birthday. Mum and Dad had laughed at the name but she hadn't cared then and she didn't care now. Susan soothed her, quietly humming the lullaby of her childhood, before putting her back in the pram.

She walked on past the post office and down the hill towards the markets. Everyone was shouting at her but she walked through them, parting the crowds as she stared straight ahead. Ugly faces pressed against hers and then, in an instant, she was at her mother's graveside. The white marble headstone reflected a warm, golden light. A vase of red roses wilted as she looked at them. She knelt on the wet grass and took them from the vase. Laying them gently on the ground, she drank the fetid water. It tasted of milk. Her baby began to cry again and, as she stood up, a sharp pain stabbed her back. Invisible hands grabbed hers and she struggled to be free, to pick up Angel Face.

"Susan, Susan. Are you all right? Wake up."

She opened her eyes to see a frightened look on Roy's face. She sat bolt upright and he held her tightly to his chest. "She's coming, Roy. Our baby's coming."

He released his hold and looked into her deep blue eyes. "You're sure?"

Susan nodded. "Bring my case down. We need to go."

He ran up the stairs two at a time and, within seconds, was back down again with the carefully packed suitcase in one hand. By the time he had put it in the boot of his car, Susan had her coat on. She stopped to look around the kitchen, absorbing every detail.

"Is something wrong?" Roy asked. The urgency in his voice bordered on panic.

She smiled. "Nothing at all. I was just thinking that the next time I'm here I'll be a mum, and you'll be a dad."

He took her hand and kissed it. "Come on, Mrs Jessop— soon to be Mummy Jessop. The roads are going to be bad until we're closer to town. I don't want our baby born in the car."

The plan had been to go to the hospital in Susan's car, because she would be more comfortable, but the Spitfire was on the drive and her car in the garage. With the narrow lane behind them, the road was relatively clear. Black tracks in slushy snow contrasted with the dazzling white of the fields. Susan watched as eager sheep followed a trailer of hay, jostling together for the food, their woolly coats turned grey by the snow. Roy gripped the steering wheel with whitened knuckles. All around, the snowy world continued to turn as if it were an ordinary day. With the waiting over, and the moment they had looked forward to finally here, she felt detached from reality.

"This doesn't feel real," Roy said. "It's as if the world has gone into some sort of suspended animation and won't start turning again until she's born."

"I was just thinking the same thing. I wonder why we're both so sure it's a girl." The calmness in her voice took her by surprise. She spoke as if nothing unusual was happening, with the sort of voice that might ask Roy whether he wanted chips or mashed potato.

To her relief the main road was free of snow. Braking to a halt at a junction, Roy took her hand and then accelerated away, her hand beneath his on top of the gear stick.

Susan shuffled in her seat.

"Are you having a contraction?"

"No. Maybe it's a false alarm." She took a deep breath and held it for a moment before breathing out slowly. "I take that back. That was definitely a contraction."

He increased the speed. Neither of them uttered another word until he had parked the car at the hospital and switched off the engine.

"Love you." They spoke simultaneously.

* * * *

"You wait here, Mr Jessop. Keep your wife's case with you until she has been examined and we know this isn't a false alarm." The nurse turned on her heel. Susan followed her. The doors of the labour ward closed slowly on their hydraulic hinges, taking his beautiful wife from his sight. The weight of responsibility had been lifted from his shoulders, and he sank gratefully onto a plastic chair. Half past eleven. Mum would be home from church and having coffee and biscuits with Dad. The plan had been for him to phone them when the baby was born. It seemed a ridiculous plan now. He wanted to tell them they were at the hospital and everything was fine. Mum had said they were wrong to be so sure the baby was a girl.

"What about a boy's name?" she had asked him. "Have you thought of one?'

A perfectly reasonable question but, no, they hadn't. She would be called Emma Siobhan. The nursery had been painted in lemon because the next baby might be a boy.

He leaned forward, his elbows on his knees, hands clasped together. Two nurses burst through the doors, forcing him to his feet, his eyes hungry for news. They walked straight past him and he resumed his position, rotating his thumbs, three times in one direction and three times back.

The nurse who had told him to wait put her head around one of the doors. "We'll be a while yet, Mr Jessop. Why don't you go to the canteen and buy yourself a coffee."

"Is she all right?"

"Your wife's fine. She's in good hands and baby is on his way. Pass me her suitcase, will you?"

He did so and the nurse disappeared into the forbidden world of the labour ward.

The nurse—or midwife—or whoever she was had said, 'baby is on *his* way'. Did she know something he didn't?

He bought a coffee and a bar of chocolate from a lady in the uniform of the Women's Royal Voluntary Service. Pans clattered in the kitchen, breaking the silence. Empty tables and chairs stood in regimented order. Four chairs to a table. Eight tables by six. Forty-eight tables. One hundred and ninety-two chairs. A smell of potatoes and gravy hung in the air. There were a few other customers, some in white coats, others in everyday clothes, their garments identifying them as either doctors or hospital visitors. A sign on the wall informed him that dinner would be served between one o'clock and three o'clock. He screwed up the wrapper of his chocolate bar and threw it onto the table. The WRVS lady came and took it away with a sniff of disapproval. Anxious to return to the uncomfortable chair outside the labour ward, he drank the lukewarm coffee in one draught.

* * * *

Diana set the tray of coffee and biscuits on the table, turning up the radio to cover the sound of Henry sucking on dunked biscuits. Next Sunday would be different. By then she would have a grandchild and they would be at Roy and Susan's house, or they would be here with the baby, visiting. Either way she wouldn't be listening to the offensive sucking.

"Did you say Roy was taking Susan to the hospital on his way to work tomorrow?"

"I said he was taking her to the hospital. I think he'll want to stay with her, don't you?" Henry leaned back in his chair.

"Yes, I suppose so. Unless she doesn't want him to."

"Why wouldn't she want him to? I presumed they would want to be together. They're very close. You must agree with me there."

She heard Henry's voice of reason and even that annoyed her. Deep down she knew her mood was nothing to do with the biscuits, or the sucking, or Henry's calmness. She was worried sick about the birth, needing to know that everything would be all right.

"I'll give them a ring."

"What for?"

"To ask if there's anything I can do."

"Sit down and finish your coffee, dear. Susan's a healthy young woman. She's not poorly. She's going to have a baby, the most natural thing in the world."

"You would say that." Diana sat down again. "I'm sorry,

Henry. I can think of nothing else."

"I know, love. And no-one is more excited than I am. We just show it in different ways. If you want to ring them, go ahead."

As she left the room Diana put her hand on her husband's shoulder, gripping it momentarily. He took another ginger biscuit from the plate.

She returned within a minute, her face pale with shock as she slowly lowered into her chair.

"What is it?" Henry asked. "Is something wrong? What did he say?"

"Nothing."

"What do you mean? Didn't he say anything, or is something wrong?" His eyes widened, his calm exterior stripped away.

"There was no reply."

"That's good, isn't it? Of course it's good. The waiting will soon be over now. Are you all right?"

"Yes. Yes, of course. Odd really. Now it's happening I feel... Oh, I don't know how I feel."

"I think I'll take a turn round the garden with my pipe, if you don't mind."

Diana looked up at her husband of thirty-four years, and nodded.

Moments later he was standing on the snow-covered lawn in his slippers, with clouds of smoke billowing around him. She watched him take a handkerchief from his pocket and wipe his eyes. If she wasn't much mistaken, he was crying.

* * * *

With nothing to do, Roy observed the detail of his surroundings. Framed prints of Monet's Water Lilies and Van Gogh's Sunflowers broke the monotony of the plain paintwork. A strip of plastic, eight inches deep, ran along the walls, giving protection from damage by trolleys. Scuff marks proved its efficacy. Time passed with excruciating tedium. He had been there for an hour and a half.

The nurse's head popped around the door and he jumped to his feet.

"You can come and sit with your wife, Mr Jessop."

He followed her down a corridor lined with doors to the left and right. He had assumed Susan was just the other side of the first doors, but the place was a labyrinth. A cleaner mopped the floor, moving her tripod sign of 'Wet Floor' with one foot as she worked.

An atmosphere of cocooned efficiency ruled the world this side of the swinging doors.

"Is she all right? What's happening?"

"She's fine, Mr Jessop. I'm the midwife in charge of your wife. Baby will come when he's ready, but we've put her on a drip to hurry things up a bit. I've spoken with her obstetrician and she advised it, as baby is overdue."

Roy thought it a contradiction in terms to say 'Baby will come when he's ready' and then say, 'we've decided to hurry things up a bit'. 'He' again. Very odd.

They turned right into a side ward. Relief flooded through his body at the sight of Susan sitting up in bed.

"I'll be at my desk if you need me. Pull the red cord behind the bed if it's urgent, although I don't expect it will be, not for a while. Lunch will be here soon."

Roy sat beside her, making circular motions with his thumb on the back of her hand. Her other hand had a needle inserted into a vein. White adhesive strapping held it in place. The liquid, held high on a frame, dripped through a valve, down a tube and into her bloodstream.

"That looks painful."

"Is does, doesn't it? But it isn't." Her face contorted. She squeezed Roy's hand so tightly his fingers went white before she relaxed and loosened her grip. "But that was."

He marvelled at her. He couldn't take his eyes off the young woman who had transformed his life in every way. His thoughts returned to the day he'd walked into the Threlfalls and met the girl who used to dance in a gilded cage at the 'In Time' disco. Now, less than a year later, she was his wife and about to become the mother of his daughter.

"What are you thinking?" she asked.

He shook his head at the question. "I don't know. Everything—and nothing. I just want this over with, and to know you're safe, and the baby's safe."

"Me too," she laughed. "There's nothing to worry about, Roy."

"You're right. It's just so quiet here. It seems weird."

"Sister told me it would be busy enough tomorrow morning. Apparently three women are to be induced, but I'll be in the post-natal ward by then."

Lunch came. Susan nibbled between contractions but Roy couldn't eat a thing, his appetite taken by futile worry. A midwife asked him to monitor the contractions, how often and how long. They gradually increased in length and intensity and the time between them shortened.

A clock on the wall became their focus. At two o'clock the drip was removed but the canula was left in her hand 'just in case', although in case of what, no-one said. Her blood pressure was taken every half hour. The midwife said the foetal heartbeat was strong but that baby was taking his time. By four o'clock each contraction lasted for thirty seconds. Susan was taken to the delivery room and given an injection of pethidine to ease the pain. Roy held her hand, his palms bleeding as her nails dug into his flesh. It hurt, but not as much as the pain etched on Susan's face. She writhed in agony, twisting and turning on one side, then on her back, and then on her other side.

"Despite all the contractions, Mr Jessop, she isn't ready to push yet. I'll give her another shot of pethidine. I'll be going off duty soon but the next shift will have your wife's notes."

Roy didn't like the way the midwife spoke over Susan, as if she were insensible. He didn't like the way things were at all. Ignorance and terror combined to silence him. He had no authority in this parallel world where life and death hung in the balance. Lives that had not begun sometimes ended here. Susan and their baby were at the mercy of the midwife. He was terrified. The drugs closed her eyes, dulling her senses but not the pain.

An older nurse introduced herself as Midwife Helen. She took Susan's pulse and blood pressure and then listened to the baby through her Pinard horn. Roy was asked to wait outside, the serious look on Midwife Helen's face imprinted on his mind, despite the smile that sought to hide her concern.

Another corridor, another plastic chair, another Old Master's print on the wall. The minutes ticked by, each an hour long.

As Midwife Helen walked towards him, he knew something was different, and not in a good way. The other midwife had always just popped her head round the door with a 'you can come in now, Mr Jessop'. As he jumped to his feet the chair tipped over.

"What is it? What's wrong?"

"You wife's blood pressure has escalated to a dangerous level and the baby's showing signs of distress. The consultant obstetrician is on her way. Please try not to panic, Mr Jessop. All will be well, but it's probable that a caesarean operation is necessary. The baby is still too high, and your wife's cervix has not dilated as much as we would have expected by now."

Roy righted the chair and sat down again, his legs unable to support the weight of anxiety.

"Can I see her?" He looked up at the little woman. Her years of experience shone through caring eyes.

Before she could answer, a tall, thin woman in flat shoes and thick stockings passed them, walking quickly into the delivery room.

"Not now. That's Miss Sugden, the consultant. I have to go, but I'll let you know as soon as a decision has been made."

More minutes passed as hours before Midwife Helen re-appeared. "We're setting up a theatre team. All will be well, Mr Jessop." She looked at her watch.

Roy automatically looked at his. Eight thirty.

Two porters ran down the corridor, wheeling a trolley into the delivery room. Less than a minute later they were running back with Susan, hastily followed by Miss Sugden and Midwife Helen. Roy ran behind them, barely conscious of the faces that turned to stare. Suddenly, swinging doors shut in his face. He looked up to see the illuminated words 'THEATRE. DO NOT ENTER WHEN LIGHT IS ON.' He staggered back several paces as though hit by a sledge hammer. All he knew, all he cared about, would live or die behind those doors. He ran his fingers through his hair and leaned against a wall, his eyes closed.

* * * *

"I'm telling you something's wrong, Henry." Diana replaced the receiver and returned to the lounge.

"You don't know that. I'm sure we'd know if anything had happened. I keep telling you, bad news travels fast. Look how you fretted when he went to France, and all for nothing."

She sat on the edge of the armchair, her fists clenched. "They've been out all day. They must be at the hospital."

"Yes, love. I agree. And I don't profess to know a lot about babies, but I remember Roy took his time. He'll phone, as he said he would, when the baby's born. All will be well."

"I know. I know. I can't rest. Do you think I should phone the hospital, just to confirm they're there?"

Henry sighed deeply. He was just as anxious as Diana, but felt he must, as Rudyard Kipling had said, 'keep his head when all around were losing theirs'.

"No, Diana. I don't think you should. We know they must be there, but go ahead if that's what you want to do."

Quick steps took her back to the hall. As her hand reached towards the receiver, it rang.

"Roy, is that you?"

"Yes, Mum. It's a girl. We have a daughter."

"Henry! It's a girl."

Henry was at her side, his arms around his wife.

"Is everything all right?" she continued.

"Yes, it is now. It had to be a caesarean. She's a big baby. Susan's sleeping now. Oh, Mum. What a day. Put the kettle on in about an hour. I'll come and tell you all about it. I have to phone Jimmy and Jill. They'll call Chaz."

"You can do that from here," Diana said, but the line had

gone dead. "He hung up. Says he'll be here in about an hour for a cup of tea."

"To hell with a cup of tea. I need a whisky."

CHAPTER FIVE

Consciousness slowly won over exhaustion and anaesthesia. Sensibility struggled to the surface as Susan opened her eyes. She lay on her back. The window to her right had its blind pulled part way down. To her left a locker, with a water jug and plastic cup, provided the only furniture other than her bed. The door to the single room had an oval pane of glass. Lifting her head from the pillow, she could see she was alone. No other beds—no baby—no Roy—no clock on the wall. Her stomach hurt and it seemed as big as ever. Her head flopped back on the pillow and she stared at the ceiling. In her head, an image of her baby formed, wrapped in a green cloth, and being held out by a smiling woman in a green gown.

The door was pushed open. "Ah, Mrs Jessop. Awake at last."

"Where's the clock?" Susan whispered, her throat dry and sore.

"You're in a post-natal ward, Mrs Jessop. The clock was in the labour ward. Baby will be brought to you soon."

"What time is it?"

The nurse looked at the watch pinned to her uniform. "Half past twelve. Your lunch will be here soon and baby will want feeding."

"Did I have a girl?"

"You did indeed, Mrs Jessop. A fine big girl. Nine pounds five ounces to be precise. I'm not surprised you had a bit of difficulty." The nurse helped her to sit up, plumping her pillows and setting the back rest. "Would you like a drink of water?"

Susan nodded and the nurse poured a small amount from the lidded jug. She tried to sit up a little more, but the searing pain across her stomach pushed her back.

"Press down with your hands, love. You've had a big operation. Push yourself up that way. That's it. You'll be right as a bobbin in no time. Sister put you in this little room so you can rest. The main ward can get a bit noisy with all those babies. If you need the toilet pull this cord and one of us will take you in a wheelchair. No need to go traipsing up and down the corridor."

Susan sipped the water, and then the nurse helped her take off the theatre gown and put on her nightdress.

A second nurse came in, followed by a little trolley being pushed by yet another nurse. Susan's whole body melted at the sight of her baby. Her emotions overwhelmed her, knowing she would give her life for this little part of her own being. Her exhaustion evaporated and all pain was ignored as Emma Siobhan Jessop was laid in the crook of her arm. Smiling at her baby through tears of joy, she marvelled at the long, dark eyelashes. Closed eyelids kept secret their colour. Tiny fingers, tipped with perfect little nails, gripped with strength around her little finger. Emma yawned. Dark hair wisped around, not knowing which way to turn. Susan gently stroked the head that instinctively turned to her mother's breast. Wordlessly and expertly, a nurse helped her arrange her nightdress so that her baby might take her first feed.

Afternoon visiting was permitted between three and five o'clock. Evening visiting, restricted to fathers only, the half hour between six thirty and seven. Roy and his parents were at the hospital at two forty-five. Diana had despatched Henry to the florist in Barwick-in-Elmet earlier in the day. As they waited he was almost hidden by the bouquet of pink chrysanthemums.

The doors opened and they filed in. Roy knew where to find her. Some sixteen hours earlier he had put her things in the locker before kissing her lightly on the forehead and leaving.

"Ah, Mr Jessop." Both Henry and Roy turned to their name. The ward sister in her dark blue dress approached.

Roy's heart sank. "Is something wrong?"

"No, no. Nothing's wrong." She spoke briskly. "Mother and baby are doing well but your wife is extremely tired. Please keep your visit brief and quiet." She smiled towards Diana and Henry. "Are you Mrs Jessop's parents?"

"These are *my* parents, Sister. My wife has no family—at least, no parents."

"I'm sorry to hear it, but I'm sure you'll give her all the support she needs. It will take a while for her to be back to strength. She had a long and difficult labour, and then a major operation."

"I know. I was here." Roy felt irritated by the suggestion that Susan might want for anything. "There's no question that she will have anything other than the greatest support." He was anxious to see Susan and Emma, and walked away. Diana and Henry grimaced before following him.

Roy paused briefly at the side of the clear-sided cot before kissing Susan on the cheek.

"I love you both," he whispered. Her pale face with dark, dark rings under her eyes smiled warmly. She looked awful. Even without the sister's warning, Roy wouldn't let his parents stay for long. "How are you feeling?"

"Okay. Tired. Glad it's over."

Diana and Henry, eager for the first sight of their granddaughter, peered into the cot with sighs of delight.

"You can pick her up if you like," Susan said.

Diana looked at her daughter-in-law. "Are you sure?"

"Of course I'm sure. Roy, you lift her out for her first daddy cuddle."

Roy lifted his daughter. "You don't know it, Susan, but I had a cuddle last night."

"No, I didn't know. I don't remember much at all. I can't believe I had such a perfect pregnancy and then made such a mess of giving birth."

Henry pulled two chairs forward for himself and Diana. Roy placed his daughter in her grandmother's arms with gentleness and care. Sitting on the edge of the bed, Roy held Susan's hands in his. "It wasn't your fault, love. Never think that. We have a healthy, strong daughter, and that's all that matters." He lifted her hands and kissed them both. "Now I need you to be stronger so you can come home and we'll be a proper family."

"Can I come home with you now?"

"Not today. You need to rest, but I'll have a word with Sister and see what she says." They watched as Diana passed Emma to Henry. His father held her as if afraid she would break, all the time smiling broadly. He seemed unable to take his eyes from the miracle in his arms. Emma opened her eyes. They gasped.

"They're so blue, Susan, just like yours," Diana said. "I mean, I know babies have blue eyes, but look, Henry, just look at the colour."

"It's a family thing. My mother and I were very alike. Dark hair and blue eyes. That's the O'Malleys for you."

"We should go now, Diana," Henry said. "Susan looks tired and we should let them have time on their own, these two." He looked towards them. "I mean these three."

Roy took Emma and laid her back in her cot, tucking the blanket around her. "I'll see you back at the office, Dad."

"No rush. You stay as long as the Sister will let you. Babies aren't babies for long, you know."

"Try to rest, dear. We'll see you soon," Diana said.

They kissed Susan on the cheek, and left.

"Why does everyone keep going on about resting? I feel fine, really. I've had a baby, that's all."

"You're wonderful, Susan Jessop. You had a hard time of it, though, and you do look a bit tired." Roy saw a hint of a frown cross her face and changed the subject. "I spoke to Jimmy last night. He says he and Jill will come to see you when you're home."

"Then I'd better be home by the weekend."

"Maybe you will be. It's only Monday today."

"I was expecting to be in for two or three days at the most. That's what they said at the ante-natal clinic."

"I know. But that was for a normal birth. They may want to keep you longer."

Her frown deepened. "They won't even let me walk to the bathroom. They take me in a wheelchair. I had to roll onto my side before I could get out of bed and they had to bring a step for me."

"You'll feel better every day, love."

She laid her head back on the pillow and closed her eyes. "I wish my mum was here."

* * * *

Diana and Henry stepped outside into the cold January air. They hadn't spoken since leaving the ward but neither of them had any doubt as to where the other's thoughts lay. With the exception of the day Roy had been born, Henry could not recall being happier.

Diana's thoughts had turned to more practical matters. "I need to go shopping. Emma's such a big baby she'll need the second size clothes straight away. Are you going straight back to the office, or do you want to come with me?"

"You go, love. Have you enough money on you?"

"I have my cheque book." She pulled on her gloves. "I'll come to the office when I'm finished. Tell Roy he must come to our house for dinner." She turned and gave him a peck on the cheek. "See you soon, Grandpa."

Henry chuckled. "And you, Granny."

Diana set off towards the Headrow as Henry made for the Scarborough Arms.

* * * *

Roy was right. Susan did feel better every day. A nurse removed the dressing on the third day, causing more than a little discomfort. With her back hunched, she walked gingerly to the bathroom. Every footstep jarred her body. A nurse carried her wash-bag, a clean nightdress and a towel.

"Take your time, Mrs Jessop. Pull the cord if you need any assistance and please leave the door unlocked."

There had been no mirror in her room. When she looked at her reflection she barely recognised the face that looked back. Her lips were as white as her cheeks and her hair lay flat and lank. Leaning forward, she pulled her lower eyelid down towards her cheek, revealing pale flesh. The whites of her eyes were a yellowish grey. Standing up as straight as she dare, she breathed in until a sharp pain pulled her back to a hunch. Everyone had said she looked so much better. *What must I have looked like three days ago?* If she were to be discharged for the weekend she would have to put on a bit of make-up.

She stepped into the warm water, lowering herself in before resting her back on the slope of the bath. Her breasts seemed to start just below her collar bone and ached more than ever. It would be a long time before she could wear normal clothes or fasten her jeans. The stitched red line started just below her navel and disappeared from view over her swollen abdomen. Swishing the water around, she washed the congealed blood from the wound before closing her eyes, not wanting to look at her body. Fingertips explored the length of the line to just above the point where her pubic hair would have started, if the nurse hadn't shaved it off. She lay there for some time, considering which might be the easiest way to get out of the bath.

The water had cooled by the time the nurse returned. "Twist yourself around onto all fours before standing up."

Susan took her advice, and her hand, before stepping over the side of the bath.

"Will you help me wash my hair in the sink, please?"

The nurse looked at her watch. "No time today, Mrs Jessop, but you can have a shower tomorrow and do it then. It'll be more comfortable than leaning over a sink. I'll leave you to dress."

Susan gathered her possessions and made her way to her room.

As she approached the open door, a nurse called from further down the ward. "This way, Mrs Jessop. We've moved your things."

Susan looked inside her room with dismay. Her bed was stripped down to its plastic-covered mattress. Emma's cot and the cards and flowers had all been removed. No-one had said anything about moving. And where was Emma? Where had they taken her? Her pace quickened.

"Here we are, Mrs Jessop." The nurse had led her to a ward, stopping at the foot of the only vacant bed and looking in the cot to make sure the sleeping baby was Emma. "All your things are in the locker."

"No-one said I—"

"Sister thinks you need a bit of company now you're so much better."

Susan sat on the edge of the bed and pressed down with the palms of her hands, swinging her legs onto the clean sheet.

"I'll be back in a minute with that dressing. You sit back and relax."

She frowned, feeling she had been tricked into going for a bath so they could move her out of her room and into the main ward. The woman in the bed opposite smiled and Susan smiled back.

The nurse returned and pulled the curtains around the bed. "Good, very good. Stitches due out on Monday, then we'll see about you going home."

"Monday? You must be joking. I want to be home for the weekend."

"Having a party, are we?" The nurse laughed.

"No, of course not. I just want to go home, that's all."

"This isn't a prison, Mrs Jessop, but you had a difficult birth." She spoke quietly. "If you take my advice you'll stay until Miss Sugden discharges you."

"I want to go home now." Susan raised her voice. The nurse pulled back the curtain. There were six beds in the ward in total, and Susan became acutely aware of the staring faces of the other five mothers. The nurse checked the clipboard of notes at the end of the bed before lifting Emma from the cot and passing her to Susan.

"Time for a feed, Mrs Jessop."

Susan glared at her. Just because Sister thought she should have company didn't make it a good idea. The nurse had pulled back the curtain, making it obvious that privacy wasn't considered necessary for breastfeeding. With her eyes fixed on Emma's fine black hair, Susan tried to decide whether or not she liked the tickling sensation. She had expected the sucking to hurt but it didn't. It just tickled a bit.

As Roy arrived for afternoon visiting Susan burst into

tears.

Pulling up a chair, he sat by her side. "What is it, love? Emma's all right, isn't she?"

Susan nodded. He passed her a tissue.

"I hate it here. I want to go home," she hissed through gritted teeth.

"Why have they moved you?"

Susan shrugged. "Sister's idea—apparently I need company."

Roy looked around the ward. All the mothers had visitors and were chatting happily. He kept his voice low.

"Have they said when you can come home?"

"Not before Monday—unless I walk out. It's up to Miss Sugden."

Roy didn't know what to say, and so he said nothing. He wanted Susan to stay here and rest, to take the advice of the experts.

He had come in Susan's car just in case they were discharged. The carrycot was on the back seat. He had clothes for Emma and Susan.

Emma stirred. Susan carefully slid out of bed. Holding her baby against her chest, with her head resting on her shoulder, she shifted her weight from one foot to the other in a swaying motion. "There's nothing wrong with me or with Emma. She's a good baby, and strong. I don't see why the district nurse couldn't come round to our house to take my stitches out."

"Have you suggested that to anyone?"

Susan shook her head. "No, I only just thought of it."

"Mind if I have a cuddle?"

She smiled and passed Emma to him before climbing back onto the bed.

"I had a bath today but there wasn't time to wash my hair. If I were at home I could do it in the shower. It feels awful."

The ward sister approached them. "Mr Jessop, you shouldn't be picking baby up all the time. It's not hygienic."

Roy frowned. "She's my daughter, Sister, and I'll hold her

if I want to."

"And she is in *my* care."

He laid Emma back in the cot. Ignoring the sister, he kissed Susan on the cheek and whispered, "I'll be back soon. Start folding those cards up, and empty your locker."

He left the ward without another word. Susan grinned sweetly at the sister, who returned a look of satisfaction.

CHAPTER SIX

At every bump in the road and at every corner, and each time Roy braked, Susan held her stomach as firmly as she dare. Her muscles, once so firm and tight, had ceased to exist. The familiar half hour journey couldn't go fast enough, every mile taking her closer to home.

Roy parked near the front door and took the carrycot from the back seat. Susan stepped thankfully into Orchard Cottage. With Emma fast asleep and tucked up in her blankets, Roy put the carrycot on the dining room table, leaving the door ajar. As he gently put his arms around her, his kindness overwhelmed her. She was home in every sense.

His strong arms lifted her as if she were no weight at all, and carried her to the sofa where he knelt at her side. "Try to sleep, love, while you can. I'll listen for Emma and wake you when she needs a feed."

She closed her eyes and, within seconds, had drifted off.

Roy watched her flickering eyelids until they stilled, and her breathing softened to a quiet rhythm. Standing up slowly, he crept from the room and closed the door behind him. He used the phone in their bedroom to call his mother.

"She's not strong yet, Roy. You must turn the central heating up to make sure they're warm enough."

"I know."

"I think she should have stayed in hospital a bit longer."

"She hated it there."

"But Roy—"

"Mum, I need to phone Jimmy to tell him we're home. Will you call Dad to say I won't be at the office today?"

"Yes, of course. Do you have something in the house for dinner?"

"Yes, Mum. We have everything we need. I have to go."

"I'll pop in later."

"Not today, Mum. Maybe tomorrow."

"Well, if you're sure there's nothing I can do."

"Really, Mum, we're fine. See you soon."

He pressed the receiver button to terminate the call and dialled Jimmy's number. No reply. Of course there wouldn't be. He'd be at work. He dialled Doctor Hirst's number and informed the receptionist that they were home, and would need the district nurse to call.

Creeping downstairs as quietly as he could, he tip-toed into the dining room, looking and listening, as Emma made little sucking noises. A little hand escaped from beneath the blanket. He smiled as she flexed her perfect fingers. Lifting her out, he wrapped her in a blanket and carried her upstairs to the nursery. "Look around you, little princess. This is your bedroom. Mummy and Daddy have been waiting for you, and now you're here."

Emma opened her eyes briefly and then closed them again as he turned her to face the window.

"This is your garden, Emma, where you'll play in the summer. Daddy will chop all the weeds down and we'll have a lawn to play on."

Susan's hand on his shoulder startled him.

"You made me jump. Can't you sleep, love?"

She shook her head. "I thought I would, and I did for a little while, but I'm sick of being told to rest. I'm fine now I'm home, honestly, I am."

He put Emma in her cot and turned to her. Taking care not to squeeze too tightly, he enveloped her in his arms. She felt as fragile as a china doll as she rested her head on his shoulder. "We're a proper family now. What do you think of that?"

Susan smiled as she looked into his eyes. "I have to pinch myself to know it's true. I want this moment to last forever." Emma stirred. They held hands, watching her as little noises gave way to tiny baby cries.

"You sit in the chair, love. I'll pass her to you."

As Emma suckled, Roy took a clean nappy, vest, dress, and socks from the chest of drawers. He laid them out neatly.

"I can do that, Roy. You don't have to."

"I know I don't have to, but I want to. I don't want to be

one of those dads who brag about how many children they have and how they never changed a nappy."

"A cup of tea would be nice."

"I'll put it on a tray and bring it upstairs." He kissed the top of her head.

Susan smiled as she listened to his retreating footsteps. She was quite sure her father had never changed her nappy when she was a baby. Her mum had done everything. On reflection, she thought theirs had been a strange marriage, with no proper home. Her dad hadn't loved her mum, not like Roy loved her and Emma. The pub had been the only home she had known. Perhaps that was why she had liked going to Jimmy's house so much. She and Jimmy were such different people, and yet they had many things in common. They were young to have no parents and they both had money. They shared a wonderful friend in Chaz. She had Roy, and Jimmy had Jill. Her friends would visit at the weekend. They hadn't been for a while, and she wondered if Jill had patched things up with her mother. Jimmy kept very quiet on the subject, which Susan took as his agreeing with his fiancée. They were engaged and living together all the time now, but with no immediate plans to marry. They would probably get married when they decided to start a family.

Translucent, veined skin stretched across her breasts. They ached like mad. Emma didn't seem very interested and fell asleep with her mouth still open. Susan changed her nappy and laid her in the cot. As she tiptoed downstairs, Roy emerged from the kitchen with a tray.

"Take it in the lounge, will you, love," she whispered, "and put a saucer on my cup. I was on my way down to tell you she's asleep. If I don't wash my hair soon I'll go crazy."

* * * *

The following morning Roy was clearing the snow, finishing the job he had started when Susan had gone into labour, when the sound of a car took him from his task.

Nurse Valerie had arrived. "Good morning, Roy."

He threw the shovel into a pile of snow.

"Don't let me stop you," she called as she let herself in.

He had wanted to show off his daughter, pleased to have an excuse to stop digging. But maybe Nurse Valerie wanted to speak with Susan on her own and maybe, just maybe, he would rather be out of the way. He retrieved his shovel and carried on with his work.

Nurse Valerie unclipped her uniform hat and placed it on the kitchen table before hanging her blue gabardine coat on the back of a kitchen chair. The blue, short-sleeved dress and crisp, white apron gave further evidence of her profession.

"So how was the first night at home, Susan?"

"Fine. She's asleep. She had a feed at eight o'clock and again at two in the morning. Roy slept through the two o'clock. I woke her for a feed at seven thirty."

"And how about you?"

"I'm okay. Better now I'm home. I was just going to get dressed," Susan said, knowing it to be a lie, but what she thought Nurse Valerie would want to hear.

Valerie took a notebook from her bag, and wrote something down. "I understand you had a caesarean?"

"Mmm."

"I'll need to check your wound, and then I'll have a peek at Emma. I have to weigh her."

She followed Susan up the stairs, bag in hand.

With her dressing gown untied, Susan lay on the bed, shuffling on her bottom to pull up her nightdress.

"Didn't they put a dressing on?"

"Oh, erm, yes. I took it off when I had a shower yesterday. Is it all right? The wound, I mean."

"Very neat, I'd say. It'll shrink and fade with time. I'll dress it now and leave you a couple of spares. Keep it as dry as you can." Gentle hands applied a dressing.

"I don't know what to wear. I'm fed up with maternity smocks, but everything else is still too tight. Jeans are out of the question."

"Don't worry, Susan. It takes time, especially after a

caesarean. Wear whatever's comfortable. You don't want anything rubbing on your stitches. Stay in your dressing gown if you want. That's what you'd be wearing if you were still in the hospital. Now, where's this baby of yours?"

Valerie took a little sling from her bag and put a sleeping Emma in it, attaching a spring scale, and holding her up. "What did you say her birth weight was?"

"Nine pounds five ounces."

The nurse put Emma back in her cot. "What does it feel like when she feeds? Does it hurt?"

"No. She's very gentle. It just sort of tickles. Why?"

"Babies usually lose a bit of weight in the first few days, but Emma has lost more than I would have expected. You may need to supplement with some bottle feeding."

"But she's so content. She'd cry if she were hungry. That can't be right. My breasts are bursting, they're so big."

"It isn't your fault, Susan. Mother's milk often doesn't start to flow with a caesarean. She should be waking at least twice in the night. I think she may be getting lazy, and not feeding properly."

"I didn't buy any bottles," Susan whispered.

"I have a sample in my bag. We'll give her a try, shall we?" She produced a packet of dried milk and a bottle. "Let's go downstairs. You bring that lovely daughter of yours."

Taking Emma from her cot, Susan followed the nurse. She rocked her baby from side to side, holding her tightly. She had failed to feed her, and Emma was fading. She had failed at the most basic task of motherhood. Tears filled her eyes as she watched Nurse Valerie pour boiling water into a bottle, a mark on the side showing how much to add. She then tipped in the contents of a packet, replaced the teat and shook the bottle before holding it over the sink to run cold water over the glass. The nurse then shook a few drops onto the underside of her wrist. "Sit yourself down, Susan. Let's give it a try, shall we?"

Susan could barely believe her eyes as Emma sucked greedily, her little cheeks working fast to take in the nutritious liquid. But then she coughed the teat from her mouth, and milk spurted across the kitchen floor. Susan shrieked.

Roy came rushing in from the garden. "What is it? What's wrong?"

"Nothing's wrong, Mr Jessop."

"Susan? What is it?"

"I haven't been feeding her properly and she just threw up the packet stuff."

Nurse Valerie waved away her words. "Her little tummy has taken a shock, that's all. Try her with a little more."

The baby sucked on the bottle.

"There we are. Clever girl, Emma." Nurse Valerie's calm, professional voice acted like a salve.

Susan kept her eyes steadfastly on her daughter's face. "I thought my milk would be better."

"Lots of mums choose to bottle feed these days. The new formula milk is very good and you can measure how much she's taking." The nurse turned to Roy. "You'll be able to take your turn with the night feeds, so Susan can sleep."

"I don't want to sleep."

"I'll stay here, while your husband goes for some bottles and formula milk." She turned to Roy. "Is that all right with you?"

"Of course, yes. Where do I go?"

"The chemist in Seacroft will be nearest. Tell them you need bottles and a sterilizer, and formula milk for a newborn."

Roy grabbed his keys and was gone.

"I expect he's pleased to have something to do," said the nurse. "New dads can feel a bit left out."

Susan made no reply. Emma sucked the last drop of milk, evidenced by the sound of air being sucked through the teat. Valerie took the bottle from her and put it in the sink. "Sit her up now. That's right, support her under her chin with your left hand and rub her back with your right." Emma gave a belch. "Now you can put her down for a sleep."

"Maybe she's still hungry."

"She'll be fine for now. Let that settle. We don't want to give her too much all at once when she's not used to it."

Susan put her in the carrycot on the dining room table. "You can go if you want to. You don't have to stay with me.

Roy won't be long."

"Are you sure?"

"I'm sure you have lots of other people to see. I'll be fine."

"I'll call again on Monday to see how things are going and, if your wound has healed, I'll take the stitches out. Read the instructions on the formula milk carefully, and phone the surgery if you need me for anything. Anything at all." Valerie fastened the clasp on her bag before putting on her gabardine and hat.

After shutting the door behind the nurse, Susan went into the dining room to check on Emma. The only sound was that of Nurse Valerie's car as she set off down the lane. Wandering into the kitchen, her forefinger hovered over the radio switch for a moment, but she decided against turning it on. The music might wake Emma. Roy would be back soon and she ought to be setting the table. Looking around, she noted the spotlessly clean room with satisfaction. Everything was so neat and tidy, just as he liked it. With a deep sigh, she walked through to the lounge. The sofa looked inviting. She lay down on her side, her sagging belly resting on the feather cushions.

For the first two days and nights after Emma had been born, Susan had only been able to lie on her back. She was clearly recovering from the operation. Everything would be fine when Roy returned with the bottles and milk.

Without warning, tears flowed like torrents, tickling her cheeks and flowing sideways over the bridge of her nose and soaking the cushion. Her dream of being a perfect mother had been well and truly shattered. She was useless.

* * * *

With three bulging carrier bags on the passenger seat, the clear blue sky persuaded Roy to take the roof down. Folding the canvas carefully, he knew his car would have to go. A two-seater sports car was all very well for a bachelor, but those days were over. He had no regrets, but the opportunity to have the wind in his hair and the sun on his face was too good to miss.

The nurse was with Susan and the few minutes it would take to put the roof down wouldn't make any difference.

The chemist's assistant had been very helpful. The bags contained everything they needed for Emma, plus a couple of dummies and a bottle of gripe water, *'just in case'*.

He knew every bend of the winding road and had always enjoyed the drive from Seacroft to Barwick-in-Elmet. The wood to his right was known as Tom's Coppice. To his left, and beyond a low hedge, the expanse of snow brightened the day. Low winter sunshine had turned the road into a sparkling ribbon, stretching before him as he came out of the bend. He screwed up his eyes and leaned forward to take his sunglasses from the glove compartment. Searching with his left hand, he took the next long, gentle curve of the road.

A horn blasted. Bang! Spinning, spinning, spinning, trees, road, hedge, road, trees, road, all flashed before him with impossible speed. He flew through the air, his eyes closed. He would die, and never see Susan or Emma again.

Landing with a sickening thud, several seconds passed before he attempted to move. Something warm trickled over his forehead. He opened his eyes, and tentatively moved each limb in turn. He put his hand to his forehead. Blood trickled through his fingers.

"You okay, mate?" Turning towards the shout, Roy realised he was in a field, and his car was upside down in the hedge about thirty yards away. He staggered to his feet, his blood-spattered clothes covered with mud and snow.

"Yes, I think so. More than can be said for my car. What happened?"

"Clipped my tractor, you did."

"No-one else hurt?"

"No, and it'll take more than a little sports car to dent my tractor. It's Roy Jessop, isn't it? Henry and Diana's lad. Your head looks nasty."

Roy took a handkerchief from his pocket and held it to his forehead. Blue lights flashed beyond the hedge where the top of a tractor cab was just visible. The contents of the carrier bags were strewn over the field of melting snow. He staggered forward. "My baby daughter needs the milk."

Two policemen approached from a gateway, picking their way over the ploughed field. The tractor driver stepped towards them. "Norman Grayling. That's my farm." He pointed towards a group of buildings in the distance. "Over there, Barwick Grange."

Roy looked at his shattered watch. "What time is it?" The two policemen looked at each other.

"You taking the mickey?" the taller one said. Roy looked at them blankly. "If you want to know the time, ask a policeman. Is that your game?"

"No. No. My watch is broken. I need to go home." Roy picked up a packet of milk with his free hand. "My wife and my baby need these things. It's urgent. She's a newborn baby." With his handkerchief back in his pocket, he picked up a carrier bag and started to collect the scattered shopping. Blood poured from his head, staining the snow with a bloody trail.

"Concussed if you ask me."

Norman nodded.

"Right, yes. Thank you, Mr Grayling. Can we presume that's your tractor?"

"Aye. It is. He was over the white line—clipped my front wheel, that's all. I reckon the sun dazzled him."

"I think you'd better come with us, young man." The policeman took Roy by the arm. "We can call an ambulance from the car. Not been drinking, have you? Wetting the baby's head? What's your name?"

"Roy Jessop. I haven't been drinking, and I have to go home, I tell you, with the baby milk." He shook himself free from the officer's grasp. "My wife will be worried sick."

"And just how are you going to do that, Mr Jessop? Your car's in the hedge."

"I'll walk. I live in the village. Orchard Cottage."

"You go with the officers, Roy. I'll take the shopping to your wife. Go on, now. You're bleeding all over my field."

Feeling dizzy, he took out the blood-soaked handkerchief and held it again to his head. Only then did he notice his grazed knuckles and ripped jacket. A trouser leg flapped about, ripped from above his knee to the hem, revealing a jagged gash in his calf. Blood oozed through the laces of his shoe. Nodding in resignation, he followed the officers.

* * * *

Diana had put a lot of thought into the simple menu. Chicken casserole, followed by treacle sponge pudding would be easily transported and warmed up without detriment to the quality. She packed plenty of newspaper around the pots. A pint of milk and a packet of custard powder were placed in a smaller box. She had prepared enough for four, but if Roy and Susan didn't want to eat it today, everything could go in the fridge for tomorrow.

Henry stood on the kitchen doormat, stamping wet snow from his boots. "It's melting fast now, slippery underfoot, though. You'll need to watch your step. You should put some wellies on."

"I'll be all right. I'm only walking from the house to the car, I'm not going for a hike. You'll need to be careful carrying the boxes. Be sure to keep them upright."

"Do they know you're doing meals-on-wheels?"

Diana grinned. "No. But I'm sure they'll be pleased. I've done Roy's favourite, which happens to be easily transported."

"Don't tell me." Henry put up his hand, silencing his wife with the palm of his hand. "Chicken casserole and treacle sponge pudding." They laughed, and Henry kissed her on the cheek as he lifted the larger box from the table. "At least we don't have to drive to the hospital to see them. I don't know about you, but I'm glad they're home."

Diana carried the smaller box to the Jaguar, and they set off on the short journey through the village, turning down the narrow lane to Orchard Cottage.

Henry tutted when he saw the tractor lumbering in front of them, spitting lumps of mud from the deep treads of its wheels onto his car.

"You can't stop there. You're blocking the lane," he shouted.

The tractor driver looked towards Henry before taking three muddy bags from the side of his seat. He leaned back in the cab and switched off the diesel engine.

"I say…" began Henry.

Norman Grayling walked towards the car. "Hello, Mr Jessop."

Diana saw Susan at the window, and waved.

"I'm afraid your Roy's been taken to hospital," continued the farmer. "Bit of a prang in his car. He asked me to bring the shopping."

"What?" Diana leaned across Henry. "What was that about a hospital? What's going on, Henry?"

Susan opened the window. "What's the matter?"

"Are you young Mrs Jessop?" Norman asked.

"Yes."

He walked his muddy boots across the little front garden to the open window.

"Name's Norman Grayling. Your husband's had a bump in his car. He'll be all right—cut his forehead a bit. He asked me to drop these off. They've taken him to the hospital to be stitched." He handed the three muddy bags through the window to an ashen-faced Susan, before climbing back in his tractor and driving away.

Henry drove forward a little before reversing into the drive.

Susan shut the window, and was at the kitchen door as Diana approached.

Susan unpacked the bags quickly and pushed the muddy, blood-stained boxes into the waste bin. The inner bags of dried milk were intact. She transferred the powder into a plastic box, retaining the directions from one packet that wasn't too badly damaged.

Diana dispatched Henry to the hospital with strict instructions to phone as soon as he knew anything. Both she and Susan wanted to go with him but agreed it wouldn't be right to take Emma out in the cold weather. It seemed worries were never far away.

Susan's decision to bottle feed had been a surprise, but

was no more than a vague question in the back of her mind. As she stepped into the kitchen she heard Emma crying.

"Would you make up a bottle, please, Diana?" called Susan. "Everything's there."

"Of course. You go upstairs and see to her." Diana put the kettle on and read the instructions carefully, delighted to have been given something to do. Emma's cries had stopped and within a few minutes she was on her way upstairs with the bottle.

"Here we are. You sit in your chair, Susan."

Emma nestled in the crook of her mother's arm, sucking contentedly on the teat.

"She wouldn't have the dummy." Susan kept her eyes on her baby. "She pushed it straight out with her tongue."

"Some babies won't. Roy never did. He cried for the first two months and then found his thumb."

"It's all my fault." Susan stifled a sob.

"What is? What do you mean?" Diana quickly knelt at her side.

"I should have stayed in hospital. They could have helped me with the feeding and Emma wouldn't have lost so much weight, and Roy wouldn't have gone out to buy bottles, and he wouldn't be in hospital." Her tearful, blotchy face looked up. "What if he dies? I'll have killed him. What have I done? I'm no good as a wife, and no good as a mother. I'm just a stupid girl. It's all gone wrong. You must hate me."

Diana blinked. Any resentment she may have felt against Susan evaporated in a second.

"Listen to me, Susan. Roy will be all right. You're the best thing that ever happened to our family. We all love you, and you'll be a super mum. You had a hard time of it but you're home now, and Roy will be here soon. You have a healthy baby. What more could any of us want?"

Emma paused in her feeding. Air bubbles rushed noisily into the bottle before she continued her rhythmic sucking. Susan took a deep breath, sighing away her tears and wiping her cheeks with a forearm.

Diana shifted, sitting sideways, next to the nursing chair.

"When I came home from hospital with Roy I was terrified. The war was on and he was quite small. Five pounds two ounces, he weighed. My family lived in Sheffield and they were being bombed a fair bit. No-one warns you about how you'll feel, suddenly so responsible for this little person who is so entirely dependent upon you. It's frightening. No-one gives you a book and says, 'Here you are, this is what you do with a baby'."

Susan gave a thin smile. "Did you think about having more?"

"More than thought about it. I had four miscarriages after Roy. Maybe, these days, they could have done something about it. But not then. Roy's very special to us."

"He's everything to me. He wants more children. We talked about it in France. Madame Fournier made us laugh. She said, *'You will 'ave lots of babies'.*"

Diana drew breath, but stopped herself from asking if Susan would like more. It was too soon to think of that.

Emma sucked on the air of an empty bottle.

"Here, let me take her. It's about time I had a cuddle. You can get dressed and then we'll see about lunch. Henry and Roy will be back soon."

* * * *

Not in a million years could Henry have guessed he would be waiting for Roy in the Casualty Department. Not that day. The nurse had assured him he would be called when he could see his son. His hands shook as he recalled the sight of the Spitfire, upside down in the hedge.

As it had turned out, Diana had been right to persuade him to have the day off—more than she could have known. Susan had looked so pale, and now there was some question of Roy staying in hospital. Suspected concussion, the nurse had said, and told him to wait until Roy's head had been stitched. What the hell had he been doing out shopping, anyway? They had everything they needed for the baby. Roy had said so only the day before when Diana had asked him.

"Mr Jessop."

Henry stood up quickly and followed the nurse, passing six or more cubicles before she swished aside the curtains that concealed his son.

A chill ran from his head to his feet, draining the saliva from his mouth.

"Bloody hell, Roy. Whatever happened?" Henry never swore in front of his wife, but had she been there, he might have slipped up.

"It's not as bad as it looks, Dad. Did the farmer take the milk to Susan?"

"What?"

"The farmer. I think he said his name was Norman."

"Oh, yes. Yes, he was at the cottage with some shopping."

"The doctor wants me to stay in overnight."

"How do you feel?"

"Okay, until I try to lift my head off the pillow."

"You're going to have a bloody great scar on your forehead. I don't know what your mother will say."

"Or Susan. I'll need clean clothes to go home in. I daren't let Susan see these rags. She'll have a fit."

"Susan wanted to come, so did your mum, but I persuaded them to stay in the warm. Bloody good job I did, too. No point bringing little Emma out. What were you doing at the shops, anyway?"

"Keep your voice down, Dad. I went to buy bottles for Emma. Susan couldn't have come with you. She would need to get all the stuff organised."

"I thought she was going to...you know?"

"She was. It's a long story. Well, not long, but she's not, not now. I went to the chemist in Seacroft and was on my way back when this happened." He put his hand to his forehead and winced.

"Your car's buggered."

"It doesn't shuprise me," he slurred. "The poleesh shed they'd shend it to a garage."

"I think I'll push off, son. Your mum and Susan will want

to know how you are. We'll phone later, and I'll come back tomorrow." Henry stopped speaking. Roy was asleep.

He almost ran to the staff nurse's desk. "I think you should come. I don't like the look of him and he's fallen asleep." He followed her back to the cubicle, trying to keep pace with her shapely legs and black stockings. Her flat shoes didn't do them justice. The sound of Roy being sick jolted him to the seriousness of the situation, and a wave of guilt passed over him. His step faltered as the curtain closed between him and the stockings and the sick.

The leather seat of his car gave a comfortable ride as Henry considered how best to word his report to Diana and Susan. They would know soon enough just how bad his injuries were, but at least they wouldn't see all the blood. Christ Almighty, but that had shaken him.

The curves of the road switched the sun from side to side. He lowered the sun visor against the glare. Brake lights ahead slowed him until he came to a standstill. He drummed his fingers on the steering wheel. After several minutes he realised no traffic was coming through in the opposite direction. Someone sounded a horn. He sighed, and considered turning off the engine but the heater was keeping his feet nice and warm, so he let it run. Thoughts of Diana's chicken casserole made his stomach rumble. He should have phoned from the hospital. They would be expecting him to bring Roy home.

The deep growl of a powerful engine brought his attention to the road ahead. A low-loader lorry, its yellow lights flashing, came towards him. His stomach fell. White knuckles gripped the steering wheel as he attempted to still the tremors that jangled every nerve in his body. The contorted wreck that had been Roy's Spitfire took away all thoughts of food. It hadn't looked so bad in the hedge. The car was a write-off and Roy was lucky to be alive.

The car immediately in front of him set off slowly. Henry took off the handbrake and selected drive in the automatic gear box.

Diana's anxious face peered from the window.

He waved and saw her anxiety turn into a frown.

Susan's pale face stared at him as he wiped his feet on the doormat. For once, Diana said nothing. He had been expecting a torrent of questions.

"Sorry I forgot to phone. He'll be home tomorrow. Nasty gash on his head and a bit of concussion. Nothing to worry about."

"I was about to ring the hospital," Diana said. The accusation came across loud and clear. Years of experience told him he was in the dog house. She wouldn't say too much in front of Susan but there was no mistaking that brittle edge.

"Yes, well, I said I'm sorry. I told Roy we'd phone later to see how he was, and I'll go back in the morning to pick him up."

"So he'll definitely be home tomorrow?" Susan asked.

"I presume so. There didn't seem much wrong with him to me."

The two women looked at each other.

"I'll phone the hospital now, Susan." Diana left the room, closing the door behind her.

Henry looked straight at Susan. "Sorry, love. I should've phoned."

"Don't worry, Henry. I'm sure he'll be all right. Would you like some lunch? It's still in the oven, keeping warm."

"Just a little portion, then. I don't have much appetite."

"That's not like you. Are you all right?"

"Of course I am. Never better. When I've had a bite to eat, I'd like to see young Emma."

Diana's voice could be heard coming from the hall. Her words were indistinct, but the pitch grew disturbingly high. As she came back into the kitchen, Henry's fork suspended between his plate and open mouth. He was in for it. The nurse must've told her about all the blood.

"It seems you're right, Henry." Sounding calm and relaxed, there was even a hint of warmth in her voice. He hadn't been expecting that.

His fork completed its journey and he savoured the tender chicken. "That was grand. Is there any more in the pot,

Susan?" With his appetite restored, Henry wiped the corners of his mouth on a napkin. Thoughts of treacle sponge pudding and a nap filled his head—after he had had a little cuddle with Emma, of course.

"What did they say?" Susan asked.

"Just that he's doing well. He's in a ward now. They want to monitor him for twenty-four hours, that's all. He should be home tomorrow afternoon. Although I should warn you Susan, he's had fourteen stitches in his forehead and twelve in his leg."

"I knew it had to be more than a little bump with all that mud and blood on the shopping bags. I put them in the waste bin."

"Henry, I want you to go home and fetch some overnight things for me."

"What about my pudding?" he spluttered. "And I'd like to see my granddaughter, if you don't mind." He didn't understand why Diana sounded so overwrought. Little Emma was perfect and Roy would be home the next day, so why all the fuss?

"Yes. Yes, of course. There's no immediate hurry, I suppose."

"You don't have to stay," Susan said. "I'll be all right now the bottles are sorted out."

"I know," Diana said. "But in the early hours, if Emma won't settle, you may be glad of some company. It's just for one night."

"Is that okay with you, Henry?" Susan asked.

He shrugged.

"You can go to work tomorrow, as usual," Diana said. "And I'll phone you at the office when Roy's ready to come home. That way you're already in town and Roy will be home more quickly."

Henry's shoulders sagged in defeat, but then his spirits lifted as Susan served the treacle sponge and custard. "I'll need to take him some clothes. His are a bloody mess."

"Henry!"

"I mean they're covered in blood, my dear."

Later that night, as Diana lay awake in the guest bedroom, she reflected on the day's events. Had Henry played down the extent of Roy's injuries to stop her worrying? Was he trying to protect Susan from the truth? Or had he, as she suspected, simply got it all wrong? The staff nurse on the ward had advised against visiting. Roy had been vomiting, and lost a lot of blood. He'd had a transfusion and was being carefully monitored. She couldn't have told Susan all that. The good news was that if he improved as was expected, he would be allowed home on the morrow, and so, when she'd come off the phone she had been able to truthfully say that Henry was right.

Diana marvelled at her daughter-in-law, understanding the earlier flood of emotion. Susan had sought to protect her from the extent of Roy's injuries by hiding the carrier bags, and blamed herself for them. Meanwhile, the dear girl needed cosseting.

CHAPTER SEVEN

Susan rushed forward and hugged Roy as Diana gasped in horror.

"I'm all right. Really, I am. It looks worse than it feels."

"You look like Frankenstein," Susan giggled.

Diana flopped into a chair with her head in hands.

"Come on, Mum, there's no need to be so dramatic," Roy said over Susan's shoulder.

"Pull yourself together, Diana," Henry cajoled her, his hand rubbing her back with affection. "The lad's all right, isn't he?" He fumbled in his pocket, and produced a screwed up piece of paper. "Here are the instructions. A list of things to watch out for."

Diana looked up and took the list from him, reading it intently before passing the paper to Susan.

"Have you seen this, Roy?" Susan asked. He shook his head. "Okay. If you're sick, or dizzy, or have a severe headache, or are light sensitive, or go into a deep sleep, I have to take you back to the hospital. Otherwise, you just need to rest. Although, how I'll take you to hospital if you're asleep, I don't know. So that's both of us being told to take it easy." She tilted her head towards the hall. "And if I'm not mistaken, our daughter's waking up. Perhaps someone should tell Emma that her parents are a pair of wrecks."

Over the following week Roy's accident caused something of a role reversal. Instead of Roy caring for Susan, she looked after him. So far there had been no problems. She had no complaints. In fact, she could already see she had been in danger of feeling sorry for herself, and the accident had given her a jolt. Diana called every day but Susan made sure there was nothing for her to do. Nurse Valerie had called and told her she shouldn't be lifting Emma until she had healed a bit more. Susan listened to the advice, and ignored it. What was she supposed to do? Wake Roy up and ask him to lift her out of the cot? Not very practical. Roy slept a lot but not in a way that worried her. He wasn't unconscious or anything.

She gave Emma her bottles day and night, changed her and winded her. Her need to know Emma was safe was far greater than her need for sleep, and she preferred to watch over her rather than risk not waking up if she should cry.

Fifteen pink congratulation cards arrived from Ireland. Patrick, Maggie, Rose, Alf and Hettie, and even Sam Braithwaite, all sent their greetings and congratulations. A parcel containing a delightful little dress and matching bonnet arrived from France with cards from Jeanette and Anton, and Chaz and Jérôme. Diana put a birth announcement in the Yorkshire Post, and Billy Oldroyd and Johnnie Frogett, customers at the Threlfalls ever since she could remember, had left a card at the auction rooms with two ten pound notes. Emma was one week old, and already Susan couldn't imagine life without her.

She liked Henry and Diana. In fact, she more than liked them, she loved them. They were her family, along with the O'Malley's, the Fourniers, and Jimmy and Jill—all of them so much more than friends.

Jimmy and Jill were due to arrive any minute, and Susan hastily applied some make-up and a dash of lipstick.

Thoughts of her mum were never far away since Emma had been born. At the thought of her, her mood darkened with regret, wishing her mum and dad could see their granddaughter. For all his faults, her dad had loved her in his own way. When the weather picked up a bit she would take Emma to Ireland. Gran would like that.

The sound of a car door being slammed interrupted her train of thought and took her to the window. Jimmy and Jill had arrived, carrying several parcels, all wrapped with pink paper and ribbon.

* * * *

"Do go through. Roy's in the lounge giving Emma her bottle," Roy heard Susan say.

Jill gasped as she went in.

"Christ, man," Jimmy said, "what happened to you?"

They relayed the story of the past week, each giving their own perspective.

"So I could say you were both in stitches," Jimmy quipped.

"Don't make me laugh, Jimmy." Susan held her stomach. "It hurts." She took Emma from Roy. "I'll just take her upstairs and change her. You can come with me if you like, Jill."

With the females on their way to the nursery, the two men exchanged serious glances.

"I haven't said much to Susan. It's no good thinking about what might have happened, but I was lucky."

"What about the car?"

"Haven't seen it. Not since the accident. It's up to the insurers, but a sports car is no good for a family man. I had every intention of changing it."

Jimmy nodded in agreement. "What will you go for?"

"An estate car, I think. Maybe a Volvo."

"That's certainly different."

"The immediate problem is that I've been told not to drive for two weeks, and Susan can't drive for another five weeks because of her operation. We'll have to rely on my parents. It's the one disadvantage of living out in the sticks."

"Jill and I still aim to move to York. Jill's done a bit of painting at Vine Street, and I've put a few screws in the staircase to stop it creaking. That sort of thing."

"Will you marry—you and Jill?"

"There's no rush. It's up to her. She still isn't speaking to her mum."

"That's a shame. My mum fusses a lot, but she's been a big help."

"Susan likes her, doesn't she?"

"Yes. What's Jill's mum like?"

"She's okay with me face to face, but Jill says she thinks I'm not good enough, and that she's a snob. I haven't seen her since they fell out."

"I suppose I'm lucky not having a mother-in-law." Roy linked his fingers and twiddled his thumbs around each other.

Jimmy looked directly at him. "You would have liked Susan's mum."

"I'm sure I would. I was forgetting you knew her."

"She was a good friend to my mum. Susan looks just like Auntie Siobhan."

The conversation paused, and the room fell to a comfortable silence, until Susan and Jill came downstairs to join them.

"She's asleep," Susan said. "I've put her in the dining room to be sure I hear her when she wakes."

"Do you think you've changed, Susan?" Jimmy asked.

With a sideways movement of her leg, Jill kicked him.

"It's all right, Jill," Susan said. "Jimmy can ask me anything. The answer has to be 'yes', doesn't it? Of course I've changed. Everything has changed, and for the better."

"It's just that I never imagined you as a mum."

"Me neither. I have to pinch myself to know it's true." Susan blinked and looked towards Roy before turning her attention to the pile of pink parcels. "Now, what have we here?" She ripped at the paper like a child on Christmas day, revealing a teddy bear, a rag doll, and a dress. Delight lit her face with childlike happiness.

The afternoon passed in amiable conversation. Susan made sandwiches and a pot of tea. Jimmy and she laughed about their childhood together, telling the others how they used to play in Vine Street, and of the door in the bedroom that used to connect to Granny Florrie's house.

"You know Susan and I were born on the same day? Our mums were on the same ward," Jimmy said.

"I didn't know that!" said Susan. "I thought they met in the playground when we were at Elder Road Juniors."

Jimmy shook his head. "Mum told me. They didn't become friends until we were at school, but she remembered your mum from the hospital."

"How weird. I never knew. Do you remember Miss

Hughes?"

"I do. She was lovely, in her old-fashioned way."

"She knew Alf." Susan's face fell as almost-buried memories threatened to surface. Jimmy clearly saw it. A shadow crossed his face. They had shared so much—too much. Some things would never be a topic of conversation. Jill and Roy didn't seem to notice.

"I've brought my camera." Jimmy brightened. "When Emma wakes I'd like to take some photographs. I could send a print to Chaz."

* * * *

Diana wished she could drive. The bus service from Barwick-in-Elmet to Leeds was both infrequent and unreliable.

Experience had taught her the best time to broach a controversial subject with Henry was just after breakfast.

He put his paper down and lifted his cup from its saucer, so she took her chance. "I'm thinking of learning to drive."

His jaw dropped so far and so quickly he almost lost his upper denture.

"I said, drive, Henry. Not fly."

"But why? Where do you want to go?"

"Nowhere in particular, but it would be nice to have a little car. I could go to see Emma if the weather were bad and you were at work." Henry continued to stare at her as if she were mad. "I could do the supermarket shopping on my own." She saw his eyebrows raise a little, for he hated the weekly chore. "I could pop into town and not have to rely on the buses."

He put his cup back on the saucer and leaned back, his hands before him, fingertip to fingertip. "It wouldn't be easy for you, at your age. The roads are very busy these days."

"Henry!"

"But—"

"I was thinking of learning in an automatic, so I wouldn't have to worry about gears."

"You've given it quite bit of thought, then?"

"Yes, and I thought you'd be all for it."

Henry stood up quickly. "Put your coat on."

Diana was too surprised to say anything. Spontaneity from Henry was unheard of.

"Where are we going?"

"Not far." She noted his serious face and tried to guess what he was thinking. She knew him so well and yet, right at that moment, she couldn't read his thoughts at all.

Within minutes they were travelling towards Leeds. He indicated left and they turned into a garage forecourt. Rows of second-hand cars, with prices pasted to their windscreens, stood neatly to attention, like soldiers awaiting orders. Henry drove on to the back of the garage where the ground was muddy. Surely he wasn't going to park there and expect her to walk back to the forecourt? It was a scrap yard. Bits of cars were stacked up all over the place. He slowed to a halt. "Look around, Diana. What do you see?"

"A mess. An untidy mess. Why have you brought me here? Aren't we going to look at the cars?"

"Look at the one in front of you."

She stared for a few seconds and then dropped her face into her hands. The sight of Roy's Spitfire took her breath away. She gasped for air, her hand patting her chest.

"I don't want you to drive, Diana. I'd never know a moment's peace if you were out on the road."

"Take me home NOW!"

Henry reversed, executing a three-point turn before driving back to the road. As they travelled the familiar route Diana noticed a battered section of hedge. Pale branches, stripped of their bark, contrasted with the dullness of the hedge and the field beyond.

"Is that where...?" Her voice was calm, almost a whisper.

He nodded. She hated the casual manner of chance, and the way it nonchalantly changed lives. She could have felt cross with Henry, but in the short journey she had seen a different side of him, a side that quelled her anger. Henry must have been badly shaken when he'd seen the car in the hedge. He must have seen it on his way to the hospital and she realised he had minimised Roy's injuries to protect her and Susan from knowing what might have been. With everything that had happened, and her staying the night with Susan, she had forgotten to be angry with him.

The intense emotions of the twenty-four hours surrounding Emma's birth had affected them all. Only at the distance of a week later, could she see that they all had each other's well-being at heart. She had a lot to be thankful for, and if the thought of her driving upset Henry, she wouldn't bother with it.

* * * *

The vast expanse of the Volvo bonnet spread before him. The contrast with the Spitfire could not have been greater. Roy felt as if he were driving a tank. His close brush with death had been something of a catalyst, bringing into sharp focus his mortality and the thin line between life and death.

He could have returned to the office the previous week, but hadn't wanted to go with stitches in his head looking—as Susan had put it—like Frankenstein. Inwardly, he admitted he had enjoyed being at home with her and Emma. He had waited for two hours at the hospital to have his stitches removed, for a job that took only five minutes. At least the wound on his leg didn't show. His dad would be thinking he'd gone home.

Miss Tanner had opened his mail and set it out in three piles on his desk. The pile to the left, she explained, could wait. The pile in the middle was sale catalogues for his perusal, and the pile to the right needed his attention. She brought him a cup of coffee, making no comment about his scar, for which he was extremely grateful. "Good to have you back, Mr Roy."

Turning the pages of his diary, he noted she had booked in three valuations, and there was an auction in Selby on Friday. The normality of the room came as a welcome change. He worked his way through the right-hand pile of mail. Miss Tanner knew which clients expected a personal response. She was good at her job.

Susan was doing a good job as a mother, and Emma was thriving. With the turmoil of the first week behind them, life at Orchard Cottage glided into routine. He would have been happy to do his share of the night feeds, but Susan always saw to it.

He had been reluctant to leave them after breakfast. His appointment at the hospital had forced him into town, but now he was at work he was glad to be back. Looking across the room to his father's desk piled high with paperwork, he shook his head. How anyone could work in such chaos was beyond him, and yet Jessop's Auctioneers was a successful business.

Familiar footsteps climbed the stairs. "Ah. Good to see you back, son. I saw your coat on the stand. How are your lovely wife and my beautiful granddaughter?"

"Both well, thanks, Dad."

"I must say you look better without the embroidery." Henry chuckled.

"Okay, okay, very funny. Now for some work. Anything to tell me?"

"No, I don't think so. Brenda's kept the wheels turning. Speaking of which, how's the new car?"

"Different. Everything's different." Roy saw a frown cross his father's face. "Don't look so worried. Everything's fine."

"Oh, yes, quite. I know how a baby changes everything."

"I was ready for the changes brought about by Emma. I didn't know babies changed cars, though." He smiled and opened the first catalogue, fixing his eyes on the list of paintings. "You and Mum have been fantastic. You do know that, don't you? Susan and I are very grateful."

Henry coughed and shuffled some papers.

Roy thought he saw the trace of a blush at his collar, and returned his eyes to the catalogue.

* * * *

Susan had been looking forward to having the house to herself. Emma had been fed and changed and was sleeping soundly. The breakfast dishes were in the sink. A bucket of nappies needed washing and there was a pile of ironing on the dining room table, but they could all wait. She threw her dressing gown to the floor. Making sure the bedroom doors were wide open, her head sank gratefully into the pillow. The duvet snuggled around her in heavenly luxury. An hour would do it, if only her head would stop spinning. She worried she might not wake when Emma cried. She worried about keeping the house tidy. She feared Diana and Henry would think she wasn't good enough. Her mind leapt from one worry to another in rapid, disjointed thought, making her head ache. Mental and physical exhaustion joined forces, and she drifted from daydreaming to dozing, and then to shallow, flickering sleep.

Emma lay in the big old pram at the Threlfalls, sleeping soundly as smoke curled around the wheels and up over the sides. Susan watched as her mother gently rocked the pram. Her wraith-like figure smiled before fading into the smoke…

She sat bolt upright, jolted from her sleep. A glance at the bedside clock told her she had been asleep for no more than ten minutes. She dashed to Emma's room to find her daughter sleeping soundly.

Nappies fluttered in the back garden, and the washing machine was spinning another load when Diana called around. Susan had showered, dressed and put on her make-up. Switching off the iron, she filled the kettle. "Take a seat in the lounge, Diana. Emma will be waking soon and you can give her a bottle, if you like."

"Are you sure I can't do anything else?" Diana sounded disappointed. "I could iron a few shirts."

"No, it's all right. I can manage. I like to iron Roy's shirts. If I came to your house you wouldn't let me iron Henry's shirts, now, would you?"

"Of course I wouldn't. You're quite right. I don't mean to interfere."

"You weren't, but if my ears are right, Emma's waking up. I'll warm a bottle while you bring her downstairs."

Love poured from grandmother to granddaughter. Anyone would think Diana had had six children the way she held her so confidently. Emma relaxed in the arms of her grandmother, enjoying the comfort of the milk. "There's a mother and baby group at the village hall tomorrow morning. You could pop along and meet a few of the other mums."

Susan hesitated. "I'm not sure that's my sort of thing."

"It's up to you, of course, but with Roy back at work you might find country life rather boring."

"I don't think there's much chance of boredom. Looking after Emma takes most of my time, along with all the washing and ironing and housework. When the better weather comes I'm going to have a go at gardening. I actually quite like the countryside—I especially like Provence. There's plenty to do here and, anyway, Emma sleeps most of the morning. Maybe I'll think about it when she's a bit older. I'll have the all clear for driving soon, so we can go into town. Don't worry about me, Diana. I'm fine. Really I am." She felt as if she were gabbling, and closed her mouth.

"If you say so, but you know where we are if you need us. Henry and I go to the supermarket once a week. You can always give me a list if you want anything."

The sound of sucking air drew Diana's attention to Emma. She put the empty bottle on the coffee table and in one movement, raised the baby to a sitting position.

"I'll take her back upstairs." Susan took her. "I'm sure you have lots to do."

"Yes, yes. I'll be off. You don't want me under your feet."

Before Susan could protest, she had gone, closing the door behind her. From the window, she watched her mother-in-law's receding figure walk briskly down the lane. She was glad she had gone, and hated herself for it. A pang of jealously clenched her teeth as she thought of Roy back at work. Back to normality. A mixture of tears, mascara and foundation smeared her skin. She sniffed and put Emma in her cot before returning to the ironing. At least when she was on her own she didn't have to pretend to be happy.

CHAPTER EIGHT

March 1970

Maurice Cawthorne couldn't recall ever having lied to his wife before. There were things he hadn't told her, but he had never actually lied. He hadn't mentioned Jill's phone call to his office staff, or that he was meeting her for lunch. He had told Anthea he was going to his tailor—which he was not. Looking around, he noticed, for the first time, the red, white and green decor of the Italian restaurant. Bizarre shapes of wax had melted down the Mateus Rose wine bottles which served as candle holders.

Once upon a time he had admired Anthea for her standards but, at that moment, he despised her for them. They were the sole cause of this dreadful fallout with Jill. She had said she might be a little late. Drumming his fingers on the marble-topped table, he shifted his weight on the wrought iron chair.

Anthea's friends were unlikely to go there. The place was too informal for their taste. A quick scan of the clientele confirmed his opinion.

He had never thought of himself as an observant person, and hadn't seen Jill enter the restaurant but, as she approached the table, his eyes were drawn to the plain band of gold on the third finger of her left hand. He felt the blood drain from his face, his jaw drop, and the weight of Anthea's wrath drop onto his shoulders.

"You look a bit pale, Dad. Are you okay? Mum hasn't been nagging you about me, has she?" Jill took a seat opposite him, resting her hands on her lap.

"N-no. Nothing like that."

"What, then? You look as if you've seen a ghost."

"Is it real, I mean, is it a real one?"

"Is what real?"

"Your wedding ring?"

She didn't reply straightaway, just looked into his eyes,

blinking rapidly. Lifting her hands to the table, she turned the shining ring with the fingers of her right hand, and pushed her engagement ring up to it tightly.

"Yes, Dad. Jimmy and I were married this morning at the registry office in Leeds." She spoke softly.

A waiter gave them each a menu.

Maurice accepted the card with trembling hands. "Dear God in heaven."

"I hope you and Mum can be happy for us." She paused. "It's not like you to refer to the Almighty, Dad. You're not religious, and neither is Mum. The whole idea of the big church wedding thing, you know—I didn't want it."

Maurice leaned back on his chair, rubbing his hand over his mouth in involuntary gesture. "No, I don't know. Your mother always says that when the ungodly pray it's already too late for divine intervention. And she's right. It's too late for any intervention, isn't it? Godly or otherwise."

"Jimmy and I are happy. We're looking for a house in York. In fact, he's scouring the estate agents now. I'm meeting him in an hour, so we'd better order some food."

"I'm sorry, love. I seem to have lost my appetite. I wish you and Jimmy well but, you see, from the day you were born I've dreamed of walking down the aisle with you, and now that'll never happen."

"Oh, come on, Dad. There's no need for histrionics. It's not as if I've died or something."

"No. But you're our only child. You mean everything to us and…"

"And you wanted me to have the wedding you and Mum wanted, not what I wanted."

Maurice saw her eyes glisten, her jaw set with determination. He saw her swallow back the temper which, as a child, she hadn't been able to control. He saw that she had wanted to tell him kindly, and that he'd pre-empted her plan by noticing the ring. Maybe if she had worn gloves, or he simply hadn't noticed, their meeting could have been different, and he could have stayed on good terms with her. But that wasn't how it had happened. He was acutely aware that an invisible line had been crossed and he'd lost her.

"I do hope you and Jimmy are happy, but I have to go home to tell your mother."

"And I'll tell you exactly what she'll say. First on her mind will be, 'Oh Maurice, what will our friends say?' Then it'll be, 'Is she pregnant?' Thirdly, 'How could she do this to us?'"

The waiter returned, order pad and pen in hand.

Maurice felt tired. The truth of her words made a heavy burden. He stood up, squeezed her shoulder with an affectionate grip, and left.

Maurice revved his engine before switching off the ignition and pulling on the handbrake. Heavy feet carried him to the house, knowing that Anthea would be waiting for him, and his news would release a torrent of vitriol. He'd once asked how she knew when he arrived home, and she had explained that she was familiar with the sound of his car engine. It had to be true, because, no matter how quietly he pulled into the drive, she was always standing in the kitchen with her fingers splayed on the table. He had fleetingly thought of changing his car and not telling her, just for the hell of walking into the house undetected. But then he balanced it against the inquisition for making such a large purchase on his own, and decided it wasn't worth the hassle. He would be in for some hassle now.

Anthea was standing in the kitchen in her usual pose. "Look, Maurice. An invitation to Caroline Dean-Fellowes' wedding. It's at the Minster, and afterwards at Fellingham Country Club. She's marrying that M.P. fellow, you know, what's his name?" She looked at the card. "That's it. Charles Xavier Hetherington. Isn't it wonderful? I shall need a new outfit. You'll have to buy a morning suit. When you go back to your tailor you can order one. It'll come in for Jill's wedding." She seemed to notice his discomfort. "What's the matter? Aren't you well?"

"I'm perfectly well, dear. Sit down. I have something to tell you." He pulled a chair from the table, scraping it across the floor, knowing the noise would annoy her, but not caring.

He sat down heavily.

Anthea's face creased to a frown. She sat opposite him, her hands clasped together on the table.

He was aware he had her attention, that his manner conveyed he had something important to say, and that she knew she wouldn't like it.

He put his head in his hands. "Jill and Jimmy were married this morning at the registry office in Leeds." He heard her chair creak a little and her breath leave her with a groan as if it were her last. A palpable silence followed and he dared to look up. Her eyes were closed, her forehead creased, her lips set in the ugly lines of grief.

"And you were invited, but not me?" Her words were a monotone of controlled anger.

"No, Anthea. I wasn't there. You mustn't think that." Maurice was horrified, but he wasn't going to be the butt of even more anger than he deserved. "I went to meet her for lunch, I admit. But I had no idea."

"Is she pregnant?"

"I don't know."

"I suppose he was with her, showing off that he had taken her from under our noses. That nobody of a boy."

"No. He wasn't. I think she said he'd gone to the estate agents. They're looking for a house in York."

He wished she would cry, or show some sort of normal reaction, instead of all the hate, hate, hate.

"How could she do this to us? Whatever have we done to deserve this, Maurice? I ask you."

He shook his head in resignation.

"So you didn't go to your tailor, then?"

"No. I admit I misled you there, Anthea, and for that I apologise."

"I suppose they'll buy some awful, little terraced house in the student area. I'll never be able to hold my head up in society again. I shall reply to the Dean-Fellowes and say we are unfortunately away at the time of the wedding. We'll send a gift of course. We shall have to book a holiday."

* * * *

"How did it go?" Jimmy asked.

She shook her head. "We didn't have lunch. He was too preoccupied with how he was going to break the news to my mother to say anything much." She threw her head back in feigned defiance, her red hair falling about her shoulders.

"No regrets?"

"None. How did it go at the estate agents?"

"Very well. We have three houses to look at this afternoon. One in Haxby and two on Huntington Road. I have the details in my rucksack. Are you sure you want to do this?"

"Of course I am. This is a happy day, Jimmy. A day for looking forward, not back. Where are we going first?"

"Huntington Road. One's occupied, and I have a key for the other. The one in Haxby is empty."

"I thought we agreed to look for somewhere in York. Haxby is a little way out." Jill sipped her coffee.

"I know, but it's to the north of the city, and not far from work. I liked the look of it." Jimmy released the clips on his rucksack and took some papers from an envelope. "What do you think?"

She took the papers. Her eyes widened in delight. The picture of an old stone house with mullioned windows had a solid look about it. "It looks gorgeous. Bigger than I thought. Can you afford it?"

"You mean can *we* afford it, Mrs Hanson. It needs some modernisation, so the answer to your question is yes, but the modernisation will have to wait. It all depends on whether we could live in it as it is for a while."

"What about the houses on Huntington Road?"

He passed her the remaining contents of the envelope, and watched as she looked through them. "Do you want something to eat?"

Engrossed in her reading, she didn't answer straightaway, then, "Sorry. Did you say something?"

"I asked if you wanted something to eat. You said you didn't have anything with your dad, and I could do with something. How about a wedding breakfast in a coffee bar?"

Jill laughed. "Okay, why not?"

The first house they viewed on Huntingdon Road was a typical nineteen twenties semi-detached. It had three bedrooms, a bathroom, kitchen, lounge and dining room, and the owner was keen to point out the solid brick construction. They looked around under the close scrutiny of Miss Falstaff, who told them she had lived there all her life, and was making a heart-wrenching move to Bournemouth to look after her widowed sister.

They thanked her as they left.

Back in the car they looked at each other and burst out laughing.

"I couldn't live there." Jill giggled. "I'd be afraid of becoming as boring as the walls."

Jimmy took her hand and kissed it. "I can't imagine you ever being boring."

They drove a little further and parked outside the next house on their list. It had a small front garden and, from the outside, looked similar to Miss Falstaff's house, but inside was a different story. This house had a new kitchen and bathroom, and although of similar age and dimensions, it had a bright, clean air to it.

"I could live here," Jill said, as she wandered around the ground floor." Her footsteps on bare floorboards echoed around the empty rooms.

"Me, too, but there's a problem," said Jimmy, standing in the large bay at the front of the house. "There's no drive. Nowhere to park, only on the road. Not many people owned a car at the time these houses were built."

"I suppose we could knock down part of the garden wall and park on the lawn," Jill suggested.

"Maybe. But this is only the second house we've looked at. There's no hurry. I don't want us to buy somewhere and then want to move in a couple of years."

"You're right. Come on. I'd like to be in Haxby before dark."

Jimmy locked the door and they set off, driving north,

and away from the city. "We could call to see Susan on our way back. It's not far out of our way."

"Should we phone first?" Jill was busy reading the information from the estate agents "She might not be at home."

"She won't mind if we just pop in, and if she's out I'll put a note through the letter box to say we called. I haven't seen her for weeks, not since just after Emma was born." Jimmy smiled broadly. "I think she might be interested to know we were married today."

"Do you think she'll be annoyed we didn't invite her?"

He laughed. "Probably."

Jill returned her attention to the description of the house in Haxby. They would be there soon and would know whether the description lived up to reality.

* * * *

Stone architecture gave a reassuring timelessness to the town centre of Ilkley. The triangular flowerbed that served as a roundabout filtered the traffic of three roads. With Susan at his side, and Emma in her carrycot on the back seat, Roy followed the signpost to Leeds. The day had been an anniversary of sorts. The last time they had been there they had travelled in the Spitfire, barely boyfriend and girlfriend, and now they were married with a beautiful daughter. So much had happened since the day he and Susan had sold the paintings from the Threlfalls. Good and bad.

Susan had had everything organised—bottles and nappies, clothes and creams. She had taken so naturally to motherhood after what they referred to as a tricky start. It could only be a matter of time before she became more organised at home. He drove with his hand over hers on the gear stick. Her hand felt thinner, almost fragile. As he turned to her pale face, she smiled warmly. Such a wonderful wife. He had no complaints, and yet he worried about her being on her own so much. She had tried the mother and baby group in Barwick, but said they all knew each other and she felt left out.

He had even asked if she would like to move back to town. If only she weren't so thin and pale. His mother had noticed it and he had told her not to worry.

His mind switched to the oil paintings in the back of the car. He had sold one at a good profit, bought two as an investment for himself, and another on behalf of a client. Buying and selling works of art, particularly paintings, was becoming an increasing part of the business, and a part he enjoyed. At the auction he had spoken to Stan Hinton, who had introduced him to Thomas Barraclough. Stan had pointed him out on his last visit to Ilkley, but Roy had had no dealings with him.

"I've told Thomas all about you," Stan had said.

Roy had given him a business card. "Perhaps we could meet another time, Mr Barraclough. I'm here with my family today, a sort of working day out."

Thomas Barraclough had nodded his assent.

Roy was keen to make new contacts in the art world. He saw it as the future. Furniture auctions were changing. Modern houses with fitted furniture had no place for old-fashioned bedroom suites. Big furniture items sold very cheaply, making little commission, and creating a lot of work for shifters. If they specialised in art, and kept the property side of things, Jessops Auctioneers would be much more profitable. He considered how he might broach the subject with his father. It would need careful handling. He didn't want his father to think that because he had made him a partner, he wanted to change things for the sake of it. If his dad insisted on keeping the furniture side of things they would have to be more selective. They couldn't keep shifting pianos that nobody wanted.

Emma had slept for most of the day, her contentment disturbed only by hunger. Daylight had given way to darkness as they turned into the lane. The car parked outside Orchard cottage didn't have any lights on. A figure could be seen pushing something through the letter box.

"Who's that?" Fear clipped Susan's words.

The figure turned and they saw Jimmy's cheerful face in the headlights. He put up one hand to shield his eyes from the glare.

Roy swung the Volvo into the drive, and Susan jumped from the car before it had come to a standstill and ran to hug her old friend.

Ten minutes later Susan was giving Emma a bottle of milk and Roy had made a pot of tea. "So what brings you out of Leeds on a Saturday, then?" Susan asked.

Jill was sitting on her hands. Jimmy took her left arm, and she held her hand forward. "We thought you'd like to know."

Susan's jaw dropped. "Congratulations to you both."

Roy stood up, shook Jimmy by the hand and kissed Jill on the cheek. Emma cried in protest as Susan stood up, so Roy took her and she resumed her feed.

Susan hugged Jimmy, and then Jill. "When was this, then? Why didn't you tell us?"

"This morning, and we didn't tell anyone, so don't be cross. You didn't miss a party." Jimmy grinned. "I'm surprised you didn't notice Jill's ring. You were always so observant."

"What? Not even your parents, Jill?"

"No, not even them. A sore point, I'm afraid, but we do have some other news."

"You're not pregnant?"

Jimmy laughed. "Oh, typical you, Susan. Straight to the point but, no, you're wrong. We've seen a house in Haxby that we're hoping to buy. It's a wreck, but we love it."

"But what about Vine Street? You can't leave number sixteen."

"Why not?" Jimmy looked to Jill and then to Susan in total surprise. "We have no ties to Leeds. York has been our plan for some time. We both work there, and travelling each day is a pain."

"Jimmy's right, Susan." Roy put the empty bottle down and held Emma over his shoulder, rubbing her back. "What's the point in travelling back and forth all the time?" The baby gave a loud burp. "I think Emma agrees." He turned her to face Susan. "I'll take this little lady upstairs. Won't be long."

Susan's face relaxed. "I'm sorry, Jimmy. It's all such a surprise. A nice surprise, but it's just that I never thought about you leaving Vine Street. That house has always been there as part of our lives. I remember going there for the first time for your birthday, and our mums chatting, and my dad being cross when Mum and I were late back. Living in a pub wasn't like having a house. And then there was the door through to Granny Florrie's and, oh I don't know."

"But that's all in the past, Susan. Memories. Good memories, but the past."

Susan blinked rapidly, squeezing her lips together. "Tell me about the house in Haxby. This place was a wreck when we first saw it, so I know what you mean."

Their friends described the house and their ideas for its renovation. When Roy came back downstairs they talked of the work that had been done at Orchard Cottage. The conversation divided, with Jimmy talking to Roy about the practical side of the building work, while Susan and Jill chatted happily about colour schemes and furniture shops.

The girls made sandwiches and more tea and the time slipped by. Shortly before midnight, Jimmy and his new wife said their goodbyes and Susan watched the rear lights of their car disappear down the lane. Tears pricked her eyes. Turning into Roy's arms, she hid her face in his chest.

"Come inside, love. It's cold out here." He released his hold and led her by the hand into the bright lights of the kitchen.

* * * *

"What do you think?" Jimmy asked as he drove.

"I think we've had a lovely day. A very busy day, and perhaps not quite a traditional wedding day, but I've enjoyed every minute of it," she paused. "Well, perhaps not every minute. I wish things had gone better between me and Dad. Inevitable I suppose."

"Do you think I should go and see them some time? I would, if you thought it would help."

"No—not yet, anyway. Maybe when we move to Haxby and we're all sorted out, we could invite them over."

Jimmy took his hand from the steering wheel and sought hers, squeezing it affectionately. "You mean *if* we move to Haxby, Mrs Hanson. I'll phone the estate agents in the morning and put our offer in. Don't set your heart on it too much. There are the surveys to be done and all that stuff. The place may be about to fall down, for all we know."

"Oh, Jimmy. Ever the practical one. Well, I can dream about it. I can think about curtains and carpets and furniture."

Yellow street lights flashed across the car between shadows, glistening on the wet road. The windscreen wipers swished over the noise of the engine. While Jill's imagination furnished the house in Haxby, Jimmy's thoughts returned to his old friend. "What I actually meant was, what did you think about Susan?"

"Susan?" Jill's tone expressed surprise. "She seemed fine to me. Not too cross that we didn't invite her."

"I didn't mean that. You didn't think she seemed a bit strange, then?"

"No more than usual. But you know her better than I do. Maybe she's just tired."

Jimmy stared at the road, eyes focussed, but his deeper thoughts were with his childhood friend. "She seemed not quite with it, sort of distracted, if you know what I mean."

"Not really. But like I say, you know her better than I do. Better than anyone, probably. Even Roy. Are you worried about her?"

"Maybe. Maybe it's my imagination. A lot's happened in the last twelve months, I suppose. Housework isn't her strong point, is it? There was washing piled up everywhere, and the sink was full of dirty dishes when we arrived. I saw Roy quickly load the dishwasher after he put Emma to bed."

"They have a lovely house, and Emma's gorgeous. I wouldn't worry too much, Jimmy."

"Maybe you're right. I've always worried about her. I suppose it's become a habit." He flicked on the indicator and turned into Vine Street. "Home sweet home for my beautiful bride." He parked the car directly outside number sixteen and carried Jill over the threshold. "What do you think of the honeymoon venue, Mrs Hanson?"

"I think it's exactly where I want to be, Mr Hanson."

Jimmy almost dropped her as he slipped on the pile of mail. Laughing together, they picked up the letters.

Jill froze, the laughter falling from her face.

"What is it, love?"

"My father's handwriting."

"Open it, then."

Her shaking hands tore at the envelope. They read the brief note together.

Dearest Jill,

I had hoped to see you but perhaps it is for the best that you are out. At your mother's request I brought your clothes etc. They are in the back yard. I wish you a happy future.

Dad. X

Jill rushed to the back door with Jimmy close behind her. The key was in the lock and she flung the door open. Without a word passing between them they carried the two suitcases and eight cardboard boxes into the house.

"That just about says it all." She looked inside one of the boxes. "She's even sent my school photographs. God knows how he fitted it all in the car."

"I'm sorry, Jill."

"Why should you be sorry?"

"I'm the cause of all this, of you falling out with your parents."

She walked around the boxes that stood between them. Lifting his arms onto her shoulders, she hugged him. "You must never say anything like that again. If Dad's too weak to stand up to her, that's his loss. You and I have everything we want and I have no regrets, not one. For all they knew we might have been away on honeymoon and all my things would have been out in the yard for weeks." She kissed him on the lips and started to giggle.

"What? What's so funny?"

"I was just thinking maybe we do need a bigger house. I don't see all this lot fitting in here."

Jimmy grinned. "Come on, Mrs Hanson, time for bed."

CHAPTER NINE

Orchard Cottage
Barwick-in-Elmet

Dear Chaz,

Sorry I haven't written earlier. Jimmy and Jill called yesterday, and you'll never guess what. They are married. They just went and did it. Their witnesses were people who worked at the registry office. Don't you think that's really romantic? Jill has fallen out with her parents, but I suppose they'll make it up one day when they're over the shock. She pretty much told me that her mum doesn't think Jimmy is good enough. Isn't that horrible? I've never met her but I don't like her. It makes me like Jill more because she's prepared to fall out with them for Jimmy. I'm lucky I suppose, Diana and Henry are really nice.

I seem to be busy all the time with Emma, and cleaning and cooking and washing and ironing. You wouldn't think so if you could see the house, it's always in a mess, no matter how hard I try. It makes me wonder how on earth my mother managed to work in the bar all the time when I was a baby. Your mum would laugh at my attempts at cooking. I go to Diana and Henry's house most days now. It's better than Diana coming here, because I can tell she wants to start tidying up and that makes me feel useless, which I am when it comes to being a housewife. I wish I could sleep more. I'm scared of falling asleep and not hearing Emma cry. Silly of me, I know. The trouble is, when I do fall asleep I have horrible dreams, so it makes me doubly afraid of doing so.

Jimmy and Jill are buying a house in Haxby. They say there is no point in staying in Leeds when they both work in York. They're right, of course, but I can't bear the thought of never going to the house in Vine Street again. Please write soon.

With love from your friend,
Susan. X

Chaz smiled broadly as she read the first part of the letter. Gradually, her face became more serious. She had hoped for a recent photograph of Emma, but there was none. Jimmy had sent a picture soon after she had been taken home, and Roy had had stitches in his forehead. She handed the letter to her mother, who held the flimsy paper in one hand as she stirred a pan of soup.

"Quelle surprise. Jimmy est marié. Il est bon, n'est pas?"

"Wonderful news. When Dad comes home we'll open champagne and toast their marriage. I'll go to Aix on Saturday and buy a gift—something easy to post." Chaz always thought and spoke in English when Jimmy or Susan was the topic of conversation. Her mother spoke a mixture of the two, keen to practise the language she had never truly mastered.

"Good idea, ma petite. Buy somet'ing from all of us. Jimmy is what ze English call a dark 'orse, I t'ink."

"What do you think about Susan not sleeping? That can't be good. And she doesn't mention Roy at all."

"Sometimes I t'ink we will always worry about that girl." Her mother sighed and handed the letter back. She tasted the soup and added some salt. "Maybe you should write to Jimmy and ask 'im. 'E 'as seen her recently."

"You're right, Mum. I'll do that after dinner."

Dear Jimmy and Jill,

Congratulations! I received a letter from Susan today and was delighted with your news. My mum says you are a dark horse, Jimmy! She and Dad send their love. Do you have any photographs? Susan also told me you intend to move to Haxby. It all sounds very exciting. Jérôme and I are house hunting but with no particular hurry. We will be arranging our wedding next year, but haven't fixed a date yet.

When you saw Susan, did she seem all right? She said in her letter she wasn't sleeping well and I don't know why, but it set alarms bells ringing in my head. She was always such a city girl, and I'm not sure that being out in the countryside is good for her. I'm starting to sound like my mother, but maybe that isn't a bad thing. I hope you can tell me I'm wrong about all this.

Mum and Dad say you and Jill are welcome here anytime, but I'm sure you know that already.

Write soon,
With love,
Chaz. X

* * * *

"I worry about them, Henry." Diana refilled his coffee cup.

"Why's that, love?" Henry knew what she meant. His question was more to buy a little time than to seek an answer. He saw Roy almost every day and knew his son was unhappy. He couldn't put a finger on it but the lad didn't smile unless he was talking about Emma. He didn't run up and down the stairs two at a time anymore, and his desk wasn't as tidy as it used to be. He sighed a lot too, as if the burdens of the world were on his shoulders.

"It's hard to say, but it's not right. That much I *do* know. Why does she never want me to help? I walked down there yesterday. She was out, and so I peeped through the windows. Honestly, Henry, you never saw such a tip. The kitchen was in chaos and there was laundry stacked up in front of the washing machine. The ironing board was up in the dining room and the lounge had coffee cups and dirty plates everywhere."

Henry took another mouthful of toast and marmalade to further delay the need to reply.

Diana continued. "Roy can't be happy about it. You know how he likes everything neat and tidy."

"You're right, love, but I don't see what we can do. If you say anything it'll come out that you've been noseying through the windows."

"How could she go out and leave the house in such a mess, I ask you? I expect she'd gone shopping in Leeds."

Henry knew she was right. Susan often called in at the auction rooms, and she and Roy would go out for lunch.

"Give her time, love. It's been a big change for both of them. She likes to wander around the shops, buying things for Emma."

* * * *

Roy was discussing his appointments diary with Miss

Tanner when the revolving doors turned. He looked up to see Susan struggling through with the pram. She wore no make-up and her shoulders sagged beneath a coat that looked too big. He put his arm around her and kissed her cheek, protecting her from the disparaging eyes of the receptionist. She was barely recognisable as the girl he had fallen in love with. Her smile didn't light her face like it used to. Everything had been all right until Emma had been born. Not that he blamed his daughter. He adored her. Without her, he doubted Susan would stay with him. When had everything gone so badly wrong?

He crouched down on his haunches and smiled at Emma, tickling her under her chin. She wriggled in delight, dimpling her fat cheeks. He recognised the pink pram set that had been knitted by Hettie Lawrence. "Good to see you both. Shall we go?"

Susan looked at Brenda over his shoulder. "Yes, please."

"Tell Dad I'll be back later." He grabbed his coat from the stand.

Brenda picked up the phone receiver and passed on his message as Roy manoeuvred the pram through the doors, closely followed by Susan.

"And where would my two favourite girls like to have lunch?"

"I don't think Emma minds where she is as long as she can have her bottle." Susan pushed the pram towards the town centre. "I have everything in the holdall. Her milk will be warm enough. I put it in the thermos flask."

"You're so good, Susan. The perfect mum. Emma always looks lovely."

"But I don't, is that what you mean?" He noticed resignation in her words—a helplessness.

"No, I didn't mean anything of the sort. You're my lovely Susan—my wife." With his hand on the pram handle, he forced it to stop.

Susan looked down at her feet.

"What is it, love?"

She raised her head slowly, her gaze piercing his.

He dreaded her reply. The few seconds of silence seemed to hold the future and he wished he hadn't asked the question.

A wan smile flickered across her lips. "Nothing. I'm a bit tired. That's all." She blinked rapidly. "I'm sorry the house is such a mess. I do try, you know."

"I couldn't care less about the house." As the words left his mouth, he knew them to be true. The untidiness wasn't important. The triviality of it all hit him between the eyes. "Come on. We'll have lunch in Lavell's restaurant and then I want to buy you some new clothes." They set off, walking more quickly, with Roy keeping his hand on the pram handle. A sideways glance detected her frown but he said nothing. He had said enough for one day.

Susan had given Emma her bottle and was settling her back in her pram as the waiter approached with their lunch. Roy watched as she pushed the food around her plate with a fork.

"I'll have to go as soon as I've eaten. I have an appointment in Headingly at half past two and need to call back at the office first." He looked at his watch. "I had hoped they would be a bit quicker here."

"I thought I might drive up there later, to call on Alf and Hettie. That's why I put Emma in the pram set. I thought Hettie would like to see her wearing it."

"I'm sure she would. But before you go, have a look in the ladies' department and try to find a coat you like. You haven't bought anything for yourself for ages."

She looked surprised, as if the thought were inconceivable. "No, I suppose not."

"Do you remember that one you lost on our first date?"

"I bought it in Dublin. Patrick was with me." Her face softened at the memory. "Patrick chose it, really. I was going to buy a black one, but he insisted I bought the blue because it matched my eyes. He said they were gentian. That's a flower, isn't it?"

"Yes, and he was right. Maybe you could find another in the same colour."

Susan picked at her salad.

"No time for a pudding for me." Roy wiped the corners of his mouth with a napkin.

"I haven't seen him for ages."

"Who?"

"Patrick. I might walk round to see if he's in."

"It's a fair walk. Why not drive up, before you go to see Alf and Hettie?" He stood up and kissed her on the cheek. "Must dash. Have you enough money on you to pay the bill?"

She put down her fork. "I'll put it on the account."

Roy took the escalator to the ground floor and walked through the perfume department. Stepping out onto the pavement, dazzling sunshine made him screw up his eyes. He couldn't care less whether it rained or shined. His thoughts were as far from his appointment in Headlingly as they could possibly be. Susan dominated his thoughts. He knew she wasn't eating properly. Emma slept through most nights, or so Susan told him, but she was still tired all the time. He felt helpless. If she wasn't looking after Emma properly it would be a different matter, but he couldn't fault her there.

Brenda Tanner looked up with sympathetic eyes. He hated that. Sympathy was the last thing he needed.

"A Mr Hanson telephoned. He asked if you would ring him back." She held up a piece of paper.

"Did he say what it was about?"

"No. I asked, but he said it was a personal matter."

Roy frowned, and then relaxed. "Oh yes. I know. It'll be Jimmy Hanson. Thanks. I'll ring him now."

"It's a York number. That's his extension below the main number. Don't forget your afternoon appointment in Headlingly. Mr Henry's out, by the way."

This was Brenda's way of telling him he could make the call in privacy. Roy took the paper and went upstairs. He presumed his father had gone to the Scarborough Arms.

"Hello. Is that you, Jimmy?"

"Yes."

"Good to hear from you. How are the newly-weds?"

"We're fine, thanks. Listen, Roy, I know it's none of my business—but I had a letter from Chaz today and we're all worried about Susan."

Roy's hand gripped the receiver. "Why? Why would Chaz be worried about her? She hasn't seen her since our wedding. Susan's fine. We just had lunch together."

"Susan wrote to Chaz. It's nothing specific, just a feeling, really. Susan said she wasn't sleeping well. I thought she looked tired."

"We're fine. Really. Nothing to worry about. Why don't you and Jill come round for lunch on Sunday?"

"That would be good. I'll reply to Chaz and tell her there's nothing to worry about."

"See you Sunday, then. About one o'clock."

"I look forward to it, and I know Jill will, too. Thanks."

They said their goodbyes and Roy replaced the receiver slowly, the click echoing with finality. A full stop. A line drawn. No longer able to dismiss the facts with wishful thinking, he didn't know whether he felt relieved or saddened. Both, perhaps. He rested his elbows on the desk, head in his hands.

After a while he leaned back and rubbed the palms of his hands over his face, pulling his cheeks down so hard it hurt his eyes. He had invited Jimmy and Jill for lunch without consulting Susan. Jimmy was her closest friend so she couldn't possibly object to him coming for lunch, he reasoned. Jimmy knew her better than anyone. He had seen through her act, and been concerned at what he'd seen. The fact that he had taken the time and trouble to telephone spoke volumes. Jimmy was obviously worried about her, and Roy knew his worry was well founded, despite his denial.

His father's footsteps on the stairs jolted him back to his working day. He looked at his watch. Quarter past two. He was going to be late for his appointment in Headingly.

* * * *

Thomas Barraclough rocked back and forth on the balls of his feet. He didn't like to be kept waiting, and this art expert fellow would know that before he was much older. He rubbed the gold cufflink in his left sleeve with his right forefinger.

From his position in the bay window he could see the driveway and front garden. Snowdrops brightened the hedge bottom, and a hint of colour peeped from daffodil buds. He would have to contact the gardener in the next week or so, and discuss his plans for the herbaceous borders.

A Siamese cat flexed its body around his shin, and he stooped to pick it up. It hissed at him and then mewed loudly.

"You bad-tempered cat, Elouise. I don't know why I put up with you. You only want food. But we must wait. You, for your fish, and I, for Mr Jessop." He sighed and brushed cat hair from his trousers with the back of his hand. "Go and play with Alexia if you don't want my affection."

A clock chimed its single stroke of the half hour, diverting his attention. Taking a key from the mantelpiece, he wound the mechanism, at the same time staring at his reflection in the mirror above the fireplace. Nature had not been kind to him. Long, thin strands of hair fought a losing battle to cover his scalp. Turning to one side, he checked the straightness of his parting before carefully putting the onyx and gold clock in its ordained position. To its left a hinged box in the same onyx and gold balanced the miniature vase to its right. He had bought the three pieces at the same auction— one of his earliest investments. He shuddered as he recalled the tirade of abuse his mother had hurled at him when he had told her how much he had paid for them. She had been wrong to accuse him of wasting money. The clock had been worth ten times what he had paid for it, even then. But her words still rang in his ears.

"You are a fool, Tom lad, and a fool and his money are soon parted."

With hindsight, he saw her obsession with money as the first symptom of her depression.

"We Barracloughs are working class. You should remember that, Tom lad. We make cardboard boxes. We have our own business, true enough, but we're still working class. Buying stuff we don't need isn't for the likes of us. You should put your money away for a rainy day. What your father would have said I can't bear to think. God rest his soul."

Well, he had a big factory, and there hadn't been a rainy

day. Even if there had been, his investments had been far more profitable than the interest rates of a bank.

Manufacturers always needed boxes, and he, Thomas Barraclough, was the man who provided them. Mother was not there to call him 'Tom lad' and criticise his investments.

He hated his surname. An invisible shudder ran through his body whenever he heard it. 'Barraclough' was so very common. If he had known he was going to become so well-known, so respected, he would have changed it when he was twenty-one and able to do so without asking mother's permission.

Her depression had been a terrible thing to live with, for both of them. He had been sympathetic and had considered himself to be a good son. He could have done no more. That was the trouble with depression. Everyone in the family suffered.

He had paid for her to see the best psychiatrist in Leeds, but Mr Feany had only been able to say that tangible reasons were unlikely to be found. With hindsight he might have questioned her treatment, but had accepted there was little likelihood it would have made any difference.

The doorbell rang, relieving him of his uncomfortable reverie. He touched his cufflinks, left and right, before opening the door.

Roy Jessop proffered his hand. "I'm so very sorry. I'm thirteen minutes late."

Thomas didn't answer, and kept his hands to his sides. He wanted to humiliate the man, thereby giving himself an advantage if there were any bargaining to be done. The precision of the apology was unexpected. By saying he was 'thirteen minutes' late, Jessop had shown himself to be a man who paid attention to detail, a man not accustomed to being late. If he had said he was 'a bit late', it would have been an entirely different matter.

"Mr Barraclough? I do have the right address, don't I?"

"Come in. The drawing room is to your right." He stood aside, watching with approval as Roy wiped his feet on the coconut mat. Eloise and Alexia ran towards him, and rubbed their moulting fur around Roy's legs.

"Take no notice." Thomas pushed one of the cats with his foot. "They're a pair of tarts, showing their affection to a complete stranger in the hope you have some food for them."

Roy brushed the cat hair from his trousers as best he could before following Thomas into the drawing room.

"I hear you are something of an expert on paintings, Mr Jessop?"

Roy looked thoughtful. "Is it a painting you want to sell?"

"Sell? Good Lord, no. I want to buy. Stan Hinton told me you were the best around here."

"That was very kind of him."

"I hope not. I hope he was telling the truth, not paying you a kindness. I was there when he acquired two Charles Cannon paintings last year. You'll recall he introduced us recently at Ilkley."

"Yes. I remember. Cannons don't come on the market very often."

"I don't want a Charles Cannon. I'm interested in investing in the impressionists. I admire their skill, whilst having doubts about their messy daubing. Something of an anomaly, don't you think?" He turned to the mirror and checked his hair.

"What exactly is it you want me to do, Mr Barraclough?"

"I'm a collector, and an investor. I want you to find impressionist paintings that will increase in value. Can you do that?"

"Yes. But I'm a businessman and have to ask what's in it for me?"

"A finder's fee, plus expenses, within reason. I would also want you to do any negotiations. Buy at auctions, that sort of thing."

Roy nodded. "I'm sure we can work something out to our mutual advantage."

"Then there's no more to be said." Thomas took a business card from the onyx box and gave it to Roy. "Telephone when you have something." They shook hands and Thomas closed the door behind his visitor. Alexia and

Elouise dashed to his side, depositing yet more of their pedigree hair on his trousers.

"All right, all right, you mercenary tarts. I'll feed you, but don't expect any cuddles. You don't deserve my affection."

* * * *

Roy drove back to the office. He had recognised Thomas Barraclough as soon as he had opened the door. It was interesting to hear that Stan Hinton and Barraclough had discussed his expertise. Stan had said he was the best in the area. Thomas Barraclough was a strange man, his bony handshake surprisingly firm. He was obviously rich. Roy made a mental note to ask his father about him, and where his money came from.

As he walked from his car to the office his mind turned to the galleries of Aix en Provence and the wealth of impressionist paintings he had seen there. There was no shortage of artists in Aix, and some of them were very good.

From his studies at Leeds University and his art degree, he knew the first impressionists had been shunned by the purists of French art. The 'messy daubing' of Cézanne, Van Gogh and their contemporaries had been snapped up by the nouveau riche of England in lucky naivety. Thomas Barraclough wanted him to discover fashionable artists of the future. It was an exciting project. The pure light of Provence attracted artists just as much today as it had in the early impressionist movement.

Running up the stairs two at a time to his office, he realised, with a pang of guilt, that he hadn't given a thought to Susan or Emma since the moment he had stepped into Thomas Barraclough's house.

His father was at his desk, eyes closed and hands clasped across a rising and falling chest.

"Have you heard of Thomas Barraclough?"

His father sat up straight and coughed. "Who?"

"Thomas Barraclough. I'd say he was in his early forties. A bit weird."

"Cardboard boxes."

"What?"

"His father started a small business making cardboard boxes—worth millions now, I shouldn't wonder. Can't say I know him. He's a funny bugger, though, apparently. Some say he's a shirtlifter, but I wouldn't know about that. Why do you ask?"

"He was my appointment this afternoon. He wants me to buy impressionist paintings for him."

His father frowned and shuffled some papers on his desk. "Make sure he pays you. Tight as a duck's arse, that one."

Roy laughed.

"You may laugh, Roy, but I'm not wrong."

"I'm sure you're not wrong, Dad. It's just—oh, never mind."

"It's good to hear you laugh for a change."

His face dropped with the truth of his father's words.

"Your mother and I are worried about you, and about Susan."

"Why's that, Dad? There's nothing to worry about. We're fine."

"If you say so."

"Yes. I do say so." Roy clenched his fists. First Jimmy, and now his dad. They were right of course, so why was he denying it? And why did the truth annoy him so much?

CHAPTER TEN

Susan signed the bill and handed it back to the waiter. He separated the carbon copy, folded it and put it back on the plate. She gave him a pound note.

"Thank you, Mrs Jessop. I hope we see you again soon." He pulled her chair away from the table as she rose.

After checking Emma's blankets were tucked in place, she steered the pram through the dining area, weaving her way through the waiters and waitresses as they set the tables for afternoon tea.

Lavell's had a reputation for high quality clothing, and without thinking she pushed the pram towards the children's section. The new summer stock would be on the shelves and she intended to buy something especially pretty for Emma. Taking a pink and white dress from the rail, she touched the embroidered flowers at the hemline and held it up.

"It'll fit her by the time summer's here, Mrs Jessop."

Susan turned quickly.

"I'm sorry. I didn't mean to make you jump."

"It's okay, I was miles away. You're right though, she's growing bigger by the day. I'll take it. Put it on the account, please."

Susan followed the assistant to the counter, and signed the bill before placing the bag in the pram.

The ladies' department was on the second floor. A short ride in the lift took her to a riot of colour in summer clothes. Skirts, lightweight jackets, blouses, dresses, swimsuits and bikinis filled the rails beneath fluorescent lights. The cheerful fashions clashed with her mood. Roy had told her to buy something for herself, and she wanted a warm, black coat.

"Excuse me."

The assistant looked up from her work. Jealousy rose within Susan's chest as she saw the words 'Trainee Assistant' on her badge.

"Do you have any winter coats left?"

"A few, madam." She pointed toward the back of the store. "They're over there. They've all been reduced so you may be lucky."

Her melancholy mood lifted when she saw the red 'Sale' tags. Touching the fabrics and checking the sizes and prices, she selected a fine worsted coat in black. As she put her arm in the sleeve Emma started to cry. She rocked the pram with one hand, but the crying grew louder. With a sigh, she returned the coat to its hanger, and put it back on the rail. The coat would have to wait.

She lifted Emma out of the pram. Her face was bright red and her forehead hot and damp. Realising she would have to take her straight to the doctor's surgery, she put her back in and wrapped the blankets around her. A knot grew in her stomach as she gripped the handle, whitening her knuckles with a mixture of fear and anger. What she really wanted was the freedom to walk round town without having to work out how many nappies and bottles to take. She wanted to laugh with Chaz and have a conversation about pop music and clothes and makeup. Tears of self-loathing streamed down her cheeks as she placed the carrycot on the back seat of the car. Emma was kicking and screaming, and the thought of the drive to Barwick-in-Elmet filled her with horror. Driving from the car park, she decided to take her to the hospital instead. It would be quicker. Emma never cried like that. Something was badly wrong.

She parked on Portland Street and took Emma from her carrycot, throwing the holdall over her shoulder and running to the hospital entrance, her daughter clutched tightly to her chest. Heads turned to the crying baby and her distraught mother. The queue at reception parted to allow her to the front. She gave Emma's name, address, and date of birth.

The nurse typed everything onto a form. "And what's the problem?"

"She's hot and she's crying. Can't you see that? She doesn't usually cry. She's a good baby."

"Please take a seat. Doctor will see you as soon as possible." She put the form to the back of a box containing several others. Susan was about to say she needed to see a doctor straightaway when the nurse stood up and leaned forward, touching Emma's forehead.

"If I were you I'd take off her hat and undo her coat. It's very warm in here." The nurse sat down again, dismissing her with 'Next please'.

Emma screamed louder than ever. Susan untied the pink ribbon of her bonnet. Her hair was wet with sweat. Taking a cloth from the holdall, she wiped her head, then took off her leggings and unbuttoned her coat. Even her chubby little legs were sweaty. She stood up, put Emma to her shoulder and swayed from side to side, humming a lullaby. The screams subsided into sobs and within five minutes her baby had fallen asleep. She sat down again and resigned herself to a long wait.

Tiny red spots appeared on the back of Emma's hands, and when Susan pulled down the front of her clothes she saw they were all over her body. With rising panic she went back to the reception desk, making her way to the front of the queue.

"I'm sorry to bother you but she's come out in a rash. I'm very worried." The nurse left her desk and peered at the baby, touching her forehead with the back of her hand. She lifted an eyelid.

"She's asleep, not unconscious. I don't think there's anything to panic about, dear. Doctor will see your baby when it's her turn."

Susan waited for almost two hours and was about to use the public telephone to let Roy know what was happening, when Emma awoke. Susan took a bottle of milk from the holdall and Emma was sucking greedily when a nurse called, 'Emma Jessop.' The nurse took the bag and they followed her through the double doors to a cubicle.

"Doctor will be with you soon."

A further twenty minutes passed. Emma finished her feed and gave a large burp. Susan waited with no option but to listen to the moans and groans from neighbouring cubicles. Names were called, medical histories recited. *Yes Doctor. No Doctor. Thank you very much, Doctor.* She was fed up. Apart from the rash there didn't seem to be anything wrong with Emma.

Roy would be home, wondering what had happened to her.

"Sorry to have kept you waiting, I'm Doctor Finan." She seemed too young to be a doctor, not much older than Susan. "What seems to be the trouble?"

"She was crying and crying and she has a rash."

"Let's have a look, shall we?"

Susan gently eased Emma's arms from the sleeves of her jacket, took off her cardigan and pulled up her vest. The doctor ran her fingers over her chest, and she wriggled and opened her eyes.

"Are my hands cold, little one?"

Susan watched intently as the doctor checked behind her ears and at the back of her neck. She took a thermometer from the pocket of her white coat and placed it in Emma's armpit.

"She doesn't feel hot now, but I'll check her temperature. Has she been ill at all, off her food, anything like that?

"No, Doctor."

"Has she been coughing at all?"

"No, Doctor."

"Well, it doesn't look like measles. The rash is raised, but I'm quite sure it's nothing more than a heat rash. She has a lot of clothes on, Mrs Jessop. Have you been outside with her, or indoors?"

"We were in a shop..." Susan's voice trailed off. It was her fault.

"Leave the cardigan off, Mrs Jessop. That lovely jacket is quite enough to keep her warm." She looked at the thermometer. "Perfect. If you're still worried in the morning, take her to your G.P. Now, if you'll excuse me, I have a lot of patients to see."

Susan folded the cardigan and put it in the bag. Holding Emma closely, she walked straight past the queue for the telephone, and out into the evening air. Lying her down in the carrycot, she draped a blanket loosely over her.

"Good girl, Emma. I'm afraid you have a useless mother."

Emma gave a smile, sucking in her cheeks to make little kissing noises.

Tears welled in Susan's eyes. She wiped them away with the back of her hand and sniffed. "We'll be home with Daddy soon, I promise." She ripped the parking ticket from the windscreen and set off. The rush hour traffic had gone. Roy would be worried about her. She should have phoned.

As she approached Orchard Cottage her worst fears were realised when she saw Henry's car. Diana's figure was silhouetted in the lounge window, peering out, before turning quickly. Roy opened the car door before she had chance to apply the handbrake, his face etched with a mixture of fear and relief.

"I'm sorry. I should have phoned." Susan stepped out and hugged him. With his arms around her, she felt his desperation.

"Where've you been? I've been frantic."

"Let's go inside, shall we? Your mum and dad can go home now." She released herself from his grip and opened the back door of the car, lifting Emma out.

"I rang Alf and Hettie to see if you were there, and I rang Jimmy. I was about to call the police." Roy followed her into the kitchen.

"Sorry to cause such a panic." She saw relief flooding the faces of his parents. "I took Emma to the hospital."

"Why? There's nothing wrong with her, is there?" Diana asked.

Susan put the carrycot on the table. "No. Nothing at all. She was crying and all hot. Turned out she had too many clothes on."

Roy let out a sigh. "I have to make a couple of phone calls. Cancel the blood hounds. Won't be long."

Susan felt awkward, feeling his parents' eyes upon her.

Roy could be heard dialling, and then saying, "It's okay. Yes. She's home. I'll have to go. I need to call Jimmy to tell him she's back. Thanks, Alf." The phone clicked and he dialled again.

She looked around the kitchen. "I see you've been busy, Diana. Everywhere looks much tidier than when I left."

"We were worried. We didn't know where you were."

"I know, and I'm sorry. I should have phoned."

Henry looked at Diana. "Come on, love. We should go now, leave Roy and Susan on their own. It's been a difficult few hours for all of us."

"Of course, yes."

He held her coat as she put it on. "We'll be off, then."

"Are you sure you won't stay a while?" Roy had returned to the room. "I've finished on the phone."

"No. Your dad's right. We'll go home. You'll be wanting to see to Emma." Diana smiled into the carrycot. Emma was wide awake and starting to whimper. "See you soon." She pulled on her gloves as Henry held the door for her.

"Thanks for coming." As the door closed behind them Roy turned to her. "I'm sorry, love. I rang them to see if you were at their house and the next thing I knew they were here." She watched as he took Emma from her carrycot, holding her closely and breathing into her hair.

"I never made it to Alf and Hettie's."

"I know. Alf told me not to panic. He told me about the time your dad rang the police when he thought you were missing."

She looked down at her shoes. "I'd forgotten about that. I was upstairs asleep."

"Alf told me you were perfectly capable of looking after yourself and, if anything had gone wrong, we'd have heard about it." He held Emma over his shoulder, supporting her with one hand, and cupped his other hand under Susan's chin, forcing her to look up at him. "You did the right thing, Susan. You were worried about Emma."

"I wanted to phone you, but was called in to see the doctor and then, when I came out, there was a queue and..."

"Don't worry about it. You're home and you're both safe. And, anyway, I have a confession to make." He put one arm around her and kissed her on the forehead. "I've invited Jimmy and Jill for lunch."

"That's nice. When?"

"This Sunday."

She released herself from his arm. "Oh, Roy. It'll take me

ages to tidy up."

"No, it won't. Mum's done most it, and I'll help with the cooking. Anyway, it's only Jill and Jimmy. They won't mind if we're a bit untidy."

"You're right. Of course they won't mind. But still, I'd like to make an effort."

"I could take tomorrow off work, if you like."

"Oh, no need for that. It's only Thursday. I have two full days to organise myself."

* * * *

Sunday morning dawned. Roy lay in bed with Emma sleeping in her cot. Music drifted up the stairs mingled with the sound of chinking cutlery and glasses. When he had arrived home on Friday the house had been tidy, dusted and cleaned. He had bathed Emma, and after dinner Susan had made a shopping list while he'd put their daughter to bed. On Saturday morning she had been to the butchers and greengrocers in Barwick-in-Elmet and bought everything necessary for lunch. She still looked pale, and too thin, but some of her sparkle had returned.

Slipping quietly from the bed, he put on his dressing gown and crept downstairs.

"Anything I can do?" He slipped his arms around Susan's waist as she peeled potatoes.

"No, all under control here. Is Emma still asleep?"

"Mmm. I'll take a shower and see to our little princess when she wakes." Roy felt her body stiffen. "What's wrong? What is it?"

"Nothing." She gripped the edge of the sink. "Dad used to call me his princess. It reminded me, that's all. You go for your shower. Emma could wake at any moment."

Roy went upstairs slowly, pulling wearily on the banister rail. He felt tired, despite a good night's sleep. They had made love the night before. He was a happily married man in every sense, and yet he knew everything could change in a flash. Susan's reaction to his calling Emma a princess was proof of that, if proof were needed. Half of him wished he hadn't invited Jimmy and Jill, despite it having sparked a change in Susan.

* * * *

They arrived shortly after one o'clock, bringing a bottle of wine and a bunch of spring flowers. Wearing her make-up, Susan felt relaxed and happy. Jimmy complimented her on how lovely she looked, adding to her self-confidence.

"Something smells good," Jill said.

"Dinner will be ready in half an hour."

Roy and Jimmy had a beer, Jill chose a glass of red wine, and Susan insisted on drinking only water. "Until I've served the main course."

Prawn cocktails were followed by roast beef, Yorkshire pudding, roast potatoes, carrots and peas. The apple pie she had prepared the night before warmed in the oven. She and Roy sat at opposite ends of the dining table with Jimmy to her left and Jill to her right. Emma woke for her feed just as they finished the main course and now lay happily in her pram beside Susan.

"I didn't know you could cook, Susan," Jimmy said as he leaned back in his chair, patting his stomach.

Susan turned to Roy. He winked at her. "I can't. Not really. I have a big recipe book and followed it to the letter. Anyway, enough of that, how are things going with your house in Haxby?"

"Very well, and quite quickly. The surveys have been done and we'll be moving in as soon as the paperwork's finished."

"Jimmy's putting the house in Vine Street on the market," Jill added. "We'll move to Haxby as soon as we can."

"Really? I thought you said the house was a wreck. We couldn't move in here straight away. We stayed with Roy's parents."

"I know what you mean, but we'll do it one room at a time."

She was incredulous. "But that'll take ages."

"I know. But there isn't any structural work to do. The survey was surprisingly good. It needs a damp-proof course but otherwise it's just a matter of decorating."

"A bit more than that, love," said Jimmy. "The kitchen and bathroom are functional but will need ripping out. They're very old-fashioned."

"I know, and it'll be like camping out at times, but the better weather will be here soon." She turned to Susan. "I think you had more to do here and, of course, you were expecting Emma."

Susan frowned. "What do you mean?"

"Well, I don't think I'd like to do it if we had a baby on the way." An awkward silence followed, lasting a few seconds.

"I want to ask you a favour, Susan," Jimmy said. "I wondered if, after we've moved, you would pop in to Vine Street when you're in town and pick up the post."

"Of course I will. I love that house." Susan turned to Emma, staring at her with unfocussed eyes. "I'll pick up the post and phone you if anything looks important."

"I could ask Alan. He lives in Granny Florrie's old house."

"I won't hear of it. It's no trouble," Susan insisted, dismissing his suggestion with a wave of her hand.

"I'll let you have a key, then. There shouldn't be much. I'll be writing to people with our change of address."

Susan blinked, turning to Jimmy. "Have you heard from Chaz lately?"

Her question clearly caught him off guard. "Y-yes. She wrote a couple of weeks ago. She said you'd written to her."

"Yes, I did, but I haven't had a reply."

"She said she and Jérôme were house hunting. I'll write to her tomorrow and tell her you've learned to cook."

"I was thinking we might go to Provence for a holiday," Roy said.

"Really!" Susan's eyes sparkled with delight. "You never said anything about it to me. When can we go?"

He laughed. "I don't know yet—and it would be a

working holiday for me. I have a client who wants me to buy impressionist paintings for him. I thought a trip to Provence might be a good idea."

"A trip to Provence is always a good idea as far as I'm concerned. What do you think, Jimmy? You and Jill could come, too."

Jimmy nodded. "How about it, Jill? A belated honeymoon."

"I'd love to see Chaz and her family again. I only met them briefly at your wedding."

"It's settled, then. What are we waiting for?"

"Whoa, Susan," Jimmy laughed. "Some of us go to work, you know. Jill and I will have to check it out tomorrow."

"And I'll have to sort out my diary," Roy added. "But we'll go as soon as we can. I have the feeling my client won't want to wait for results, and I'm on a finder's fee with this one."

"I'd like to go to Ireland as well," Susan said. "Gran asks me to go in every letter."

Conversation flowed between the friends, from Haxby to Provence to Ireland and back again. With the meal finished and daylight fading, Jimmy and Jill prepared to leave.

"I'll be in touch when Jill and I have sorted out some dates at work."

"Good. I can be fairly flexible. I like to be around on auction days—finger on the pulse and all that."

"Are you sure we can't help with the washing up, Susan?" Jill asked.

"I won't hear of it. Everything will go in the dishwasher. You have to be at work tomorrow and I have all day to fill."

CHAPTER ELEVEN

May 1970

Susan numbered the dates back from June the fifth, the earliest date when everyone could take two weeks holiday. Seventeen days to go. An exhibition of impressionist paintings in Aix on June the twelfth had sealed it for Roy who, in theory at least, could take time off whenever he wanted.

Since the day Jimmy and Jill had been for lunch she had kept the house clean and tidy, scrubbing the kitchen floor every day. That morning, being Wednesday, she would clean the bedrooms, and in the afternoon she would go to town. She had discovered that all she needed was a strict routine, and the self-discipline to stick to it. Roy had said she was obsessed by housework and told her to rest more. Emma slept right through the night and for two hours in the morning and afternoon. But sleep didn't come so easily for her. She would crash onto the pillow at night, falling into a sleep filled with dreams, waking an hour or so later. The dreams evaporated as she woke, leaving her upset without knowing why. She would lie awake, listening for Emma, and then fall asleep shortly before it was time to get up.

Working quickly to complete the housework, Susan looked forward to her afternoon of shopping. Emma needed lots of new clothes for the holiday. Sometimes, when she went to town on Wednesday afternoons, Diana would look after Emma. Looking out of the window at an overcast sky, she decided to drop Emma off at Lark's Hill Drive.

Four hours later, with her kitchen floor scrubbed, and bedrooms immaculately clean, Susan strapped Emma in her seat in the back of her car, putting the holdall of clean nappies, bottles, and clothes in the boot. As she checked her make-up in the rear view mirror, large raindrops hit the windscreen. In the direction of Leeds, a black sky confirmed her decision to drive to her in-laws' house. She would only be a couple of hours.

To her surprise a car she didn't recognise stood in the drive. As she pulled on the handbrake, Diana stepped from the house with a lady at her side. Susan wound her window down.

"Hello, Susan. I didn't think you were coming today. You didn't ring."

"No, sorry. It doesn't matter. I'm just going to town for a few things so I won't be long."

"Jenny called by. We're going to Roundhay Park. A spur of the moment thing."

"Good for you, but what if it rains?"

"We're going to the Tropical House. It's always warm in there."

"I'll pop in on my way back, if you're home."

"Good, I look forward to it. I'll be back about four o'clock."

"I doubt if I'll be that long looking at the sky." Susan drove off. The knot in her stomach belied the cheerful conversation with her mother-in-law. Surely a couple of hours to herself wasn't too much to ask? She gritted her teeth. The sky darkened, worsening her mood as she turned on the headlights. Wipers dashed back and forth across the windscreen at full speed, struggling to cope with the downpour. Pushing the carrycot on its wheels around the shops was going to be awful. She considered turning back, but then the rain stopped as suddenly as it had started. The sky magically cleared and the sun came out.

With Emma sitting up, and supported by pillows, Susan bought three dresses, several pairs of socks, and a sun hat. She had learned her lesson, and when Emma's eyes began to close, she took away the pillows, and tucked a thin blanket around her.

She had parked at the Merrion Centre. As she pushed the pram down towards Briggate, a familiar voice called her name. She turned to see Alf Lawrence.

"Hello, Alf. How are you?"

"Not so bad. All the better for seeing you and this little lady. What brings you to town?"

"Oh, just a bit of shopping for Emma. We're going to see Chaz next month, so she needs some summer clothes."

"Will you come and see me and Hettie sometime before you go? She'd love to see you and little Emma here." He peered into the pram. "She's like you—and your mother."

"I will, and I'm sorry I haven't called. The pram set Hettie knitted was lovely. Emma wore it a lot, but it's too small, already."

"I'll tell her to start knitting again, then," Alf chuckled.

"I'll give you a ring to make sure you're at home—maybe one day next week."

"You do that, Susan. Hettie's usually in but I still like to walk around the town. Can't change the habits of a lifetime."

They went their separate ways. After a few paces Susan turned to see Alf had also turned. They waved to each other before walking on. The sun had dried the pavements and Susan crossed Briggate to walk in the sunshine, passing the corner of Thompson Square and the ground where the Threlfalls had once stood. Thistles grew in the stony ground. The building had been demolished after being declared unsafe and beyond repair by the insurers. The high wall to the side and the gates still stood, serving no purpose other than as a boundary.

Susan paused. Images of climbing over the wall with Maggie and Roy sprang into her mind. She felt the heat of the flames on her back and heard the crashing of the beams as they fell through the floors. She closed her eyes and smelled the smoke that had killed her father.

A long sigh brought her back to the present. She ought to sell the land. Roy had mentioned putting it up for auction. Walking more slowly, her steps took her towards the Parish Church.

An undertaker in his black top hat stood at the door, preventing interruption of the service within. Susan pushed Emma past the empty hearse, dragging it up the steps and along the path to the back of the church and her mother's grave. A bunch of daffodils rested against the headstone. She stooped to read the card. *To Siobhan, a lovely lady, from Billy.* It could only be Billy Oldroyd. He hadn't forgotten her mother after all those years. The simple gesture stabbed her heart. She never brought flowers. She sighed deeply. As the breath left her body the trees whispered under a light breeze, hushing the outside world and holding the oasis of the churchyard beneath their branches.

* * * *

Roy told himself he mustn't worry. She usually went to town on Wednesdays and had probably called at his parents' house on her way home, or gone to see Alf and Hettie, or even her old friend Maggie, or Patrick. He made a ham sandwich and turned on the television, his eyes drawn magnetically to the clock every few minutes. Why didn't she phone? If he rang his parents and they weren't there, it would mean a repeat performance of the time Susan had taken Emma to the hospital. He simply couldn't bear the thought of them fussing and worrying. It would do no good. Either she was with them or she wasn't.

He grabbed his keys and ran to his car, reversing out of the drive with squealing tyres as he roared down the lane. In less than two minutes he was in Lark's Hill Drive, stopping at the gateway to number four. Susan's car wasn't there. Thumping his fists on the steering wheel, his jaw tightened. She had seemed so much better recently. Ever since Jimmy and Jill had been for lunch she had been like the Susan he first knew—almost. He drove slowly back to Orchard Cottage, trying to think logically. She must've gone to town. Then what? The idea came in a flash. He rushed inside and dialled the operator.

"A new number please—Haxby, York—Hanson—J." His fingers drummed on the hall table as he waited. "Thank you. Yes. Sorry, I need to write it down. Won't be a moment." He found a pen in the kitchen and, with the receiver between his ear and neck, he wrote four-six-five-nine on his left hand. "Thank you." His fingers trembled as he dialled the number. If she wasn't in Haxby, she had to have been in some sort of accident.

"Haxby four—"

"Jimmy, it's Roy. Is Susan with you?"

"No. Is something wrong?"

"I don't know. She's not home and I don't know where they are."

"She has Emma with her, then?"

"Yes. I, erm, maybe not. Sometimes she leaves Emma with my parents and goes to town but it's late. I'll ring you back."

"Try not to—"

Roy hung up and dialled his parents' number. If Emma was with them, he only had to worry about Susan. Mounting panic grew in his chest as the phone rang out. "Come on. Hurry up. Answer the damn thing."

Diana answered. "Barwick two-five—"

"Is Emma with you?"

"No. Susan called in earlier, but I was on my way out and she was on her way to town. She said she'd call back later, but I haven't seen her. She said she wasn't going to be long."

He hung up. Desperate fingers tore at the telephone directory as he sought the number for Leeds General Infirmary. After an interminable wait he was put through to the casualty department.

"No. No-one of that name has been here today. No. I've checked. Emma and Susan Jessop. You could try St. James' hospital. Six-eight-nine-three-nine-two will put you straight through to Casualty, sir."

Beads of sweat ran into his eyes, his churning gut convincing him that something was badly wrong.

"No. I've checked all today's patients. No-one of that name, sorry."

The moment he placed the receiver in its cradle, the phone rang. "Susan! Where are you?"

"It's Jimmy here. Sorry, Roy. I wondered if you'd tried Alf and Hettie's number."

"Do you think she's there?"

"I don't know. Tell you what, I'll ring them, and call you

back."

Roy heard his father's car pull up outside. He leaned his back against the wall halfway to a crouching position, the palms of his hands flat against his thighs.

His mother hurried into the kitchen and filled the kettle. At least this time everywhere was clean and tidy, and she wouldn't start fussing about the place.

His father put a hand on his shoulder. "No news, then?"

He shook his head. "I've tried the hospitals."

The phone rang. Shaking hands grabbed the receiver. But it was only Jimmy.

"She's not at Alf and Hettie's. Alf saw them in town at about half past three. He said they were fine. He said to try the hospitals and if they can't help to go to the police station and report her missing."

"I'm on my way. I've tried the hospitals."

He was about to hang up when he heard Jimmy shout, "Roy! Hang on."

"Why? I have to go."

"I wanted to say I'll find Maggie's number. She'll know where Patrick lives, and then we've checked everywhere we can."

"Thanks. Let me know."

He turned to his father who was sitting at the kitchen table, a mug of steaming tea before him. "Dad, I want you to go home, and Mum, I want you to stay here. Jimmy will ring soon. Alf says I should report them missing. I'll call you from the police station. They'll take notice because Emma's with her. She could ring, either here or your house, or someone might ring to say where they are."

Diana held a mug towards him. "What about some…?" but he was gone, slamming the door before she could finish.

* * * *

"Maggie—it's Jimmy, Susan's friend. Have you seen her?"

"Susan? No. Not seen her since before the baby was born. I don't even have her address. I sent a present for Emma to Roy's office but I never heard from her. What's happened?"

"I don't know. She's missing and she has Emma with her. What about Patrick? Do you have his number?"

"Patrick's here with me. He just called in for a cuppa, so she's definitely not with him."

"Thanks, Maggie."

"You'll let me know when you find her, won't you? The trouble with Susan is she thinks she's bullet proof."

"I'll let you know."

* * * *

Siobhan Fletcher. Loving wife and devoted mother. With hands pressed to her temples, the words on the gravestone pierced a hole through her head. How could this be true? Susan was asleep. But Susan was not a baby. She was six years old and wearing a party dress.

Susan looked at her watch. With all reason crumbling, her eyes saw the watch her father had given to her mother. Pauline would be home now. With purpose in her step, she walked quickly past the markets, past the Threlfalls with its shining brass door handles and on to Vine Street. Susan climbed out of the coach-built pram and danced at her side.

Turning the key in the lock, her eyes blind to the estate agent's sign, she stepped inside, locking the door behind her and fastening the bolts.

Her mind saw the wallpaper of the fifties and the shabby eclectic furniture that had furnished Auntie Pauline's home. After wheeling the pram into the little sitting room, she wandered through to the kitchen. Only the old armchair remained but Susan was no longer in the real world. Everything was exactly as it had been when she'd first stepped inside number sixteen Vine Street. She didn't feel the soft carpet beneath her feet, and her eyes were unable to see the electric fire in the kitchen. The flames of a coal fire licked the sooted fireback. On the shelf to the side of the fireplace the radio played the familiar sound of jazz, Auntie Pauline's favourite.

Her aunt was in the kitchen. Familiarity filled her senses as she shovelled coal onto the fire and six-year old Susan Fletcher left the cosy room. As she ran up the creaking stairs, the echoing emptiness meant nothing. Dancing her way into Jimmy's bedroom, on her way to see Granny Florrie, her hand reached for the latch.

A baby cried somewhere in the distance. Susan scratched frantically at the wall, breaking her nails and scraping the skin from her fingers. Wild eyes blazed with disbelief as her knees buckled and she fell to the floor. With fists beating against the hollow plaster, her mind surrendered to the mutilations of the past. Bloodied hands covered her twisted, sobbing face. Physical and mental exhaustion triumphed. Her sobs surrendered to shallow breath, and sleep deepened into the blissful release of unconsciousness.

* * * *

Jill paced the floor, wringing her hands in desperation. If only Jimmy would ring with some news—or even ring to say there was no news. Anything but this silence. Jimmy had left an hour earlier and would have arrived in Leeds.

The phone rang. She grabbed the receiver before the second ring. "Have you found her?"

But it wasn't Jimmy. Alan, their neighbour from Vine Street, told her he had heard a baby's cries coming from number sixteen. It had been going on for hours.

A chill ran through her body as she hung up. She dialled 999.

"Police. Thank you. Yes, Jill Hanson. I live in Haxby. My number is four-six-five-nine, but the problem is in Leeds." Jill answered the interminable questions with increasing impatience. "Yes, number sixteen Vine Street. I think the mother must be ill. Her husband and my husband are at the police station. Please, please send someone round there. The baby's crying. Something's badly wrong. Is there someone who could go round there?"

"No-one who could be there quickly. A crying baby isn't

really an emergency."

"I tell you the mother's in there. She must be ill."

"Very well, I'll send an officer around. Stay by your telephone. I may need to speak to you again."

Jill paced the floor in frustration, desperate to do more. Emma would need warm milk. She lifted the receiver and dialled 192.

"Operator. Yes. Can you give me the number for Leeds City centre police station please?" As she waited, her eye was taken by Jimmy's telephone and address book on the hall table. Her thumb sought the letter 'J' in the cutaway index. He had only written 'Jill', and her parents' number. No number for 'Jessop'. She slammed the book shut and threw it back onto the table just as the operator gave her the number of the police station.

"Thank you." She dialled the station. "Hello, a Mr Roy Jessop is at your station reporting his wife as missing. Please tell him she's at Vine Street. He'll know which house. Thank you. Yes—it's very urgent."

She paced around the house, unable to sit still. Roy's parents must know Susan and Emma were missing. They would be every bit as worried as she was. The telephone and address book had fallen to the floor. She picked it up and looked under 'R' for Roy, and saw the entry for Roy and Susan, but nothing for his parents.

CHAPTER TWELVE

May 1970

Chaz stared at the shop window. 'Ésposes de Aix' had only been open for a few weeks and was the town's only specialist wedding shop. Until that moment she had given no more than a fleeting thought to her wedding dress, but the sight of the heavy veil of lace falling from a ring of silk flowers, matching those at the hemline, had attracted her attention. The high waist would make her look taller. Tight-fitting sleeves fastened at the wrist with silk buttons.

She and Jérôme would have the full Catholic marriage service with Mass, but that didn't mean it had to be a big wedding—just Susan, Roy, and Emma; Jimmy and Jill; Jérôme's parents; his aunt and uncle, and their daughters, and maybe some colleagues from school.

Pausing on her way back to her car, she looked up at the church where she and Jérôme would marry. The narrow steeple would ring its bells, and of course the sun would shine.

The following Saturday six smiling faces sat around the dining table at La Vieille Ferme. Monsieur and Madame Bercegeay and Jérôme had been invited for dinner to discuss the wedding plans. Jeanette had insisted that such a special dinner should not be served in the kitchen. Despite the formal table setting, the atmosphere in the dining room was relaxed. The women talked of guest lists, colour schemes, clothes, hats and flowers, while Anton and Monsieur Bercegeay discussed wines and champagne with Jérôme.

Everyone agreed the wedding should take place in late summer when the sun had cooled a little. Subject to Father Marron and the availability of the church, the date was set for the second of October. Jérôme's cousins would be bridesmaids and Susan would be matron of honour. After the marriage service, celebrations were to take place at La Vieille Ferme.

When coffee and liqueurs had been served, Jérôme and

Chaz slipped outside.

"Excité?" Chaz beamed up at him.

"Bien sûr. Cette robe doit être très special."

"Il est. C'est un secret."

La Vieille Ferme
Sunday 23rd May 1970
Dear Susan,

You'll never guess what. Jérôme and I have actually set the date for our wedding. Saturday 2nd October at the Church of St Xavier in Aix, and afterwards, here, at La Vieille Ferme. Mum is going into overdrive, talking non-stop about the food.

We were going to leave it until next year, and then I saw the most fabulous dress and thought, why wait? You are to be my matron of honour. No arguments now. I'll call the whole thing off if you say you won't do it. But I know you will, so that's silly. We are buying a little house near the school. You will love it. It's quite modern by Provence standards, only about a hundred years old!

When you come to Provence for your holiday we will go to Aix and you can be measured for your dress, and of course we are all desperate to meet Emma.

Please write soon. Give my love to everyone. Jimmy tells me you had a lovely lunch together recently. See you soon,

Love,

Chaz.

* * * *

Roy shifted anxiously from one foot to the other.

"I tell you, Officer, something's wrong."

"I understand your worry, sir, but you're telling me that for the past seven hours no-one has knowledge of the whereabouts of your wife."

"Yes, that's right."

"Let me just say that in ninety-nine per cent of cases, they turn up. Been to a friend's or something like that."

Jimmy stood at his side, an overwhelming sense of déjà vu riveting his feet to the floor. He had had a similar response, standing in that very spot, telling an officer his mother was missing. The memories of that night shot through him like a thunderbolt with every detail of the conversation imprinted on his mind.

Numbed by his own stupidity, he grabbed Roy's arm. "I know where she is."

Roy turned his ashen face to Jimmy.

"She's at Vine Street. I just know it." They turned from the desk and ran from the police station.

A young constable approached the sergeant at the desk.

"A message for a Roy Jessop." He had a note in his hand. "Someone rang to say his wife has gone to a house in Vine Street. Didn't say which one though."

The sergeant shook his head and returned to his paperwork.

* * * *

Screeching to a halt and without pausing to close the car doors, Roy and Jimmy ran to the door of number sixteen. As Jimmy turned the key they heard Emma's cry coming from the sitting room. The bolts held the door locked. Jimmy and Roy hurled their shoulders to the door, simultaneously falling into the hallway. Jimmy turned on the light as Roy grabbed his daughter from the pram and held her to his chest.

"In the bag, Jimmy. There'll be a flask of milk in the bag. Pour some into a bottle, quick. She must be starving."

Jimmy did as asked and Roy wiped Emma's tear-stained cheeks with the corner of a blanket.

The ensuing silence, heavy with relief, was broken by sucking noises as Emma wolfed down the milk. Jimmy caught the terrified look in Roy's eyes and ran from the room. Susan had to be there. She wouldn't leave Emma on her own. He raced into the kitchen and switched on the light. The sight of an empty chair, in an otherwise empty room, took his long legs leaping up the stairs.

Seconds later he shouted, "She's here, Roy."

Roy had his foot on the bottom step, Emma still feeding hungrily in his arms, when Jimmy began his careful descent with Susan's limp body in his arms.

"Is she alive?" Roy whispered.

"She's unconscious—and cold."

"Where's all the blood coming from?"

"Her hands, I think." Jimmy laid her on the carpet, grabbing blankets from the pram and wrapping them around her as best he could. Roy knelt at her side, still clutching his daughter. Susan's face looked translucent. Fine veins pulsed at her temples. The almost indiscernible rise and fall of the blankets gave further testament to life.

Leaving Roy with her, he went to the kitchen and dialled 999. "Ambulance, quickly, sixteen Vine Street. She's unconscious. Susan Jessop—my name is Jimmy Hanson—yes—unconscious and cold." After hanging up he returned to the sitting room with more blankets, wrapping them around her. He lifted one of her eyelids. "Susan! Susan! It's me, Jimmy. Wake up!"

The surreal scene before him stabbed at his chest. Loud sucking noises took his attention to Emma. "She's finished the milk, Roy."

Roy looked startled, as if woken from a dream. "Right...yes...thanks...hadn't noticed. What do you think she was doing? I—"

His sentence was cut off by the sound of the ambulance siren echoing from the walls of the terraced houses. Blue lights flashed through the window. Two ambulance men dashed through the open door. One of them put his ear to Susan's mouth as the other placed a stretcher at her side.

"She's breathing."

They strapped her to the stretcher. Roy stared, unblinking. Jimmy took Emma from him.

"Go with her, Roy. I'll look after Emma. Just go."

Roy blinked. "Yes...right. I'll go with her. Yes...thanks." He called over his shoulder as he climbed into the back of the ambulance. "Take Emma to my mother. Tell her what has happened."

The small crowd of neighbours dispersed.

Jimmy nodded. He needed to speak to Jill.

He laid Emma in her pram, and her cry was instantaneous and loud. "Fair enough, little girl. You've been in there for a long time today." As he picked her up and the crying stopped, he realised his shirt sleeve was wet. Holding her against his chest with one arm, he dialled his home number.

"Did the police give you my message?" Jill asked.

"No, tell me about it later. Listen. Roy's gone to the hospital with Susan."

"What's wrong with her?"

"I don't know. But please, just listen. I'm at Vine Street with—"

"I thought you would be. Alan rang."

"*Please,* Jill, just listen." His anxiety caused him to shout. It grated on his ears, and made Emma squirm. He had never shouted at Jill before and had never thought he would. "I need you to phone Roy's house. The number's in my book by the phone, under 'T'. The Threlfalls number is crossed out and it's underneath, on the next line. Roy's mother's there. Tell her I'm on my way with Emma. I have to go. Emma needs her nappy changing. I'll ring as soon as I can. I love you."

* * * *

"Do you know your wife's blood group, Mr Jessop?"

"Erm, yes. From when she had the Caesarean. She's A-positive."

"Thank you. When did she have the baby?"

"January the twenty-fourth. A girl."

The nurse hurried away without replying. Roy sat down and buried his face in his hands, consumed by helplessness, and hating himself for not guessing where she had been. With hindsight it was so bloody obvious. Poor Emma. At least she wouldn't remember anything about it.

Jimmy had been fantastic. He had realised where they would be and had carried Susan down the stairs, called the ambulance, told him to go with her and was taking Emma home. He owed Jimmy a lot.

Susan had looked terrible. What if she died? He had thought she *was* dead when he'd first seen her. The prospect of bringing up Emma without a mother terrified him.

Rapid footsteps approached, and he raised his head as a nurse took a pouch of blood into the cubicle. It hadn't crossed his mind that she might need a transfusion. There had been a lot of blood and there must have been more upstairs. Surely…surely she hadn't tried to kill herself. He walked a few paces down the corridor, physically distancing himself from the frantic efforts to save his wife.

A notice board bore cards of thanks from the happily-recovered, alongside posters warning of the dangers of germs. Giant bugs with hairy faces and large protruding eyes were everywhere, apparently only eradicated by the washing of hands at every opportunity. Framed prints were screwed to the wall. Surely no-one would steal them. They wouldn't be worth anything.

Thomas Barraclough wanted him to buy original impressionist work for him. Their trip to Provence would have to be cancelled—no matter what happened. They wouldn't be going anywhere until Susan had fully recovered from whatever was wrong with her. She must recover. The alternative was unthinkable. He walked slowly back along the corridor.

"Mr Jessop?" His pace quickened as a young doctor beckoned him. "Come with me, please." He held open a door, and indicated Roy be seated in the small, windowless room. "We can have a chat in here before you see your wife." He leaned forward as he spoke, his elbows on his knees, fingers steepled. "We're running a series of tests, but what I can say is that your wife is dangerously anaemic." He paused, as if expecting Roy to say something. "I understand she had a Caesarean section recently."

"Yes, in January."

"And how has she been since then?"

"All right—I think."

"She's very slim, Mr Jessop. Has she been eating

properly?"

"Erm, no, probably not."

"Has she been sleeping well?"

"I don't think so. I don't know really."

"Has she seen her doctor at all?"

"No. I think I'd have known if she had. She will be all right, won't she?"

"Oh, yes. Physically, that is. It could be she's simply exhausted—been doing too much and not looking after herself. We'll know more tomorrow when we have some results."

"You say 'physically', Doctor?" Roy leaned into the back of the upholstered chair.

The doctor rubbed the back of his neck with one hand, as if formulating his reply. "She's been scratching at something. Her nails are in shreds. Has she been doing that for long?"

"I don't know how that happened—sorry. Is that why she needed a transfusion?"

"Oh, no, no. We don't think so. As I said, she's very anaemic." A frown creased his face. "I'm not a psychiatrist, Mr Jessop—but I think she should see one."

"A psychiatrist? Why?"

"I think your wife has had a nervous breakdown."

Roy sank into the chair.

"Are you all right, Mr Jessop?"

He stared at the doctor, reeling from the blow that had been travelling towards him for some time.

"What I said is not a diagnosis but, with her physical presentation and apparent attempt to harm herself, we need to be sure. Treatment will be available for her."

Roy stood up and, for no reason he knew of, shook the hand of the doctor.

"Why don't you go and see her?"

He nodded. Weary feet carried him to her bedside. After pulling up an armchair, he rested his hand on her arm. Her hands were completely bandaged. The thin white blanket emphasised the fragility of her body, outlining the contours of every bone. Sitting beside her, making circular motions with his thumb on her arm, his mind was taken back to the labour ward. The bed, the needle inserted in her left arm, the white strapping holding it in place, the drip. Similar, but not the same. Then, the needle had been in the back of her hand. The liquid had been something to start off her labour. He had watched it trickle from the pouch on a high frame, through a tube to the valve and into her bloodstream. Drip—drip—drip. This liquid was somebody else's blood. He stared at the desolate beauty of her face, unable to think beyond the present. The here and now.

Flickering eyelids kept the secrets of her dreams. He rested his head on the side of the bed. Silent tears soaked the blanket.

* * * *

"You'll have to go to the hospital on your way to work, Henry."

"What for? What good will that do?"

"All they'll tell me is that she's had a comfortable night, and Roy's with her. I need to know when she'll be home, and if she'll want any help. Jimmy said she's hurt her hands. I'm supposed to be doing the flowers at church this afternoon. I can't do that if I'm looking after Emma."

Henry sighed and drank the last of his coffee. "I'll call at the office first. Ring me there if you hear she's been discharged."

Diana nodded. He put on his hat and coat.

Driving into town, he tried to make sense of the baffling events. Susan had been missing again and taken to hospital. No-one seemed to know what was wrong with her and Jimmy hadn't said how she'd hurt her hands.

He should've known Charlie Fletcher's daughter would be trouble. That old rogue never did a straightforward deal in his life. Odd really. Diana had always been so protective of Roy, but now her concern was all for Susan. She had done a lot for the girl. All she did was worry and try to help. But there again, Diana didn't know what he knew about her father. A worm of resentment narrowed his eyes. He didn't need all this trouble at his time of life.

On arrival at the office, Miss Tanner had told him there had been no phone call from Diana as he had hoped, so he was making his way through the labyrinth of corridors to ward thirty-four.

Brenda had made an appointment for him at eleven, so at least he had a genuine excuse to leave pretty sharpish.

"Dad, what are you doing here?" Roy looked worn out.

"Your mum sent me."

"The doctors are with Susan now. Is Emma okay?"

"Yes, of course she is. What about Susan?"

"What did Jimmy tell you?"

"Just that Susan wasn't well and had hurt her hands and been brought here. What is it, son?"

"She's exhausted, underweight, and anaemic. They've given her a blood transfusion."

"But there's more, isn't there?"

Roy nodded. "When she woke up this morning she didn't recognise me. She screamed and, if her hands hadn't been bandaged, she would have pulled the blood transfusion needle from her arm. A psychiatrist is coming this afternoon. Meanwhile, they're keeping her in a side ward."

"A psychiatrist? Why?"

"I don't know."

"She'll not be home today, then?"

"No, Dad. No-one has said anything very much but I have the feeling this is going to take a long time."

Henry nodded slowly. If Roy were right, Diana would be looking after Emma for a while. She wouldn't mind though, not Diana.

* * * *

Roy dialled his mother's number. "Is Emma okay, Mum?"

"Yes, of course."

"Sorry to be brief, but I'm calling from a payphone in the

hospital and don't have much change. Will you keep Emma with you for tonight? I want to go home for a shower and then go to Jimmy and Jill's house."

"How's Susan? Your dad said…"

"They're transferring her to Stanley Grange psychiatric unit in the morning. There's no point me staying here, she's heavily sedated. I'll see you in the morning. Ask Dad to tell Miss Tanner I won't be in."

He heard his mother draw breath, and hung up.

He stood on the top step, breathing in the outside world, before setting off towards the police station to collect his car. His feet dragged. The future appeared to be no more than a desert of shifting sands. People went about their business without a care in the world, when all about him was falling down—had fallen down. His gaze stuck steadfastly to the pavement. Unable and unwilling to acknowledge the streets around him, he gripped the keys in his pocket until his hand hurt.

As he turned his key in the car door, he realised it hadn't been locked. Wires hung from the dashboard. Despite being parked right outside the police station, the radio and tape player had been ripped out. With a sigh, he started it. He had expected a parking ticket, not a break-in. Either way he couldn't give a shit.

* * * *

Every room in Orchard Cottage echoed its emptiness in unbroken silence. Without Susan and Emma, he had no home. Thoughts of his daughter made him desperate to hold her happy little body, but he wasn't ready to face his parents. Mum would be all sympathy, and want him to have dinner. Dad wouldn't understand. He could imagine them discussing it. Dad would say something about Susan pulling herself together, and Mum would tell him to be more understanding.

He almost missed the note by the kettle.

Dear Roy,

I have taken nappies, bottles, and clothes etc. for Emma. I am more than happy to look after her until Susan is better.

We are thinking of you. Dad says not to worry about work. See you tomorrow.

With love, Mum. X

Roy read the letter three times. The simple words, so carefully chosen, choked his throat. How tired he felt. The idea of driving to Haxby to see Jimmy and Jill no longer appealed. He telephoned instead. His voice cracked in deep, shuddering breaths. Jimmy said there was no need to thank him and asked him to keep in touch. They would visit, of course, when he told them the time was right.

Slumped forward onto the kitchen table, resting his forehead on folded arms, he cried. For the briefest of moments he wished he had never met Susan Fletcher, then he despised himself for the thought.

CHAPTER THIRTEEN

Susan crouched on the wide and sweeping staircase, peering between the banisters, watching the customers in the Threlfalls. Her mother and father were serving behind the bar. In the far corner Gloria was laughing as she rolled about on a huge bed with a red velvet cover. Billy and Johnny were in their usual places. Maggie leaned on the bar, talking to Patrick. Gran O'Malley and Catherine McMahon were sitting at one of the circular tables drinking tea and chatting with Granny Florrie and Miss Hughes, her teacher. Auntie Pauline was making sandwiches on her kitchen table. A little girl wearing a pure white party dress with a golden ribbon tied in a bow sang and danced. Alf Lawrence walked in and put handcuffs on everyone. Her father told him to undo them or he wouldn't give him any more free beer. Alf said it was just a joke. No-one believed him, but he unlocked the handcuffs, anyway. A scruffy old man with crooked teeth took a box of matches from his coat pocket and set light to the little girl's dress. She screamed and ran around the bar, tugging at the clothes of the customers, but no-one took any notice. They kept chatting and drinking as if she were invisible. Susan stood up and ran down the stairs. The little girl smiled and stood perfectly still. She gripped the banister rail as the little girl stared, standing perfectly still, and then faded away, disappearing without a trace. Smoke billowed around the floor. Susan shouted, but no sound came from her lips. She ran from one person to another, trying to tell them they must leave, but they couldn't see her, or hear her.

Her mother's voice drifted towards her, *'Don't worry, Missy.'* Susan turned and watched as she pulled a pint. A blackness took her peripheral vision, shrinking her view until she could see only her mother's face at the end of a long, dark tunnel and then—nothing. Sounds faded as her body was forced into relaxation, powerless against the drugs that dragged her to oblivion.

She heard a man's voice. He seemed to be talking to a baby. The baby cried and cold water rippled through her body from head to toe.

A pin prick of light slowly grew to portray Auntie Pauline's smiling face. Realising she was lying on her back, Susan willed her muscles to lift her body, but nothing happened. She was paralysed. A door opened on squeaking hinges and something was wheeled into the room, bumping into the door frame and rattling metal trays. The door closed and a woman spoke cheerfully, her words incoherent. The cheerful voice moved between the bed and the window, casting a shadow on her eyelids. A cold hand touched her arm, pressing down, a discomfort registered, tightening her eyelids, and then—the black tunnel, and carefree oblivion.

* * * *

Roy had never been inside a psychiatric hospital until that week. Stanley Grange was pleasant enough in a parallel world sort of way. Perhaps he had expected a more intimidating atmosphere. It wasn't like a normal hospital and it wasn't like the real world, either.

The building had once been a very grand house, not big enough to be classed as a stately home, but big by normal standards. On the edge of parkland to the west of the city centre, patients wandered freely along the carpeted corridors. Bewildered faces smiled at him expectantly and he smiled back.

Susan had been sedated for the past week.

Roy had given Mr Feany's senior registrar as much information as he could. It was all very well for him to say she would recover, but anyone who saw Susan would think differently.

Mr Feany had requested this meeting. His secretary showed Roy into a small, chaotic room. Taking a pile of files from the only vacant chair, she indicated Roy be seated, and left.

Malcolm Feany gave a wide smile, running his thumbs inside bright red braces as he leaned back in his creaking chair.

Bushy eyebrows appeared to have fallen from his bald head and landed randomly on his forehead. Roy sat nervously before the big man. His diagnosis and whatever treatment he prescribed held the future, not only for Susan, but also for himself and Emma.

"It's early days, Mr Jessop. I will be reducing your wife's medication slowly," he boomed.

"But she hasn't eaten anything for a week. How long will it take?"

"She has all the nutrients she needs via the drip, and the blood transfusion they gave her at the infirmary means she is no longer anaemic. You need not worry for her physical strength."

"But mentally?"

"More complex. She was very distressed when she first came around, hence the heavy sedation, and until she is less sedated and I can talk to her, I'm guessing."

"And what is your guess, Mr Feany?"

"Well, the first part isn't a guess. In layman's terms she's had a breakdown." He paused, waiting for Roy's reaction.

"And in professional terms?"

"I believe she's suffering from puerperal psychosis, and if I'm correct, it's the worst case I've ever seen."

"What does that mean, exactly?"

"Post-natal depression, Mr Jessop."

Roy held his hands up, palm to palm and fingertip to fingertip, as he let Malcolm Feany's words sink in. He breathed deeply in and out before speaking slowly, his eyes fixed on the cluttered desk between himself and the big man.

"If someone had said that a couple of months ago I would've been the first to agree, but she seemed to snap out of it. I thought she was okay."

"Your wife will recover, Mr Jessop. It will take time, but she will. We no longer tell women to pull themselves together. I will reduce her sedation today, but if she starts to show signs of distress, the dose will have to be increased again. Trying to hurry her now won't be good in the long term."

Roy nodded. "How long will it be before she can talk?"

"I'd say she should start speaking quite soon—in the next day or so, provided we can continue on the reduced medication."

"Can you tell how long she'll be here?"

"I'd rather not. False hope doesn't help any more than an unnecessarily lengthy estimate. I just don't know at this stage."

"Six months? A year?"

"Not that long. No. I think we can be sure she'll be out of here in less than six months. She will need care, Mr Jessop, and it's quite possible—likely even—that she'll need medication for a very long time, possibly for the rest of her life, albeit as a maintenance dose. But let's not run too far ahead at the moment." He stood up, signalling the end of the conversation.

"I'll go to see her now, if that's all right."

"Of course, and as she becomes less sedated it's important to talk to her. She'll be able to hear, even now." Malcolm Feany's firm handshake sparked fragile hope.

He opened the door quietly. Susan's motionless figure lay propped up on a mountain of pillows. Her arm felt warmer and her cheeks had a pink tinge to them.

"Hello, love. Mr Feany says I should talk to you, but I'm not sure you can hear me, not yet, anyway. You'll be better soon, I promise, and home with me and Emma. She's a happy baby. You don't have to worry about her. I want you to be happy, too, and come home." He leaned forward and gently kissed her forehead. "My mother's looking after her. I drop her off in the morning before I come to see you. Miss Tanner has rearranged all my appointments for after twelve o'clock. After work I pop here to see you again, and then I go to my mum and dad's house at Larks Hill Drive. I'd rather cook my own dinner at home, but Mum insists I eat with them. I've managed to persuade her I'm capable of looking after Emma overnight."

He squeezed her arm gently. Not knowing what else to say, he sat beside her in silence. He thought her eyelids moved slightly in response, but couldn't be sure. He kissed her forehead again and left the room. He had an appointment with

Thomas Barraclough the following day, and needed to organise some stuff to make it look as if he had been doing something. Jimmy and Jill would be going to Provence in ten days. He could tell Barraclough that he had people in Provence doing some local research. It wasn't a lie and he didn't want to lose the chance to work for a finder's fee. Thomas Barraclough would want results and was hardly likely to consider his domestic difficulties as a reasonable cause for delay.

Leaving her lying there had felt wrong, as though he were deserting her. He closed the car door and fastened his seatbelt, staring straight ahead, his hands gripping the steering wheel. A man walked by. Roy could only see his back but he was pretty sure he had just seen the very man he'd been thinking about go into Stanley Grange.

* * * *

Jimmy's phone call had been a bolt from the blue. Chaz's instinct had told her to be on the next flight to Leeds.

Her mother and father and Jérôme tried to convince her to wait for a few days.

"It's not that we don't care," her father said. "You know we do, and we're all as anxious as you are."

"I know. I suppose I'm finding it hard to believe. I wish I hadn't posted my letter. I only posted it today saying I wanted her to be matron of honour, and how I was looking forward to seeing them."

Jérôme held her hand as they sat at the kitchen table. "Why not go in the summer holidays?"

"Oh, no, I must see her before then. I wouldn't be much of a friend if I waited that long. I was thinking of taking a flight one Friday night and coming back on Sunday evening. That way I won't need any time off school."

Her parents exchanged worried glances with Jérôme.

"What's wrong with that?" Looking from one to the other, her eyes widened. "Don't you understand?" She rarely showed any sign of temper. "I have to."

"Jimmy and Jill will be here in two weeks. They'll give us

all the latest news. Why don't you write to Roy?" Her father's voice of reason, usually so reassuring, irritated her.

"And what would I say?"

He shrugged. "That he can come whenever he wants—maybe when Susan needs convalescence?"

"I think I'd prefer to phone him, if you're all so set on my not going over there." She stood up and left the room, scraping her chair clumsily on the stone floor.

The room fell into an awkward silence.

"I do understand how important Susan is to her," Jérôme said when Chaz had disappeared. "She's told me of their early days at school in England and how Susan's been her friend from the very first day."

"Susan 'as always come to us in 'er times of trouble—and she 'as 'ad a lot of difficult times. She eez like a second daughter to us."

"I know, Madame Fournier, Chaz told me about it. She didn't know whether she should or not, but we have no secrets. I know about her father and the brothel, and the fire."

"You should call me Jeanette." She nodded. "I cannot be Madame Fournier to you and it will be too difficult for you to call me Mama."

The conversation turned to wedding plans, and a pale-faced Chaz returned to the room. All eyes turned to her as she told them of Mr Feany's preliminary diagnosis, and of Susan's sedation.

"So you were right. There's no point in my going, not yet. But I'm going as soon as she's properly awake, even if it's just for a weekend." Disappointment clouded her face. "There's no guarantee she'll be well enough to come to the wedding."

* * * *

Chaz lay awake for hours that night, her thoughts hopping from Susan to Roy, and from Roy to little Emma. The thought of Susan all drugged up filled her with abhorrence. It felt all wrong. Roy had sounded so very weary, speaking in a monotone, only brightening when he'd talked about Emma.

He had faith in Mr Feany and maybe he was right, but it all sounded very protracted. Whatever the truth of it, she wanted Susan to come to Provence as soon as possible—and with Emma and Roy. It wouldn't be like it had been when she'd stayed for a year. Susan had her own home and family now. Chaz thought of the house she and Jérôme were buying. The spare bedroom could be for Susan and Roy, with room for a cot in one corner. The wedding was just over four months away and, more than ever, she wanted Susan to be matron of honour.

* * * *

One heavy foot followed the other down the stairs. Emma was fast asleep in her cot and the bleak prospect of another lonely evening spread before Roy. He gathered up the mail and sorted the envelopes, slowly moving one behind the other, checking for clues of the sender until he came to the distinctive air mail envelope addressed to Susan.

Jimmy had phoned Chaz on Sunday and told her what had happened. He turned the envelope over and over. Should he open it? Would Susan be annoyed if he opened her mail? If he knew its contents he would know whether or not he should read it to her.

He dialled Jimmy and Jill's number to tell them of the meeting with Mr Feany.

Jimmy answered, and after giving him the news from the hospital, he asked if Chaz had said anything about writing a letter to Susan.

"Yes, but it was written before…you know."

"I thought it must have been. Do you know what it's about? Did Chaz say?"

"She and Jérôme have set a wedding date. She wrote to ask Susan to be matron of honour."

"Do you think I should read it to her?"

"I don't know. It may help. I don't see how it could do any harm."

"Do you think Chaz will come over?"

"I'm sure she will. Just as soon as the school breaks up for summer. They finish earlier in Provence than they do here."

* * * *

Susan listened intently, trying to decide whether the voices were real or part of another dream. Someone held a hand over her arm. If she tried to pull it away they would know she was awake. Two men were talking. One voice sounded familiar. Other sounds and smells told her she was in hospital. But why? She felt no pain and could move a bit if she wanted to. She didn't feel happy or sad—or anything at all really. Her name was Susan Fletcher but that was about all she knew, other than that familiar voice.

The men were talking about a place called Provence. It sounded foreign, and as if it should mean something. She frowned and the hand tightened its grip.

"I think she's coming round, Jimmy," the strange voice said. He had called the man Jimmy. She could picture Jimmy's red hair and knew he was a friend. Her eyelids were heavy. It took an effort to open them. A man with dark, shoulder length hair was the one holding her arm. The one with red hair, the one she knew was Jimmy, sat to his side, further away from her.

"Hello, love, good to have you back," the dark-haired man said.

She looked at Jimmy. He smiled and she tried to smile back.

"Hello, Susan."

She cast her eyes around the room. The walls were pale blue. A blind hid the window. The needle in her left arm had been there when she had dreamt she was having a baby. The dark-haired man gripped her more tightly. He looked at her in a loving way, and had a kind face.

She licked her lips and swallowed. "Who are you?"

The smile fell from his face. She had upset him.

"I'm Roy. I'm your husband."

She turned to Jimmy.

"I'll find a nurse," he said, and left the room. She didn't want him to leave—she didn't want to be left with the other man.

She closed her eyes. Maybe everything was a dream, after all.

* * * *

Roy sat opposite Jimmy in the canteen of Stanley Grange, stirring his coffee, staring intently at the patterns in the frothy milk. The nurse had said that patients usually regained their memory slowly, and had told him not to worry, that as Susan became more awake she would remember more. But *usually* didn't mean *always*.

"We don't know anything about paintings. Are you sure you want us to do this?" Jimmy's question took him from his thoughts.

"You don't need to know much. Unknown artists don't charge much, so you can't go far wrong. Anything impressionist."

"That's the splodgy ones, right?"

"Right."

"So how do I tell the good ones from the rubbish?"

"You need to stand away from the painting, and this may sound stupid, but it should feel as if you could walk into the picture." Roy paused.

"Go on."

"It's the perspective, you see. The picture has to have that depth."

"We-ell, we'll try. I can't say more than that. Maybe Chaz and Jérôme will come with us." Jimmy finished his coffee and put down his cup. "I'll tell Jill what you said about the perspective and so on."

"I only wish we were going with you. Thanks for coming over to see Susan."

"I wanted to see her before we went to Provence. Chaz will be asking a thousand questions."

"She didn't know who I was." The false air of normality shattered, falling like broken glass. "She knew who you were, Jimmy, but not me. If we hadn't met, none of this would have happened. I've ruined her life."

Jimmy leaned forward, looking straight into his eyes. "Don't ever think like that. You're the best thing that ever happened to Susan. You've given her so much and in so many ways. Never, ever blame yourself." He sounded annoyed. "No-one knows Susan better than I do."

Roy sighed and leaned back. "I feel as if I don't know her at all."

"She needs you—will need you, so does Emma. You love her, don't you?"

He nodded. "Too much, maybe."

Jimmy shook his head, his voice softer. "No. That's not it. I've never been much good at talking about my feelings, but I know I can't imagine life without Jill. She's given up a lot for me—falling out with her parents and everything. Think about it, Roy, what chance of happiness would Susan have without you?"

"Women, eh?" He gave a self-deprecating smile. "We'd better go. I expect you have packing to do and I need to pick up Emma. What time's your flight?"

"Early. We fly from Yeadon at seven o'clock, changing at Heathrow."

Roy took out his wallet. "Here's fifty quid. See what you can find."

"I might not come back." He grinned, and put the money in his pocket.

* * * *

Diana watched as Roy cut his food with the side of his fork while jigging Emma on his knee. He was later than usual and she had kept his dinner warm in the oven. If he wanted to talk about whatever it was that had delayed him, he would do so. She wished with all her heart that she could take the burden from his shoulders. Only a deep and true love could hurt the way he was hurting. The light had gone from his world.

Henry came in from the garden, wiping his feet with unnecessary vigour. Diana looked at him, silently acknowledging his efforts to keep the kitchen floor clean.

"What kept you?" he asked Roy. "You know your mother doesn't like keeping food warm."

Diana groaned inwardly. Henry had always been the calm one, the voice of reason, but these days he was permanently grumpy.

"Sorry. Jimmy came over from York. We went for a coffee."

"You don't have to apologise to us—ever," Diana said, shooting a glare at her husband.

He shook his head and went from the room. They heard him rustle a newspaper in the lounge.

"We're here to help, you know—in whatever way we can."

"I know, Mum. You're being brilliant, but Dad isn't happy, is he?"

"You could say we're none of us happy. He doesn't understand, that's all."

"She will recover you know." Roy put his fork down. "I spoke to Mr Feany today. That's another reason I'm late. He says it's the worst case of post-natal depression he's ever seen."

Diana nodded, averting her eyes. She cast her mind back to the weeks following Roy's birth—his constant crying and the realisation, years later, that she'd had post-natal depression. The baby blues. She had struggled, unable to understand her emotions, feeling her mother-in-law's eye upon her. Then one day it had lifted, like a misty morning turning into a sunny day. Everything had suddenly slotted into place and she had never looked back. Shortly after that Roy had found his thumb and stopped crying. There had been the sad times, of course, with her miscarriages, but not depression. That was something quite different.

"You knew, didn't you?" He sounded astonished.

"I knew something was wrong. The diagnosis was a relief, bad though it is."

"What do you mean?"

"Because we know what we're dealing with, and she will recover."

Roy nodded, pushing his plate away. "I suppose so. Thanks for dinner, Mum. I must be off. It's time this little lady was in bed." He put her in the carrycot. "Say goodbye to Dad for me, will you? I won't disturb him while he's reading the newspaper. See you tomorrow."

Diana watched his car turn from the drive before going into the lounge. Henry had fallen asleep. She took the newspaper from his lap and folded it. He would never understand. She didn't expect him to, but then not many people did understand depression unless they had suffered themselves. They would visit Susan as soon as Roy said the time was right, and take Emma. Perhaps seeing her baby would help.

As she returned to the kitchen she heard Henry cough. He would come through in a moment and be surprised to find Roy had gone, and then ask how long he had been asleep. She washed the dishes and put everything away. A quick glance around confirmed it was time to take off her apron. Henry hadn't appeared, and a quick look in the lounge told her he wasn't in his chair. She called upstairs. "Are you up there, Henry?"

When she didn't receive a reply she muttered to herself and went up to find him. The bedroom door stood ajar and, with her hand resting on the door handle, she was about to tell him he should have taken his shoes off, but something didn't seem right. She edged into the room. A chill ran down her spine when she saw his face. So pale. He couldn't be, could he? Not dead? She stared at the man who had been her husband for thirty-four years. Numbness froze her limbs. Her scalp tingled and shrank to her skull as her breath escaped in a rush. The tingling ran though her body and shut her eyes. Minutes later when she opened them he was still there. Still dead. She would have to telephone Roy, and the doctor. But there was no rush. Henry had been rather grumpy lately. By 'lately' she supposed she meant since Emma had been born. He had been so looking forward to being a grandfather, but the reality seemed to fall short of his expectations, what with Roy's car crash and Susan not coping. Odd, really. At first she had been against Susan, afraid she would hurt Roy, but somewhere along the line she and Henry had swapped places.

Emma would never know her granddad. For Emma he would just be a man in a photograph, and somehow the thought upset her more than anything, and the tears flowed.

She gripped the banister rail as unsteady legs took her downstairs. The kitchen clock ticked more loudly than usual, emphasising the relentlessness of time, telling her to start making phone calls.

Doctor Hirst said he would come straight away. Diana would have preferred to walk to Orchard Cottage. Telling Roy over the phone would be difficult, but she didn't want to leave Henry on his own. She was still staring at the phone when the doctor arrived. He confirmed that which she knew to be true, and said there would have to be a post mortem since Henry hadn't seen a doctor for a while.

She followed his clumping boots down the stairs and made him a cup of tea while they waited for the ambulance to take Henry away. He asked after Susan and Emma. She knew he was attempting to make light conversation to fill the air as they waited. She told him Susan was still in Stanley Grange and that Emma was very well. He hadn't asked for further details and she gave none. Henry would have called it a conversation stopper.

The ambulance pulled away without the need for sirens or lights or speed. Doctor Hirst insisted on taking her to Orchard Cottage.

* * * *

Roy heard a car pull up and opened the door to see his mother carrying a small suitcase. The unmistakable figure of Doctor Hirst stood at her side. His thoughts flew to Susan before logic told him that any news from Stanley Grange would have come directly to him. "What is it?"

His mother walked straight past him and into the lounge.

The doctor waited on the doorstep. "May I come in? I'm afraid it's bad news." Roy stood aside.

The doctor asked if he would like to sit down. "It's your father."

"What are you talking about? There's nothing wrong with Dad. He was reading his paper an hour ago."

The doctor's carefully worded news shook him to the core. He paced around the house, not wanting to believe any of it, willing the doctor to be wrong. His mother was in the kitchen saying goodbye to the doctor and thanking him. For what? For telling them his father was dead? He didn't believe it. How could she be so calm? He ran upstairs and into Emma's room. Hot tears blurred the face of a little girl who would never know what a lovely man her grandfather was. *Was.*

A car door closed. From the window he saw the doctor drive away. Mother was filling the kettle. Tea. The answer to everything. A cup of tea.

"Doctor Hirst thinks he probably had a heart attack." She turned to face him. "He'll have felt nothing. We have to be glad of that."

Roy pulled a chair from the table and sat down heavily, swamped by guilt. Since Emma had been born he had relied on his father more and more in the business. He should have been taking over and letting his dad take it easy, not sitting back doing the minimum. And now everything had changed.

His mother put the teacups on the table. Sitting close beside him, she put her arm around him and he laid his head on her shoulder.

"I didn't even say goodbye. I just left." Tears trickled down the side of his nose and onto his mother's cardigan.

"He was reading his newspaper, remember? You didn't want to disturb him."

"How can you be so calm, Mum?"

"I don't think it's sunk in yet. Not really."

"What will you do without him?"

"Do? I'll do what I've always done, but on my own. What else can I do? I have you and Emma and Susan."

Roy lifted his head and sniffed. His mother reached to the worktop and passed him a tissue. "I won't be able to tell her, not yet."

"You told me about your meeting with Mr Feany, but how was she today?"

"She's coming round." He wiped his face with the tissue. "She didn't know who I was, Mum. She recognised Jimmy, but not me."

"I thought something was wrong when you were eating your dinner."

"I wish I'd known, you know, that Dad was…"

"About to die? We can't live like that, Roy." She took his hand. "Look at me. We can't live every minute thinking it might be our last. None of us."

"But I'm the one who should be comforting *you*."

"You're a good son, Roy. You always have been. We shall support each other. Tomorrow will be busy. There's always a lot to do at these times."

"I don't think I can sleep, not yet."

"Me neither, but I'll go to bed, anyway. You'll be all right, won't you?"

He forced a thin smile. "Yes, Mum. I'll be fine."

After he'd heard the spare bedroom door close he went to the drinks cabinet and poured a large whisky into a cut-glass tumbler.

"Cheers, Dad. This one's for you. The Scarborough Arms will miss you but not as much as I will." The peaty liquid hit his stomach with cold comfort.

CHAPTER FOURTEEN

Two weeks later

Roy's mother looked smaller, her touch on his arm as light as a feather as they followed his father's coffin into the little church of St Peter. He'd had his hair cut short for the occasion. Dad had never said as much but Roy knew he didn't like his shoulder-length student hair-style that hadn't really been a style at all.

Three wreaths of white flowers contrasted with the dark mahogany of the coffin. Lillies from his mother, chrysanthemums from himself and Susan, and tulips from Emma.

The church was packed. His father had been well-known in Leeds. And then there were his mother's friends from church. The flower arrangers had been busy creating matching arrangements—one to the front of the pulpit, the other to the side of the lectern.

He and his mother took their reserved places in the front pew and the organ fell to silence.

"I am the resurrection and the life."

The day was something to be endured, a necessary rite, delayed for a week by the processes of the pathology department. There were a thousand things he wished he had said to his father and a few which he wished he had not.

Roy had decided not to give the eulogy. The very thought of a sea of faces staring at him had been too much. Time would tell whether he would regret his decision.

With eyes fixed on the coffin, he heard little of the service. His thoughts ricocheted between Susan, Emma and the diminutive figure of his mother at his side as she attempted to sing the hymns, managing only occasional notes. He didn't even try. Emma was being cared for by Jimmy and Jill. There hadn't been time to say much that morning when they'd collected her. After the burial, the funeral car would take him and his mother to Lark's Hill Drive for refreshments. He had no idea how many people would join them, but it would be a lot.

He had been staying with his mother, but she insisted he should go home afterwards. He couldn't be sure if she really wanted him to, but her insistence suited him. He was desperate to have some semblance of order in his life.

It was the first day he hadn't visited Susan. Malcolm Feany had said she was making good progress, and assured him that missing one day wouldn't make any difference. At least she knew who he was sometimes.

* * * *

Diana's friends from church had made copious sandwiches and pots of tea. Jessop's Auctioneers had closed for the day as a mark of respect, and to enable Brenda to attend the funeral.

She handed around the plates and serviettes. Roy felt he had all but drowned in tea since his father had died. The words still felt strange to him. Dad had died. Dad was dead. Stronger drinks were available for those who needed fortification. He sipped a whisky, nodding in acknowledgement to those who spoke to him.

"May I offer my condolences?" He turned to see Thomas Barraclough.

"Mr Barraclough, how kind of you to come."

"I didn't know your father well, but he was a respected businessman in Leeds."

"Thank you. Please tell me if it's none of my business, but did I see you at Stanley Grange a couple of weeks ago?"

"Oh, quite likely." He touched a cufflink, circling the smooth metal with the tips of his forefinger. "My late mother was a patient there. I am, erm, that is to say, I'm involved with the financial side."

Roy narrowed his eyes.

"I give them money, Mr Jessop, and I talk to the patients who would otherwise have no visitors. So may I ask why you were there?"

Roy took another sip of whisky. "I was visiting my wife. She's Mr Feany's patient."

The other man nodded slowly. "Malcolm Feany is a dedicated man in a difficult field of medicine. By *difficult* I suppose I mean unpopular. It's relatively easy to raise funds for sick babies. Mental health problems are hidden away, quite literally."

"Did my father know of your involvement with Stanley Grange?"

"I doubt it. As I said, I didn't know your father well. Maybe I shouldn't raise the matter of business today, but I'm curious. Do you have any paintings for me yet?"

"Possibly. I'll call you tomorrow, if that's okay with you."

"Certainly. I look forward to hearing from you."

The day moved inexorably on. His mother looked exhausted but Roy knew better than to suggest she sit down. The last of the mourners left at half past seven and by eight o'clock she was in her dressing gown, drinking yet another cup of tea.

"I'll be off then, Mum. I'll walk home. The fresh air will be good and, anyway, I've had a bit too much whisky to drive." He kissed her on the cheek.

"Good night, Roy. Don't worry about me. I'll be fine."

"I know. Good night." He closed the door quietly and heard her turn the key in the lock.

As he walked home it came to him that he had been wrong about his mother. With her faith in God and her memories, she had enough and was happy. Well, not exactly happy, but ready for him to go home, and for her life to resume in its new pattern. She'd had some weepy moments when she'd taken herself off to her bedroom. He had overheard her talking to his dad, telling him he had no right to avoid old age by pegging out like that, so suddenly. And yet she had tapped into a peculiar strength—organising the funeral, dealing with paperwork, phoning the bank. She had gone into overdrive with an energy born of grief. Now, with all the formalities of death over, she had moved into another phase. He saw her not just as his mother but as a person to be admired—a woman of strength and practicality. He must move forward, treasuring his memories, feeling his father's love for him as an intangible force, only recognised when it was too late.

Jimmy turned off the television as Roy opened the door.

"Don't do that on my account," he said. "Are you watching a film?"

"We've seen it before," Jill said. "How did today go? How's your mother?"

"I suppose it all went according to plan, as these things do. Mum seems to be okay. She's quite incredible, really. The bloke who wants to buy impressionist paintings was there. How has your day been?"

They spoke simultaneously, Jill saying, "Wonderful," and Jimmy saying, "Fantastic."

Roy's smile gave way to a laugh. "You enjoyed being 'in loco parentis', then?"

"We went to Roundhay Park this morning and fed the ducks," Jimmy said. "There are loads of ducklings. Emma loved it."

"I take it she's fast asleep."

Jill nodded. "Yes, she was tired out. How was Susan when you saw her yesterday?"

"Better. Well, better than she was before. She doesn't talk much. I talk and she listens."

"Does she remember what happened—you know, at Vine Street?"

"No. She says she remembers being in the cafe at Lavells with me and Emma, but nothing after that."

"Perhaps that's a good thing," Jimmy said. "We'd like to visit if you think it would be okay. Chaz wants to come and see her, too."

"I don't see why not. In fact, I think it'd be good for her." The smile fell from his face. "She doesn't recognise Emma."

Jimmy paled with shock. "What do you mean? How can she not know her own daughter?"

"She knows who *I* am, although I'm not sure she actually

remembers me. It's more as if she accepts I'm her husband because people keep telling her so. Not a true memory, if you know what I mean." He paused. "Yesterday she asked me why I kept bringing a baby to see her." A stunned silence lay between them. "Mr Feany says she needs more time, and that he's happy with her progress. I don't see any, but I don't know if that's because of the drugs. She's still sedated."

"How long will it take?" Jill asked. "Chaz desperately wants her to be at her wedding."

"No-one can say. I could go in tomorrow and find her the same, or regressed, or asking about Emma and wanting to come home."

"Doesn't she want to come home? She loves this place."

"She never asks. I talk about it, of course, but she just sits there and listens. She gets dressed each morning and goes to the common room, but only because the nurses say she must. It's quite pleasant in there."

"I could write to Chaz, and go to see Susan tomorrow morning," suggested Jill.

"Yes, that would be good. She's at her best in the morning. She doesn't know about Dad by the way, so I'd rather you didn't say anything. I'll tell her when the time's right. You two are staying here tonight, aren't you?"

Jill looked at her watch. "It makes sense, especially if we're seeing Susan tomorrow."

"Good, that's settled then. I want to hear all about Provence." Roy rubbed his hands together. "Now, where are those paintings? You did bring them, didn't you?"

"Yes," Jimmy said. "They're in the dining room."

Roy went to the kitchen and brought three wine glasses and a bottle of Chianti to the dining room. Jimmy took the paintings from their cardboard tubes and rolled them out on the table. He sipped his wine nervously as Jill squeezed his hand. "What do you think?"

Roy didn't reply. He rearranged the canvasses, piling three on top of each other and pushing them to one side. He lifted one of the remaining three, a painting of 'Place Richelme' in Aix. He held it by the uppermost corners and gave it to Jill.

Stepping away, he tipped his head to one side, narrowing his eyes. "These three are by the same artist, yes?"

Jimmy exhaled slowly. "Jacques Morel. The other three are all by different artists, but we were drawn to Jacques' work."

"I can see why. They're good. Very good. Where did you find him?" He took the painting from Jill and laid it on the table.

"On 'Le Cours Mirabeau', or 'Le Cours', as the locals call it."

"Has he had any exhibitions?" He took the painting and passed her another.

"I don't know. My French isn't up to much. He has a dog called Coco. We went into Aix on three separate days, and he was on Le Cours each time."

Roy leaned forward, looking closely at the signature in the bottom right corner of the canvas. "Jacques Morel. Never heard of him. That's good. What did you pay for them?" He laid the canvas on the table.

"I worked it out at about eight pounds each," Jill said.

Roy grinned and hugged her, and then shook Roy's hand. "You clever, clever people. I can't wait to show these to Thomas Barraclough."

* * * *

Jimmy and Jill were shown to the common room of Stanley Grange. Susan was sitting in a deep buttoned armchair, her tiny figure made smaller by the height and width of the chair. The pastel colour scheme gave an air of relaxed luxury, belying the troubles of its occupants. Patients gathered in groups. Some played a board game, another concentrated on a jigsaw puzzle, seemingly oblivious to his surroundings. A nurse moved amongst them, discreetly watchful. Music played softly.

Susan looked straight ahead with eyes devoid of sorrow. There was nothing there, the light replaced by dull emptiness.

Jimmy knelt before her. "Hello, love. How are you today?" He thought his words sounded stupid. Wasn't it obvious how she felt?

Her head turned towards him. He saw the slightest widening of her eyes. She had recognised him. "Jimmy." She leaned towards him and whispered. "Where is everyone?"

"What do you mean?"

"My mum, your mum, Granny Florrie, Chaz. Where are they?"

"Chaz is in France."

She leaned back. Jimmy could only stare as she looked down at her hands, flexing her fingers.

"I'll write to her if you like. She'll come to see you as soon as she can, I know she will."

"Why can't she come now?"

"She works at the school, remember? She's a teacher. She'll come in the holidays."

She frowned. Her hands relaxed. Tender skin with thread-like scars surrounded short, carefully-manicured nails.

"What happened to my hands, Jimmy?"

"You had an accident. You've not been well."

She closed her eyes. "Who's this with you?"

"Jill. She's my wife. You're married to Roy, and you have a daughter, Emma."

She took several deep breaths and leaned heavily into the corner of the chair.

He exchanged a worried glance with Jill, fearing he may have said too much.

"Yes, I know." She looked towards Jill and then back to Jimmy. "I'm sorry. I remember things from years ago, but more recent stuff doesn't seem real. Roy talks about Emma all the time and I try to be interested, but I can't connect with her. I hate myself for that."

"You need more time."

"I know. I know. I keep being told all that but…"

"When you're off the drugs maybe."

"I don't know why they keep giving me all these tablets."

"Susan." Jimmy spoke more loudly than he had intended. Heads turned. A nurse frowned at him. "Listen to me, Susan." He leaned forward, his voice lowered. "You had a breakdown.

Maybe no-one's actually said that to you, and maybe I shouldn't have said it, but there it is, and I can't take the words back. We want you to get better, and to do that you need to take the medication."

Her lips tightened, locking in her confusion.

"Would you like us to leave?" Jill asked.

Susan blinked and shook her head. She held out her right hand to Jimmy and her left to Jill. They held her gently as she closed her eyes.

"When I wake up each morning and my eyes are still closed, I'm a child again in my room at the Threlfalls. I can even hear the noise of the traffic on Briggate. Then, when I open my eyes, everything slowly comes back to me, right up until Roy and I were having lunch at Lavells. My memory's completely fine. When I think of Emma I get upset because it isn't her fault she has a hopeless mother. She deserves better and so does Roy. The nurses come along and see me upset and give me more tablets. After half an hour or so I stop crying, because I can't feel anything. Nothing. I'm not sad and I'm not happy. They tell me to get up and dressed and I do as I'm told. The drugs are starting to wear off a bit now and I can feel this lump of sadness building up in my stomach. They'll give me more with lunch and the sadness is taken away again. What I am trying to say is that the drugs are just blanking everything. They're not making me better at all. I sit here like a moron most of the time."

Jimmy looked at Jill who shook her head.

"Have you told Roy all this?" Jill asked.

Susan opened her eyes slowly. "No. Will you tell him for me?"

"Of course we will, but why don't you?"

Susan closed her eyes again with an almost imperceptible shake of her head. A nurse approached and rested her hand gently upon her shoulder. "Time for lunch, Susan."

They let go of her hands and kissed her on the cheek. "We'll be off, then," Jimmy said. "We'll call in at your house and have a word with Roy, like we said. He'll be here this afternoon."

"My house," she whispered.

They turned at the doorway. The nurse had linked arms with Susan. They waved, but her eyes were focussed on the floor as she moved slowly towards lunch and her next dose of tranquilisers.

* * * *

"I've already had this conversation with Mr Feany." Roy leaned against the kitchen units in Orchard Cottage.

"You mean Susan *has* told you how she feels?" Jimmy asked.

"No. Not Susan. I'm amazed she spoke to you so much. But, on the other hand, perhaps I shouldn't be so surprised. No. I noticed it myself. She is more alert before her next dose."

"And what did Mr Feany say?"

"That he has everything under control and she is on the correct dose."

"And you—what do you think?"

"It's not a case of what I think. I have to trust Mr Feany. He says he's reducing the dose very gradually and that in the long term it'll work. I've talked to Susan about it but she just shakes her head."

"So he's saying that to take her off the drugs would be worse than listening to how she feels. That he knows best and there is nothing to discuss?"

"There's absolutely no chance of her coming off the drugs in the near future. What I would like to know is when she can come home. When will she be on a low enough dose to be discharged? That's my question."

"And he can't answer that, I suppose?" Jill said.

"No. And he's reluctant to guess, other than vaguely saying months rather than years."

"I'm sorry, Roy. On the drive up here Jill and I thought we had good news for you."

"You have. From what you tell me she spoke more to you than she has to anyone."

A cry came from a monitor on the worktop. Emma had woken. "We'll get off, Roy. You'll have lots to do," said Jill.

"I'd rather you stayed. How do you feel about looking after Emma while I visit Susan? Mum wants to come with me, and I think maybe Susan will find it easier without Emma there."

"Put like that, we can't refuse," Jimmy said. "Not that we want to."

"That suits me. She's such a treasure," agreed Jill.

"You never know," Roy called over his shoulder, "the practise may come in handy one day." He continued up the stairs, unaware of the vacuum of silence behind him.

* * * *

It was Diana's first visit to Stanley Grange. She'd felt she'd been of more use caring for Emma, or had she been afraid of what she might find? She wrestled with her conscience, making an excuse of Henry's death, knowing they would have visited together.

She walked beside Roy into the common room. He had tried to warn her, but nothing could have prepared her for the pitiful sight of her daughter-in-law sitting in that big chair. She didn't know what to say.

Roy kissed Susan on the cheek. "Hello, love."

"Jimmy and Jill came this morning. He's going to speak to the doctor and tell him they make me take too many tablets, and then he's going to get me out of here. Why have you had your hair cut?" Susan's words came in a rush, babbling out as if they couldn't wait a second longer.

Grabbing the arm of the chair, Diana sat down slowly. She couldn't look at her. She could only watch her son. His love for his wife was too deep, the hurt too painful to watch.

On their journey to Stanley Grange, Roy had explained the need to reduce the dose of her medication slowly and of how Jimmy had spoken with him about it. Susan's interpretation of the conversation cast a shadow over Roy's face, creasing his forehead.

"Good to hear you so chatty, love. Mum's come with me."

"Hello, Diana. Where's Henry?"

Too shocked to speak, Diana smiled and gripped the chair more strongly. Roy had warned her that Susan was unlikely to recognise her and may not speak much. Her waif-like figure had been a shock, but nothing could have prepared her for the question of Henry's whereabouts.

"We have some bad news for you there, love." Roy held her hand, running his thumb back and forth over her knuckles. Her eyes rounded in their dark hollows, her lips shut tight. "Dad has passed away."

Diana watched her body tense and judder. Roy must have felt it through her hand. Susan opened her mouth as if to speak and then closed it again. Leaning back, she closed her eyes.

Roy turned and mouthed the words, 'Say something, Mum.'

"Henry didn't suffer, Susan. He wanted you to get better. We all do."

"Go away, Diana. I want you to go away."

Roy tilted his head towards the french doors and mouthed, 'See you outside.'

Diana straightened her back and lengthened her stride. Never in her whole life had she been spoken to like that. Roy had warned her about Susan's physical appearance but—such rudeness. There was no other way to describe it. No hidden meaning. No chance she could have got it wrong. 'Go away' was never going to be open to interpretation.

Did Susan blame her for Henry's death? What had she said that was so wrong? Her mind flitted between laying the blame at the door of mental illness, Susan's dubious upbringing in a pub, and her own Christianity, which was struggling to turn the other cheek. There had always been something about the girl. Roy knew more than he let on, she was sure of it. She admired him for his loyalty.

After a rocky start she and Susan had been good friends, or so she had thought. She slackened her pace. The initial fire in her step had quenched, giving her time to absorb her surroundings. Patients walked along the many paths threading through the grounds of Stanley Grange, some with a nurse. The plaque on a seat read 'In Memory of Edith Barraclough, 1908-1963.' She had been fifty-five. That was four years older than poor Henry. Had Edith Barraclough suffered? Was she a poor tortured soul, or had she been happy in her own world? Diana leaned back. The view from the seat took in the rolling acres of Capability Brown style landscape.

Roy had told her they were lucky to have Stanley Grange because it specialised in depression. Most mental hospitals took patients with brain damage as well as illness. She hadn't thought about it until then, but could see his point.

Her anger dissipated as quickly as it had risen. Susan was ill, not wicked. She pushed her vitriol away. Such thoughts were destructive. There had been enough of that, one way and another. Susan's past was none of her business. The girl had had a rough time and the future was more important.

She stretched her legs before her, turning her ankles in circles one way and then the other. Roy might be a long time, but she would wait.

CHAPTER FIFTEEN

The more she tried to work it out, the more her head ached. For the third time that morning Susan forced her train of thought back to the beginning.

Her name was Susan Fletcher. She lived with her father at The Threlfalls Hotel on Briggate. Her mother was dead. She should be sad or angry, but could feel no emotion at all. She even tried to make herself cry, but there was just a cloying numbness, wrapped around her like a sodden blanket.

Every detail of her childhood was crystal clear. The junior school in Elder Road, her teacher—Miss Hughes—and her friends, Chaz and Jimmy. She remembered the dirty old man who had touched her, and Alf coming to the bar. Her father had burned her party dresses that night and she hadn't been allowed in the bar again until she had been much older. She remembered acting as lookout for Maggie, and then things started to cloud. She knew Jimmy and Chaz had gone to university, and that she had had an argument with Auntie Pauline shortly before she had been killed. After that— nothing. Not in her head, anyway. Everything she had been told stayed in the shadows. Neither true nor false. And yet she had recognised Diana without knowing who she actually was. Poor Henry. Roy was very kind and Emma was a pretty girl, but how could she believe all the stuff about being married? How could she not believe it? How could she have had a baby and not remember? Her hand flew to the ridged scar beneath her night dress. Either everything she had been told was true or she would wake up and find it had all been a nightmare.

A nurse would be coming soon. If only they would leave her alone and stop the tablets she would be able to remember everything.

"Come along, Mrs Jessop. Lunchtime. Take this tablet and we'll go through to the dining room." Susan took the tablet and glass of water from the nurse. She put it on her tongue and then, with sleight of hand, slipped the tablet into her pocket. She smiled sweetly at the nurse and drank the water before taking her arm.

* * * *

Thomas Barraclough cast his eyes over the canvasses on his dining room table, aware of the tension on Roy Jessop's face. They were good. Very good. They were exactly the sort of undiscovered talent he was looking for. He touched a cufflink with his forefinger. "Just the one artist?"

"Yes, but I'll find more."

"And you say your contact in Aix found these on the street?"

"There's a street market where artists traditionally—"

"Yes, I know. Were there no others? Was Monsieur Morel all alone on Le Cours?"

"N-no. My contact sent others but they weren't good enough. I knew you were after something better."

Thomas put his forefinger to his lips, enjoying Roy's anxiety. At their first meeting, when he had set him the task of finding exactly that sort of painting, he had flattered him. Now he had to scare him a little. He considered it a necessary and enjoyable part of the game.

"Don't you like them, Mr Barraclough?"

"Yes. I think so. But I have to be perfectly honest with you, I am a little disappointed that I have no choice. I would like to have seen a selection of artists."

"I hope to travel to Provence myself in the not too distant future."

"If you don't mind my asking, Mr Jessop, why didn't you go yourself this time? Was it the unfortunate death of your father?"

"Yes and no. I couldn't go because of my wife's illness, but with Dad's death, I couldn't have gone, anyway."

"Please don't feel obliged to answer a personal question, but how is your wife?"

"I don't know. That's the truth of it." Roy ran his fingers through his hair. "When I think back to how she was when she was admitted to Stanley Grange I have to say there is an improvement, but lately she's been neither better nor worse. She seemed to be getting better, and then she turned on my mother and was extremely rude to her for no reason."

"Would you like a cup of tea, Mr Jessop? Please, take a seat in the other room. If Alexia and Elouise are in there tell them to get out. Push them off the chairs if you have to. They think they own the place."

Thomas busied himself in the kitchen. He had taken a liking to the young man, and felt an empathy with him. If he'd had a listener when his mother had been ill, someone to talk to, or even to talk *at*, it would have helped. Perhaps he could take the idea further with the management of Stanley Grange. He had their ear, and liked to think it was because he had something of value to say, and not because they felt obliged to indulge the man who had given them the money to furnish the common room. He disliked it being called *common*, it was anything but common. Malcolm Feany had suggested it be called The Thomas Barraclough Room, and while he had been flattered, he had not wanted his name on the door. On reflection, he could ask them to call it the Edith Room, after his mother.

Elouise and Alexia mewed around his legs. "Don't be such tarts, you dreadful cats. Did Mr Jessop throw you out? Good. I told him to, so don't come complaining to me." He proceeded to set a tray with two china cups and saucers with delicate yellow flowers around the rim. A matching jug and sugar bowl, with cubed sugar and tongs, and two silver teaspoons were placed with precision on the embroidered tea tray. The little teapot took centre stage. He stood back to admire his handwork before taking the tray to the waiting Mr Jessop. "May I call you Roy?"

"Of course, Mr Barraclough."

"Thomas. Never Tom, if you don't mind. Thomas." Placing a cup and saucer beside Roy, he poured the tea. "When my mother was a patient at Stanley Grange I felt isolated. I expect you do, too. You're torn between your love and loyalty to your wife and a desire for normality, at almost any cost. But there's the rub. Money cannot make her better. Mental illness, like any other, has no respect for the person." He poured a second cup of tea, with no milk, dropping three cubes of sugar from the delicate tongs, stirring for rather longer than necessary. He expected Roy to say something but he remained silent, maybe awaiting his words of wisdom.

"I come from a very poor family," he continued. "My great grandfather died in the workhouse. My grandfather was a miner in the days when profit was king and the employees of those terrible places merely facilitators of the riches of the owners. His son—my father—broke the mould. He was a man of vision, and realised that everyone who makes anything needs to put it in a box. So he started making boxes. Cardboard boxes." A smile crept over his face. "I have three factories now and produce every conceivable size and shape of packaging. Plastic, polystyrene, cardboard. Not the most glamorous of products but one which every manufacturer needs." After a sip of tea, he carried on. "I expect you're wondering why I'm telling you all this." He paused for a moment. "My reasoning is linked to my mother's illness. My success did not suit her. She hated living in this house. *Too posh for the likes of us,*' she used to say. I tried to explain that, in becoming successful, I was providing jobs for the families she knew, and that everyone gained from the way I was running the business. You see, Roy, I run a profit-sharing bonus scheme. It's linked to productivity and timekeeping. It benefits everyone involved. My workers don't take time off unnecessarily because the harder they work the better my profits, and the higher their bonus. The most beautiful thing about the system is its simplicity. Mother couldn't, or more likely wouldn't, move into the world of the employer. She simply couldn't handle it. Even when I told her I had a nurse on the payroll she said I only did it to make people work harder."

"But, that didn't make her ill, did it?"

"It worried her, and in the end, the worry took over. Of course, one can't be sure, but it's my belief that it contributed to her death. Malcolm Feany diagnosed clinical depression and

latterly, senile dementia. She simply lost the will to live, and
faded away. What I'm trying to say is that there's no definitive
answer to the myriad of questions surrounding depression. The
patient lives in another world, and I don't just mean the world
inside Stanley Grange."

"I'm sorry, erm, Thomas. I mean, I'm sorry to hear about
your mother, but my wife—Susan has post-natal depression."

"Ah, I see."

"See what?"

"That was the trigger."

"Yes. She seemed to be fine. The perfect wife and
mother, but now I see there were little signs that went
unnoticed at the time."

"And her turning on your mother, I take it you've put
two and two together there?"

"I hadn't, no. You think it's all to do with the
motherhood thing, do you?"

Thomas shrugged. "I'm not a psycho-analyst, Roy. I
merely listen and apply my mind to reasoning. What of your
mother-in-law? Where does she fit into all this?"

"Susan's mother died suddenly some years ago, and her
father died in a fire."

"And so your mother is the only parent left."

"Yes." Roy paused, clearly puzzled by the interest in his
personal life. "Susan's had a lot of trauma in her life."

"Has Malcolm Feany asked about her background?"

"No, I don't think so. He's just treating her for the post-
natal depression."

"I have a great deal of respect for Malcolm. What I have
to say now is in confidence. It's my opinion and no more. If
Malcolm has a fault it is that he doesn't always take into
account the historical background of his cases. To be fair to
the man, sometimes there is no relevant history. People can
become clinically depressed for no apparent reason. But if
there is a reason I believe it should be taken into account."

"He said Susan was the worst case he had ever come
across." Roy's words were barely audible. The teacup rattled in
its saucer as he placed it back on the tray.

"I hope you don't mind my speaking in such a forthright manner, and of matters which are really none of my business. I felt compelled to say my piece, as it were, in the hope it might help."

"He says she will recover."

"Then I'm sure she will. But tell me, Roy, does she have any treatment other than her medication?"

"No. At least I don't think so. He doesn't approve of electric shock treatment."

"I didn't mean that, dear me, no. I meant does she have any therapy?" Roy made no reply. "Does a therapist talk to her? You'd know if one did, because you would be paying for it. The National Health Service wouldn't cover it."

"Then the answer has to be no. No-one has suggested it. I would gladly pay if it would help. I'm not a rich man, but I'm not poor, either."

"Is she a voluntary patient?"

"Yes, I suppose so. What do you mean?"

"Did you sign anything as her next of kin? Is she committed to their care under the Mental Health Act?"

"N-no. Should I?"

"Good Lord, no. If she's merely being given oral medication she could leave at any time and…"

"Thomas, please. There's nothing in the world I would like more than for my wife to come home, but she's ill, and I have to go to work. My mother looks after our daughter."

"I understand. I've said too much already. It's hard to keep one's tongue when one feels strongly about something." Thomas stood up, suddenly wishing to curtail the meeting. They shook hands. "I hope we can continue with our business arrangements."

"What exactly is our arrangement?"

"Didn't I say?" He knew, of course, that he'd mentioned no figures to Roy, and had been hoping he would ask.

"No. If I remember correctly, you said you'd pay a finder's fee and reasonable expenses."

"Ah, yes. And what is reasonable? Your travel expenses to Provence and a hotel I suppose, and a fee of—shall we say twenty pounds, plus the cost of the picture I buy?"

"I'll stay with friends in Provence, so there'll be no hotel bills. I accept your offer for the three works by Jacques Morel, but a fee for future findings must be negotiable, depending on their potential. Is that reasonable?"

"I believe in fairness and that's fair. I like your honesty, although potential is impossible to quantify. We shall have to come to an agreement on an *ad hoc* basis. I'll write a cheque for the three canvasses, and you must contact me when you have more."

* * * *

Driving back to the office, Roy recalled his father's opinion of Thomas Barraclough. *'Funny bugger. Tight as a duck's arse. Some say he's a bit of a shirtlifter.* He couldn't stop himself smiling. Thomas Barraclough was fair in business, and generous with his money. As to whether or not he was a shirtlifter? He couldn't say. He was certainly effeminate, with his pretty china tea tray, and something of a funny bugger.

He would keep a record of all his expenses, and Brenda would log any relevant phone calls. She could keep a separate book with air fares, and so on. Keeping track of profits might be useful if the furniture trade continued to decline.

He felt happy in an optimistic sort of way. When he walked through the revolving doors and Brenda looked up, he realised he was whistling. He would speak with her later about the expenses account. After running upstairs two at a time, he burst into the office, his mood waning at the sight of his father's empty desk. The room didn't feel the same. Even when Dad had been in the Scarborough Arms, or out on business, his desk had held his presence. Six piles of mail, with envelopes slit open by Brenda, awaited his attention. Three addressed to himself and three to his father. He scattered them over the desk, just for the hell of it.

The art world was at his feet. A magical world that was his for the taking danced just beyond his grasp. He slumped into his father's chair. The meeting with Thomas Barraclough had been unsettling in more ways than one. He grabbed the telephone and dialled the number of Stanley Grange. He needed to make an appointment with Malcolm Feany.

* * * *

Susan wrapped the sugar-coated tablet in toilet paper before flushing it away. After washing her hands, she returned to her chair in the lounge and waited. By then she would usually have lost the ability to think about anything much. She blinked and gripped the arms of the chair, afraid someone might notice something different about her. Determined to keep perfectly still, she stared straight ahead. Several of her fellow patients had visitors. Some smiled at her as they passed through her line of vision, one man said, "Hello," and she said "Hello," back to him. She shouldn't have done that and shot her eyes to the carpet to avoid any further mishaps. Her hand found its way to her pocket and the envelope Roy had given to her the day before. The thin airmail paper made little crinkly noises as she rubbed it between her thumb and forefinger. She didn't want to read about Chaz getting married, not until her brain had caught up with things a bit more. It was the address on the envelope that both worried and intrigued her. Taking it from her pocket, she read it again.

Mrs Roy Jessop,
Orchard Cottage,
Barwick-in-Elmet,
Leeds,
Yorkshire,
England.

Roy had talked to her about going home. Maybe if she went to this Orchard Cottage she would remember it, but he kept saying she had to stay there until she was better. It sounded nice. Barwick-in-Elmet was out in the countryside. Funny that. She had never imagined herself living out of town.

With nothing else to do, she occupied her mind by counting the squares on the carpet. The geometric design in shades of brown repeated the pattern with interlocking regularity across the room. Her eyes drifted sideways. Rain pattered on the French windows, raising her eyes from the floor. For a while she watched the drops converge on the glass, drawn by gravity in twisting rivulets. Something deep inside wanted her to walk through the doors and into the rain, to look into the clouds and feel the rain on her face. But it would have to wait. Hushed conversations drifted around the room in predictable monotony. Boredom had replaced numbness. Was boredom better? It was a feeling, a something, which had to be better than nothing. But what she really wanted, what she needed, was to remember. That was the whole point in skipping the tablet. What had happened after Auntie Pauline had died? Her eyes went back to the carpet, this time without focus, as she forced her head into the past. Something had happened, something bad, but what? Maggie. Maggie was helping her, but why? No matter how hard she tried, no matter how much her head ached with trying, her memory went no further. But still, she had made some progress. If she kept off the tablets, kept pretending to take them and flushing them down the loo, it would all come back to her, and she could go home. She would remember her home and Roy and everything else that he kept telling her about. For the present, though, she would keep thinking about Maggie.

Resting her head on the chair back, a previously unnoticed set of bookshelves caught her eye. Not that she wanted to read. She hadn't read a book since leaving school. She hated reading and yet, maybe, she would have a look. There might be something interesting, and she could always pretend to be reading. After all, she was in some sort of nut house, so to do something unusual wouldn't attract attention. Well, not much, anyway.

No matter how much she stared at the page, the words wouldn't sink in. They danced before her eyes in nonsensical patterns. She had opened it about halfway through. Perhaps she should turn a page every now and then to make it look genuine. She became aware of someone approaching. The woman sat down next to her, watching her. Although she didn't want to look at the unwelcome intruder, her eyes wouldn't stay on the page. Turning her head, she thought there was something familiar about her.

"Christ Almighty, Susan. What the hell are you doing in this place?"

Maggie's voice, but not Maggie. Something had changed. She frowned. "Your hair's the wrong colour. Maggie has blonde hair."

"Not for ages you daft…"

"Who told you I was here?" she whispered, her head bursting, and her heart thumping out of her chest.

"Alf Lawrence, the copper—ex-copper now. I bumped into him on Briggate. I've been trying to ring you." Maggie's voice carried across the room. Heads turned.

Susan put a finger to her lips and stood up. Maggie followed her out of the French doors. The rain had stopped and the sweet smell of freshened grass filled her nostrils as she took the air into her lungs in deep breaths. With an unexpected sense of freedom, she linked arms with Maggie, gripping her forearm tightly.

"I want you to take me home, to my house, to Orchard Cottage."

"When?"

"Now." They walked along the path that took them to the side of the building.

"What about your hubby? Won't he want to take you?"

"No. He's gone to France. He says I have to stay here but, if I do, I'll never remember anything. They drug me up."

"You don't seem drugged up to me. What are you on?"

She set her mouth tightly. Maggie was no fool.

"Oh, I get it. You're flushing your pills down the loo, aren't you?"

Tears welled in her eyes. She tried to blink them back but they flowed silently down her cheeks.

"You can't fool me, Susan Fletcher." Maggie pulled her to a seat, ignoring the pools of rain water soaking their clothes.

A thin smile crossed her lips as she wiped the tears with the back of her hand. "Everyone calls me Susan Jessop. I know I must have cracked up, Maggie, that's why I'm in this awful place. But I don't know if I can't remember because I've gone mad, or because of the bloody drugs. Don't you see? I have to go home, to this Orchard Cottage place." She took Chaz's letter from her pocket. "Look, Roy gave me this before he went to France. The only reason I even know where I live is because the address is on the envelope. I try to picture it, but when I think of home I see either the kitchen at the Threlfalls, or a farmhouse. I think it's Chaz's house in France. Please, Maggie, I know you helped me before when I was in trouble, and I know you bought me some fish and chips."

"Christ, Susan. That was a bit different. You'd been raped. Gang raped."

She froze. Her hand flew to Maggie's arm in a vice-like grip.

"You okay?"

"No-one told me that. They all keep telling me about my daughter, about nice stuff. No-one told me anything bad had happened to me. I knew you'd helped me, but I didn't remember why. I still don't, but I believe you." The blood drained from her face. Her stomach lurched. "My daughter. Emma. Is she…?"

"She's Roy's."

"You're sure?"

"All that shit happened three years ago, Susan. Your Emma is barely six months old. Figure it out for yourself."

"Take me home, Maggie, please, now. When we get there you can phone this place and tell them I'm okay. Please, Maggie."

CHAPTER SIXTEEN

"So you say, Roy, zat you 'av an appointment with zis Monsieur Feany next week? Why do you 'av to wait so long?"

Roy sipped his coffee, and nibbled an almond biscuit. "He's on holiday."

"And is zer no-one else you can speak wiz?" Madame Fournier held out her hands, her eyes wide with disbelief.

"No-one who could make a decision. That's why I came here now, really. Nothing will change until I see him next week. I hope you don't mind my just turning up like this. I should have phoned."

"Nonsense. You are always welcome 'ere. Charmaine will be delighted to see you. When you 'ave finished your coffee you must take your bag upstairs and unpack. You are 'ere for a few days, yes?"

"I need to go into Aix to buy paintings for a client, but I can't be away for too long. My mother's looking after Emma."

"And poor dear Susan? What does she say to all zis waiting?"

"Not much. She never does, not to me, anyway. She chats more with Jimmy. Besides, I haven't told her about the appointment. I thought it best to wait until afterwards and then I can tell her what he said."

"And when she talks to Jimmy, what do zey talk about?"

"He tells me she talks about their childhood. But more importantly, that she's trying to remember."

"Remember? Remember what?"

Roy explained how Susan's ability to recall the past varied from day to day.

"Sometimes she can't remember anything after Jimmy's mother's death, on another day she will remember being with me in Lavells on the day of her breakdown. At least she does believe me now, although I think it may be Jimmy's influence. He's told her she's married to me, and that Emma's our daughter. She believes it but doesn't recall it for herself, if you know what I mean."

"And what is zis drug they give 'er?"

"Chlorpromazine. Mr Feany's reducing the dose gradually. The theory is she'll be back to where she was before the post-natal depression kicked in."

"Maybe Anton knows of zis drug. 'Is work sometimes involves such t'ings. If not, 'e will know someone who does. Now zen. Go upstairs and unpack. Maybe you would like a little rest after your journey? Take a shower if you wish. We will 'ave dinner at six o'clock when Charmaine and Anton are 'ome."

Roy showered and then lay on the bed, allowing the air to dry his body. He sighed deeply, understanding for the first time why Susan loved the place so much. She had always gone there in her times of trouble, to lick her wounds and pick up the pieces of her life. He stared at the cracked plaster on the ceiling. She had seemed so well after Emma had been born. And now...now she was in a mental hospital, drugged up and unhappy. Thomas Barraclough had sown seeds of doubt. He felt as if he didn't know anything anymore. He had had faith in Malcolm Feany, perhaps blind faith. That had to change. If she were ever to recover, completely recover, she needed to face her past and not have it pushed under the carpet.

The scent of lavender weighted his eyelids and, as he drifted towards sleep, he saw Susan standing between rows of flowers. Arid soil dusted her feet as she turned and walked barefoot away from him. He tried to follow but his feet refused to move. Emma's laughter turned his head, her arms stretched up towards him, and he lifted her onto his shoulders. She kissed his forehead and he carried her into Orchard Cottage.

The unwelcome sound of knocking dragged him to the door. The knocking grew louder. Someone was calling his name. "Are you all right, Roy? Can I come in?"

Chaz. He realised he was naked.

"No! Wait a moment."

"Dinner's ready."

He looked at his watch. Six o'clock. He had slept for almost three hours.

"Right, thanks. I'll be down in two minutes."

* * * *

After dinner, Roy walked at Anton's side as he took his customary walk around the gravel paths of the garden. The old walls released the heat of the day, making the evening almost as warm as the afternoon. The breeze had dropped and the sound of crickets dominated the air.

"Psychiatry isn't my field, you understand," Anton explained. "I am a man of chemistry. I have heard of chlorpromazine, of course. I understand it to be an excellent drug, with no addictive side effects."

"My concern is the long term." Roy fixed his eyes on the path, his hands in his pockets. "It has been suggested to me that Susan needs therapy alongside the drug, and the more I think about it, the more it makes sense. Sometimes it feels as if I don't know her at all. She told me a lot about her past when we first met, and I get the feeling it's all been one big build up."

Over dinner he had given them the details of Susan's breakdown, her treatment, and her memory loss. They had listened in silent horror as he had told them of the scene in Vine Street.

Anton sighed. "Her upbringing was certainly unconventional. She spent a lot of her time either in Vine Street or at our home. She would put on an independent air like a coat of armour. Her wilful spirit put her beyond the control of her parents from an early age. Jeanette and I saw another side to her, of course. Her friendship with our daughter showed her true nature. Without that friendship, life would have been much more difficult for Charmaine."

"What do you mean, 'her true nature'?"

"We always felt Susan liked Charmaine for her personality, and not through sympathy. She saw beyond the disability to the person, and with a kindness that cannot be faked." They walked on in silence to the end of the garden.

Roy leaned his elbows on the gate that led to the fields.

His eyes narrowed to the path he had walked with Susan in the early days of her pregnancy. "So you feel her past is the key, and that therapy is the answer?"

"It is logical to say her past was a major factor in bringing about her breakdown. As to whether it was triggered by post-natal depression? I don't know. As I said, psychiatry isn't my field. It is certainly true to say she has endured more mental trauma than most people suffer in a lifetime. If she is to recover she has to come to terms with her past, not just gloss over it and pretend it didn't happen. We had all thought Susan had put her difficulties behind her, but it seems she hadn't dealt with any of it. As to whether therapy will help—I don't know. But I will speak with someone tomorrow. Someone for whom I have a great deal of respect."

* * * *

Jeanette poured strong, black coffee as Anton filled liqueur glasses with Grand Marnier. Chaz had heard more than enough over dinner to realise she had been wrong to wait. She should have gone to her friend when she had been first admitted to hospital. Jimmy and Roy had kept all the details from her. School finished at the end of the week, and nothing was going to stop her. Nothing *could* stop her.

"Whatever you say, I'm going to Leeds with Roy."

"I t'ink zat is an excellent idea. Travelling alone is not good."

She had been expecting an argument and, for a moment, she didn't know what to say. "Well, yes, erm, when are you leaving, Roy?"

"Charmaine!" Jeanette spoke sharply. "It is not polite to ask a guest when zey are leaving. 'Ave we not taught you zat?"

"Please, Jeanette. It doesn't matter," Roy said. "I have business to see to, as you know. I need to go into Aix and browse around the artists. I would be delighted to have Chaz accompany me on my return to England, and I'm sure Susan will be equally delighted to see her."

* * * *

The streets of Aix were warming up with a clean, fresh sunshine, lighting the day with optimism. When Le Mistral blew at its most fierce it rustled the leaves of the plane trees and found its way to every corner of the narrow streets. But not that day. That day was set to be calm and sunny. The rich mineral springs of the town had created wealth, and inspired classical architecture that drew the crowds from far and wide. Shuttered windows in golden walls denied access to the sunshine that reflected its brilliance in the stonework.

Dropping him off at one end of Le Cours, Chaz drove away with a wave. Roy ordered a coffee and leaned back in the creaking cane chair. He had the day to himself. Chaz had made a detour for him and would pick him up at the end of the school day.

Artists were setting up their stalls. A busker walked by with his violin case in one hand and the lead of a small dog in the other.

The Fourniers' insistence on speaking English had given no opportunity to practise his french, unused since his last visit and, before that, since 'A' level exams. Being surrounded by the flowing sounds of the French language added to the feeling of excitement.

He took a deep breath, inhaling the atmosphere of the cafe society. With the intention of filling every moment of his day, he drank the hot coffee quickly and set off to find Jacques Morel. There would be no problem in recognising his work.

He found Jacques in the spot described by Jimmy and Jill, next to a little fountain at a crossroads. A brown and white terrier lay at his feet on an old blanket. Roy stood a few paces away, watching the artist at his easel. He was good. The natural style, even the way he held his brush, showed a natural talent unrestricted by schooling. A box of rolled canvasses lay on its side near his feet. He was scruffily dressed, in worn jeans and paint-spattered shirt. Roy guessed him to be about forty years old, but it was hard to say. The sun had aged his skin, wrinkling his eyes as they fought the light that so attracted artists to

Provence.

"Excusez moi. S'agit-il de peintures à vendre?"

"Oui, bien sûr, Monsieur."

Jacques unfurled the canvasses. Roy thought they were even better than the ones Jimmy and Jill had bought. It seemed odd that he had not had them on display. Jacques answered his question before being asked.

"J'ai oublié. La lumiere, vous comprenez? Je devais peindre."

Roy smiled. He should have known. An artist like Jacques would have to paint when the light was right. The man was a genius. He had been so absorbed in the finishing touches of his work, catching pure light of the morning sun that he had simply forgotten to set out the ones for sale.

"Ah, oui, ne me laissez pa vous interrompre. Je vous rappeler cet après midi." He didn't want to interrupt the artist's flow. He would return after lunch and buy some. The man's work was irresistible.

Jacques nodded and turned back to his canvas.

He watched for a few moments before continuing down the broad pavement, picking his way through the haphazard seating of the cafés.

The sun soared, gaining strength and shortening shadows. Writers, artists, poets, and musicians descended on Le Cours, each making a contribution to the lazy ambience of the congregated world of art. Those who were not working chatted amongst the like-minded. Some appeared to be in deep discussion, with the occasional animated conversation, arms flailing with expressive gestures.

Taking off his leather jacket, Roy paused from time to time to watch the artists at work. Some had only brought canvasses to sell. Others, like Jacques, had come to work. The style and subject matter varied, and Roy had to force himself to concentrate on the impressionists.

Two hours later, having walked the length of Le Cours, he made a mental note of those from whom he would buy. Thomas would be pleased with the quality of the paintings, if not the price. In the end he bought from three artists plus

Jacques before hurrying to meet Chaz.

On the return journey to La Vieille Ferme, Chaz talked excitedly. She had a ticket arranged for the same flight as Roy and would collect it at the airport. After that he barely listened, his mind darting between Aix and Stanley Grange.

"I see you bought some canvasses. Did you have a good day?"

"Yes. Very good."

"What's wrong then? You seemed all happy when we set off. Don't you want me to come back to Leeds with you?"

"Sorry. Yes, of course I do. My head's been in the clouds all day."

"You're thinking about Susan?"

"Yes. Exactly. I'm at a loss, Chaz, and that's the truth of it."

"I know. I've been thinking about her all day too, now I know just how bad she is."

They travelled on. Chaz parked her car amongst the hens, their nonsensical chatter so much a part of her home.

Roy went straight to his room.

* * * *

Placing his knife and fork at an angle, Anton indicated in French style that he had finished his meal. "I have spoken with a friend of mine today who is a psycho-analyst." All eyes shot towards him.

"About Susan?" Roy asked.

"Yes. We had a long lunch together and I was able to speak with him at some length."

"Can 'e 'elp?"

"Hardly, my dear. You seem to forget Susan lives in Leeds, and my friend is based in Marseille."

"Tell us what he said, Dad. What does he think of this drug they're giving her?"

"He thinks highly of it, but that she will need therapy of some sort if she is to fully recover, pretty much as Roy has been thinking." Raising his eyebrows, he looked towards him.

"Yes?" He nodded. "I gave him as full a background as I could and he came up with what I thought an interesting theory."

"Go on then, Dad. Stop beating about the bush."

"He thinks, and this is of course in confidence, because without speaking with Susan it is what he calls a remote diagnosis."

"Oh, Dad." Chaz stood up and leaned across the table, her voice raised. "Stop prevaricating. Tell us what he said."

"Please, Charmaine. Sit down. Let me speak. He thinks it likely that Susan has spent her life running away from herself, and that she doesn't like herself. Being raised in a pub meant she didn't know normal family life as a child. Her relationship with Jimmy's mother was very important to her, and to lose her in the way she did would have been devastating. Having Emma so quickly after being married, and then moving to her own home in the countryside, all these things have contributed to the precipitation of her breakdown. She has tried to be a good wife and mother, but doesn't know how to do it."

Jeanette cleared the plates from the table. "So what would 'e propose if she were 'is patient?"

"In his opinion it is essential that she has therapy. More precisely, he would recommend hypnotherapy. That way she could face her demons without further trauma. Not everyone responds to this sort of treatment, but it can be very effective."

"Bête noir." Jeanette's words were barely audible.

"What did you say, Jeanette?" Roy asked.

"Oh, nothing. Just a saying we 'ave— bête noir, 'er black beast, she 'as to be rid of it."

Roy shifted in his chair, turning to Anton. "I'm sure your friend is right. The National Health Service in England doesn't run to hypnotherapy. I would gladly pay for private treatment of course, but I don't know what Mr Feany would have to say about it."

"Does it matter?" Chaz asked. "I mean, what's important here is that Susan gets better. If you have to argue with this Mr Feany about what's best, then that's what you must do."

"You're right, of course."

"It isn't easy to argue with a doctor," Anton interrupted.

"They all have opinions and they all think they are right. When we decided to take Charmaine to Leeds as a child there were doctors in Paris who thought us quite mad, but at the end of the day, Charmaine is right. You have to do what you believe is in Susan's best interest, and not worry about the finer feelings of Mr Feany."

"That's true," Roy said. "I agree on both points, but I know nothing about either psychiatry or hypnotherapy."

Over the following days Roy drank in the atmosphere of Aix. A conversation with an artist could take his attention for a while and then he would walk on, consumed by thoughts of Susan, as alone in the crowds as she was alone in her head. The more he thought, the more he became convinced he must have a second opinion. Mr Feany's methods, by his own admission, would probably leave her on drugs for the rest of her life, blotting out the past, covering mental scars with sticking plaster medicine. That wasn't what he wanted for his wife, or his daughter. Emma mustn't have a mother who was constantly doped up, waiting for the next hospital appointment, or worse.

After Chaz dropped him off each morning he went for a coffee followed by a stroll along Le Cours. After lunch he walked to Le Parc Jourdain, and sat on one of the benches, watching the world go by. Lunchtime came and the sunshine took him for a lie-down on the grass. The sound of the breeze, fanning through the great boughs, punctuated by voices and the laughter of children, lulled him to sleep.

CHAPTER SEVENTEEN

Orchard Cottage, so inviting and so beautifully furnished, meant nothing to Susan. And yet she had known exactly which plant pot to look under for the spare key.

The wedding photograph on the television had come as a surprise. Maggie, Chaz, Jimmy, Patrick, Henry, Diana, Jimmy and Jill. They had all been there. She and Roy were definitely married. At least she remembered everyone, but the day itself, the getting married, she didn't remember a thing about.

The sound of a tractor took her to the window. The driver waved and her shaking hand waved back.

She felt sick. Very sick. The shaking that had started in the pit of her stomach had reached her fingertips.

"Tea up, love. I found a few biscuits."

The mention of food sent her flying upstairs to the bathroom. Her heaving body knelt on the floor, retching green bile to exhaustion. The shaking wouldn't stop. Maggie helped her to her feet and guided her to a bedroom, sitting beside her on the edge of the bed.

"Tell me, Maggie. How is it I don't remember this house, but I knew where to find the key, and I knew where the bathroom was?"

"No idea, but I think I should call a doctor. You're shaking like a leaf."

"No! No, please. You can call Stanley Grange and tell them I'm home. That was the deal. You promised."

"Yeah, but that was before you started going all funny on me. Look at you. You're a wreck."

Susan looked down at her shaking hands. Her head was spinning. Throwing herself sideways, her head hit the pillow and she curled into a foetal position.

Maggie wrapped the duvet around her and knelt at her side. "Okay. Have it your own way. I don't suppose you know the number, do you?"

Susan tightened her lips and shook her shaking head

from side to side.

* * * *

"Good afternoon, Mr Grayling." Diana steered Emma's new pushchair through the doorway as the farmer held open the post office door.

He took off his cap to reveal a shiny white pate. "Afternoon, Mrs Jessop. I was sorry to hear about your husband. You've had a fair few troubles lately."

"Thank you. Yes, I suppose so." She moved towards the counter, not wanting to prolong the conversation.

"Good to see your daughter-in-law's home."

Diana turned quickly. "Susan? No, Mr Grayling, I'm afraid she'll be in hospital for a while yet. I'll tell Roy you were asking about her."

"But I've just seen her at the window. Waved to me, she did."

The blood drained from her face. "Are you sure?"

"Sure as night follows day. I just drove by Orchard Cottage in my tractor." The farmer held the door open for her again as she turned the pushchair towards it.

"I must go. Thank you. Yes, I didn't know." Diana hurried out of the shop, and towards Lark's Hill Drive.

Mr Grayling must have been mistaken, but with Roy away she would have to check with the hospital first, and then call the police. It might have been a burglar.

* * * *

No-one could call Norman Grayling a gossip, so when Diana Jessop had finished her business at the counter, he held the door open for her to leave, standing to one side as she steered the pushchair though the narrow doorway and down the step.

"The usual, Norman?" Lizzy asked.

He gave an almost imperceptible nod, and she handed him a packet of Yorkshire Mixtures. He scratched his head and replaced his cap, leaving without another word. Inside his cab, he opened his sweets. The cellophane ripped, and the sweets fell onto his lap. Some spilled onto the floor.

"Shit." He unwrapped one and sucked it noisily as he picked up the others, replacing them in the bag as best he could. Looking down the road, he saw Diana Jessop on her way home. Something wasn't right. Ever since Roy had smashed up his car he had kept an eye on Orchard Cottage. He didn't know why, he just did. Susan had always waved to him, and he had been shocked to hear she had had a breakdown. Village life meant such things got around. He couldn't remember who had told him. Probably his wife. She did the church flowers with Mrs Jessop senior. It crossed his mind that looking after the baby would take her mind off losing her hubby. He waited for a few minutes, sucking his sweet, until he was sure she had had time to reach home. With ear defenders back in place, he set off towards Lark's Hill Drive.

Parking at the roadside, he walked up the gravel drive and rang the doorbell. He was about to ring it again when the door opened.

"Mr Grayling. What can I do for you?"

"Nothing. Nothing at all, Mrs Jessop. I didn't want to say anything else in the post office. Lizzy likes a good gossip."

"I'm sorry. I don't understand."

"It's your daughter-in-law, Susan."

"Yes?"

"She *is* home. I wasn't lying. I saw her at the window. She waved to me. I thought you should know, what with your son being away and all. He is away, isn't he? I haven't seen his car in the drive all week." He heard the baby cry somewhere in the house. "I'll be off then. I can see you're busy."

He retraced his steps, wondering whether or not he had done the right thing. Back in the comfort of his cab, he unwrapped another boiled sweet. What was said was said, and he had a busy day before him.

* * * *

Diana could barely believe her ears when the nurse informed her that Susan had left Stanley Grange the day before. She had taken no medication with her and they could not make her return because she had been a voluntary patient.

She replaced the receiver slowly and pressed the palms of her hands to the sides of her head to condense her thoughts. Emma's cries drifted down the stairs. She had hoped she would go back to sleep for a while. Her legs and back hurt as she went up. Pushing the pushchair and lifting and carrying Emma were taking their toll. The cot which had been bought for occasional use had become Emma's everyday bed. She loved her granddaughter, there could be no question about that. With Henry gone she had more time on her hands than ever but bringing up another child, even Roy's child, wasn't what she wanted to do. She took Emma from the cot and the crying stopped.

Back downstairs, she took her diary from her handbag with one hand and, with difficulty, found the right page. With Emma on her hip, and the telephone receiver between her jaw and shoulder, she dialled '100' and gave the operator the Fournier's number at the same time as jigging Emma. Roy was due home late that night. With a bit of luck she would catch him before he set off.

* * * *

To Maggie's relief, Jimmy and Jill were on their way over. Even when Susan had slept, Maggie had stayed awake, watching her twitch and cry. Finding Jimmy's number in the book by the telephone had been a piece of luck. She had guessed it would be under 'J' for Jimmy rather than 'H' for Hanson.

Susan seemed more peaceful and Maggie crept downstairs to put the kettle on. She put two mugs on the worktop and poured a little milk into each. A quiet tap on the back door, followed by the turning of the handle, startled her. She recognised Susan's mother-in-law from the wedding. With her eyes diverted to the sleeping Emma in a pushchair,

Maggie's face softened to a smile.

"It's Maggie, isn't it?" Diana asked.

"Yes. Susan's asleep. Did you know she was here?"

"Someone in the village told me they'd seen her at the window. I didn't believe them at first. Has she asked for Emma?"

"N-no. I hadn't thought about it. That's odd, don't you think?" Maggie saw the disappointment in Diana's eyes. The kettle switched itself off automatically. "Would you like a cuppa? Susan will probably wake up anytime soon."

"How is she?"

Maggie shrugged. "I'm no expert. I didn't know she was poorly until yesterday. She's not right, though."

Diana wheeled the pushchair into the hall, and sat at the kitchen table as Maggie put a teabag into each of the two mugs.

"Roy will be home tonight. I tried to catch him in France but he'd left. Chaz is with him."

"That's good. They're good friends, Susan and Chaz."

"Roy's worried sick. What with losing his father and trying to run the business he doesn't need all this worry about Susan."

"I didn't know, I'm sorry. Do you look after Emma all the time, then?"

"Just during the day, usually. Roy has her at night, but he's been in France for a few days on business, staying with Chaz's parents."

Maggie took a sip of her tea. "This milk's sour." She took both mugs and poured the tea down the sink.

"Never mind. Like I say, Roy's been away. I don't mind telling you I'm tired. Why older women want babies I do not know. It's hard enough when you're young. Do you have any children, Maggie?"

"Me? No."

"And what about your parents? Are they still alive?"

"No. I mean yes and no. At least I didn't think so."

Diana frowned, waiting for her to continue.

"That's why I tried to phone Susan. I have some news I wanted to tell her, and then I found out she was in that awful hospital place." Maggie went into the lounge, returning with her handbag. She handed an envelope to Diana. "I was left at an orphanage as a baby."

Maggie watched as Diana read the letter, unaware of Susan's presence on the stairs.

"Have you shown this…?" Diana looked up as she returned the letter to Maggie, stopping mid-sentence as she saw the waif-like figure of her daughter-in-law peering through the banister rails. "Susan?"

"Is that from your mum, Maggie?" Susan asked.

Maggie nodded.

"And you had it in your bag all this time and didn't tell me?"

Maggie took her friend's hand, guiding her to the sofa.

"I never asked, did I? I never said *'Hello Maggie, how are you? What brings you to this place?'*"

"She says she found my name at the council records office," Maggie explained. "She works at the telephone exchange, and when I had the phone put in she saw my name and address on a form."

"I'll get Susan some tea and biscuits. There should be some tinned milk somewhere," Diana said. "You sit with her."

Maggie watched as Susan's eyes travelled from left to right along the trembling paper. Only when she had finished and looked up did she notice that her eyes were more open than they had been the day before.

"What are you going to do? Are you going to meet her, like she says she wants to?"

Maggie paused, biting her lip. She had hoped Susan would come with her. "Yes. I just wanted to tell you first, that's all. I wanted to ask you if you think what she says in the letter is true, all this stuff about her parents making her give me up, and thinking about me every day of her life."

Susan wrapped thin fingers around her mug and shrugged. "You'll know when you see her. It doesn't explain why you were left on the doorstep of the orphanage, though, does it? Not really. I mean did she give birth in secret in the middle of the night, and did her parents snatch you away and dump you? Seems a bit far-fetched to me. And, anyway, if that had happened, how did she know your name?" She held the letter out, her hands shaking violently. "Have you told Patrick?"

"No."

A little cry from the hall diverted their attention. Maggie held Susan's wrist and took the letter with her free hand. "I think it's time you and that daughter of yours had something to eat."

* * * *

Her daughter. Emma was her daughter. The image of a newborn baby abandoned on a doorstep filled her head. Emma began crying louder. Diana was in the lounge. Whatever was she doing? The baby needed her bottle *now*. Susan jumped to her feet and took her from her pushchair. She was heavy, much heavier than she remembered. The sudden movement made Emma cry even more. "She needs her bottle," Susan said.

But Diana had a small bowl of baby food in her hand.

The highchair she and Roy had bought was set out with a chair in front of it, ready for Diana to give Emma her lunch. She hadn't known her own daughter was on solid food— shaming evidence of her failure as a mother. She put Emma in the highchair and her cries turned into a smile as she looked towards her grandmother. Susan fled the room and ran upstairs.

Wracking sobs engulfed her as she turned her head into the pillow, stifling the sound as she beat her fist on the bed.

The bed shifted as Maggie sat beside her. "It's been a while since you held her, hasn't it?"

She turned. Deep blue eyes flared accusingly. "How long? How long was I doped up in that place?"

"I don't know. Alf didn't say. Look, love, give yourself a chance. You've been through a lot, one way and another."

"Not as much as you have, and you're not a snivelling useless wreck. You did all right without a mother."

"That's not true, though, is it? I was a prostitute from the age of fifteen. I had no education worth talking about."

"And you're a really nice person."

"And now, when I'm nearly twenty-five, she writes to me and wants to get to know me. It doesn't take away the shit childhood in a home—praying to a non-existent God that she would come and take me away from the horrible nuns who did nothing but tell me I was born in sin. Like it was my fault. Emma needs you. Diana's good and kind to her, and loves her, but Emma will need your love. She only has one mother."

"But I'm no good at it."

"Believe me, a shit mother, which I don't think you are, is better than no mother at all."

Their attention was taken by the sound of a car drawing up outside. Jimmy and Jill had arrived.

* * * *

During the flight from Marseille, Roy and Chaz planned to go straight to Stanley Grange, plans which changed dramatically when Chaz called her parents to tell them they had arrived safely in Paris. They had no information other than that Roy's mother had telephoned La Vieille Ferme to say Susan had gone home. The call had been brief, giving no detail.

"Do you think I should phone home, Chaz? What if Susan's on her own?"

"She's with your mum, isn't she?"

"I don't know. Mum will be looking after Emma and, when she visited at Stanley Grange, Susan snapped at her. Mum was upset."

"You could call your mum's house. If she doesn't answer I think it's fair to presume she's at your house with Susan."

"This is the final call for passengers Fournier and Jessop. Please make your way to gate fourteen where your flight is ready for departure."

* * * *

The engine's noise lowered, signalling the descent to

Yeadon airport. Forty minutes later Chaz walked through the airport faster that she had ever walked before. Roy had run ahead to the car with their suitcases and waited for her near the car park exit. The tyres of the Volvo squealed as she closed the door and they set off for Barwick-in-Elmet. They travelled in silence, each filled with dreadful anticipation, as imagination took them from possible to impossible scenarios.

* * * *

Relief at the sight of Jimmy's car in the drive gave way to surprise. Roy hadn't known what to expect, but some sort of chaos had seemed inevitable. Orchard Cottage was in total silence when they opened the front door.

Jimmy came from the lounge, his forefinger pressed against his lips.

Chaz pulled herself up the step with one hand on the doorframe as Jimmy came forward to hug her.

"Good to see you both," he whispered. "Susan's asleep upstairs. She's okay. Emma's in the lounge with Jill. Your mum went home about half an hour ago when Maggie left."

"Maggie?" Roy's eyes widened.

"Sshh."

He lowered his voice. "What was Maggie doing here?"

"She brought her home. It's a long story."

Roy crept upstairs and sat on the bedside, watching intently as Susan's eyes darted about beneath closed lids. Whimpering cries punctuated her shallow breathing. Her once shining hair framed her pale face. An overwhelming desire to scoop her up in his arms and protect her filled every nerve in his body. He would phone Maggie later and thank her. She had left her number on the hall table. And then there was his mum. He would have to go and see her, and maybe Susan would come with him. It all depended on how she was when she woke up.

The duvet rustled and Susan flung her arms around him, clinging with a strength belying her fragile appearance. Tears filled his eyes as he stroked her hair. Her whole body quaked in his grasp.

"I remember. I really remember everything, right up until when you left me in Lavells that day."

"It's okay."

"Do you want to divorce me?" she whispered.

"No!" He leaned away from her, taking her hands and gently lifting them away. "Whatever makes you say that? Of course I don't want a divorce."

"I'm no good for you." Her gaze from big blue eyes bore into his face. "I'm no good at being a mother and I'm no good at being a wife. You and your mother can look after Emma." She blinked rapidly, her mouth clamped closed.

"Susan, Susan, Susan." He held her closely. "There's nothing to worry about. I just want you to get better, everyone does."

She pushed him away, fear on her face. "You won't make me go back to that place, will you? I won't take the drugs. I won't."

In that split second, Roy knew he could never take her back to Stanley Grange.

"No, love. I won't take you back there."

The trace of a smile raced across her lips, and her shoulders sagged. Roy swung his legs onto the bed and leaned against the headboard. She leaned into him. The quaking coursing through her body subsided as she nestled her child-like body into his side.

"Tell me what happened. How did I come to be in that place? What happened to my hands?"

He shifted his position, not knowing how to start, or even if he should.

"I need to know, Roy."

CHAPTER EIGHTEEN

Roy was in good time for his appointment with Thomas Barraclough. The traffic was light, and he knew the road well, giving space in his head for a second level of thinking.

Thinly disguised criticisms circled around like vultures, waiting for the proof of his folly to give the signal to attack. Convention dictated he should take Susan back to Stanley Grange. The decision not to do so was both his and Susan's. She had never been one for convention. The undertone of disapproval from his mother was something he had to put up with. She meant well. Chaz understood and had spoken with his mother, which had been a big help. His attempt to explain their decision had sounded like pathetic whinging. He couldn't begin to think what he would have done without Chaz. She had been Susan's constant companion, leaving him free to return to work.

Diana had said she was happy to leave Emma to Chaz and Susan's care, and that was as it should be. His fears that she may want to take over had been groundless. If he thought about it at the time, she had sounded relieved to be free of her duties.

Brenda had been her usual efficient self. He had no worries about leaving her in sole charge of the business. He fleetingly wondered what he would do when she went on holiday. It hadn't been too bad when Dad was alive. They had managed between them. On her return she had always clucked over the mess they had made of the diary. Roy smiled at the memory until the present returned to crease his forehead.

Doctor Hirst had called at Orchard Cottage. Mr Feany had been in touch and told him Susan had walked out of Stanley Grange without medication. He was a good man and had explained that Susan's shaking and sickness were withdrawal symptoms. Knowing that they would subside, and were not part of her illness, had been good news, especially to Susan. Trying to persuade her to take a lower dose had proved impossible. She had been terrified, running up to their bedroom and slamming the door. Doctor Hirst had told him to let him know if she changed her mind. Roy had been brave enough to mention therapy. The blank expression on the doctor's face had been all the answer he'd needed.

Pulling into Thomas's drive, he became aware of the figure at the bay window. He took the box of canvasses from the car and walked towards the door, raising his free hand to the bell-push. The door opened immediately and Thomas, with a cat under each arm, stood before him.

"Good God, Roy. What happened to you? Come in."

"I'm very well, nothing wrong at all. What do you mean?" Roy followed him into the dining room.

"Put them down on the table and then go and sit in the lounge. I'll make some tea. You look worn out."

Leaving the box of canvasses in the dining room, Roy looked in the mirror. Thomas had a point. He looked terrible. Older. He pushed the flesh of his cheeks upwards with the palms of his hands before taking a seat in the most comfortable-looking chair, and fell asleep within seconds.

Waking suddenly, he felt disorientated. A cat sat on his lap and Thomas sat in the chair opposite, his hands before him, fingertip to fingertip. He pushed himself to a more upright position. "I'm so sorry. Whatever must you think?"

"I'm sure you have no need to apologise, Roy. There are some excellent canvasses in that box."

"You've looked at them, then? How long have I been asleep? I'm so sorry, very rude of me. Unprofessional. Sorry."

"To answer your questions chronologically—I must say yes. Half an hour. And repeat that there is no need to apologise. How is your wife?"

Once again Roy found himself speaking candidly to Thomas. The tea went cold as he related everything that had happened since their last meeting. Thomas listened without interrupting.

"It was you who first made me think she needed more than drugs, and you were—are—absolutely right. I have no doubt about it now. Anton agrees."

"And you say these people live in Aix."

"Yes, just outside the town."

"If my memory serves me well, that isn't so far from Marseille?"

"About two hours' drive."

"Well, then, the answer's obvious. You must take her back to Aix. There will be no shortage of psychiatrists of every school of thought, in Marseille. If you can afford it, that is."

Roy frowned.

"The place is something of a favourite with the rich and famous. I'm sure your friend Anton and his colleague will guide you away from the overpriced quacks."

"I don't know. There's our daughter to consider. Susan hasn't bonded with her since coming home."

"I know nothing about maternal instincts, but surely common sense dictates that if the mother's in France and the child's in England, bonding will never take place."

"And then I don't get to see my daughter or my wife. I have the business to run."

Inhaling deeply, Thomas tapped his fingertips together. "Tell me, Roy, what is your dream?" Raising his hand, he continued, "You don't have to answer me, but you need to answer the question to yourself. Sometimes the most obvious solution is the most difficult to see." He stood up and looked in the mirror, adjusting a strand of hair. "I selected six paintings as you slept." Then he took a cheque from behind the clock and held it at arm's length.

"But we haven't discussed any of them, nor prices." Taking the cheque from him, Roy glanced at the figure. "I'm not sure. It depends on what you chose."

"I took the liberty of reading the list you'd compiled. I found it in the bottom of the box along with your documented expenses. The cheque covers everything, plus a ten per cent finder's fee. I hope you find that acceptable."

Roy looked at the cheque again, feeling slightly cheated. Not by the figure, but because, he realised, he had been looking forward to negotiating the prices.

He totted up the figures in his head, worked out the

percentages, and added his expenses as Thomas explained his choices. The cheque was for exactly the right amount, and ten per cent had all along been the fee Roy had had in mind. There would be other times for negotiation.

With the remaining canvasses in the back of his car, he turned the ignition key and checked the time on the dashboard. Brenda would be locking up in ten minutes. He might as well go straight to Barwick-in-Elmet. It would mean he could call on his mother without worrying Susan. She worried about everything. If he were five minutes late home she imagined him in a car crash. If he sneezed, she thought he had flu. Still, it was better than her not knowing who he was.

* * * *

"Roy! How lovely to see you. You look tired. How are Susan and Emma?"

"They're fine. I'm fine. Chaz is being an absolute star. Put the kettle on will you, Mum? I've only had a cold cup of tea all day." He sat in his father's chair, with one elbow on the arm, rubbing his fingers across his forehead. "I'm thinking of taking them back to Provence."

"Who?" Diana held onto the back of her chair.

"Are you all right, Mum?" Roy jumped from his seat, taking the cup and saucer from her hand. "Sit down. You've gone as white as a sheet." Guiding her to her chair, he knelt before her.

"Who? Who are you thinking of taking back to Provence?"

"Susan, obviously, and Emma."

"And Chaz?"

"Of course. Chaz lives there."

"Sorry. Yes. Stupid of me."

"I'm going to ask Anton to find some sort of therapy for Susan."

"But what about you?"

"I'll go over when I can. I have the business to run."

Grabbing his hands, she looked directly in his eyes,

squeezing his fingers. And then letting go and sinking back into the chair, her eyes focussed on some distant, invisible scene. "Sell it."

"Sell what?"

"Jessop's. Sell the business and go to France."

"But…"

"But nothing. I know you like it there and Susan loves the place. She told me so before Emma was born."

Roy returned to his father's chair.

"I'll come to visit whenever I can."

"Whoa, Mum. You're going too fast for me. How long have you been thinking about this?"

"About a minute."

Roy laughed. "Not too many details ironed out yet, then?"

"No." Diana smiled. "But I'm right, aren't I? Susan's past has caught up with her. I don't know everything by a long chalk, but I know that much. Her past is in Leeds. Leeds is the problem, in my opinion."

He drank his tea in one gulp, and then said, "I'd better be going, Mum. They'll be wondering where I am, and I like to see Emma for a while before she goes to bed."

"You will think about what I said, won't you?"

"Yes, Mum. That and a lot of other things."

* * * *

Susan didn't want to drive, not yet. She hadn't been out of the cottage since she'd gone home, and the weeks in Stanley Grange had made the world seem too big. Chaz parked Susan's car in the Merrion Centre and took the pushchair from the back. Susan lifted Emma from her car seat, gripping the handles to steady herself. Then they took the lift to the mall and walked past the once familiar shops.

"We're in good time," Chaz said. "We're not meeting Maggie until four."

"Is there time to walk down to the parish church? I want to visit my mother's grave."

"There's time. If you let me push Emma I'll be able to walk a bit quicker, but are you sure that's a good idea?"

"No, I'm not sure. But I need to do it. I don't know why, but I just do."

With Chaz in charge of the pushchair, Susan stopped to buy a bunch of white roses from a florist's stall. "Come on." Resting one hand on the pushchair, she waited for Chaz to set the pace. Crossing the entrance to Thompson Square, she stopped and looked at the site of her childhood home. Rose bay willow herb seeds floated in the air.

"Are you okay, Susan?"

She nodded. "Look." She pointed to the Yorkshire stone paving flags. "You can see where the doorway used to be. The stones are worn." Aware of Chaz's worried gaze, she walked on. "It's okay, Chaz. I'm not going to crack up on you. I'm going to ask Roy to put the land up for sale in the next auction." She set off quickly down the hill.

"Hey, wait for us."

"Sorry, I forgot." She put her hand on top of Chaz's, her confidence evaporating as quickly as it had appeared. They walked down the hill and past the markets, crossing the road to the church.

"Will you stay here with Emma? I want to do this on my own. Please, Chaz."

Chaz looked up to the clock on the church tower. "We're meeting Maggie in ten minutes."

"I won't be long, honest."

"If you're not back in ten minutes I'm coming after you, okay?"

"Okay."

Chaz would never make it up the steps with a pushchair. Her agreement meant nothing. On her own for the first time since the day she had—that was it. She'd gone there before going to Vine Street. No-one had been able to tell her that bit because no-one knew. Faltering steps carried her along the path as she forced one foot in front of the other around the church. The trees were in full leaf, offering welcome shade, unlike her last visit when...when what? Her feet stopped.

Pulling herself up to her full height, and with a deep breath, she carried on. The white headstone was within her sight. Only a few more steps.

"Hello, Mum, and Dad. You're here too, aren't you?" Kneeling at the graveside, she lay the roses down. "Sorry I've been so long. I brought you these." She blinked, expecting to feel tears in her eyes, but none came. "I can't stop. Chaz is waiting with Emma. She's my little girl. You'd like her. I wish you could meet her." She rested her cheek on the headstone that had been chosen by her father, feeling its cool smoothness. She kissed her fingers and touched the stone before stepping back. With a little wave she walked away, turning to wave again.

* * * *

"You're late."

"Sorry, Maggie. There was something I wanted to do."

"I'm glad you're late, as it happens. I only just got here myself."

A waitress approached. "Hello, Mrs Jessop. Good to see you back. We've missed you."

Susan wasn't sure she wanted to be recognised. Perhaps arranging to meet at Lavells was a mistake.

Chaz ordered afternoon tea and the waitress retreated. "How did it go, Maggie?" she asked.

"She's nice. You'll never guess what, Susan. It was pretty much like you said."

"What was?"

"When I was born. Only worse really. Her parents were strict chapel people and when they found out she was pregnant they hid her away—told people she had gone to visit a relative at the coast for the summer."

"And when you were born they left you on the doorstep of the orphanage?"

"Yes. She was sent back to school like nothing had happened. Her parents found a husband for her and she was married at eighteen. I have a half-brother and a half-sister."

"What about her husband? Does he know about you? Did she ever tell anyone?"

Maggie shook her head. "Dead. She says he was a good man but she never loved him, not really. Her parents are dead, too, but to answer your question, she never told anyone."

"So how did she know your name?"

"She said she guessed where they had taken her baby, and she wanted to know whether I was a boy or a girl. The nuns told her, and said they had named her Margaret Marks." She took a photograph from her handbag as the waitress returned, her tray laden with sandwiches and cakes.

"I'll see to it," Chaz said. She poured the tea as they helped themselves to the food. She looked sideways at the photograph of a teenage boy and girl.

"This is my brother and sister."

"No mistake there, then," Chaz said. "You and your sister are like two peas in a pod. What do you think, Susan?"

Susan nodded, taking Emma from her pushchair.

"Like you and Emma, eh, Susan?" Maggie said.

"Are you going to meet them, your brother and sister?" Susan asked.

"Clare—she's my mum—is going to tell them about me tonight. I told her it's up to them. I'm not going to tell her about, you know, working the streets. On a need to know basis—she doesn't need to, and I don't want to talk about it."

"I never thought about that," Susan said.

Maggie shrugged. "How are you, anyway? You look a bloody sight better than you did in that hospital."

"Not bad. Chaz is my guardian angel." Moving her plate towards the centre of the table, and away from Emma's eager hands, she broke off a little piece of cake and gave it to her daughter.

"Well, Chaz can't stay forever. What will you do when you're stuck out in the sticks on your own?"

Susan shifted in her seat, not wanting to talk about herself or think about the future. Instead, she asked, "When are you seeing her again?"

"She said she'd phone me tomorrow night and let me

know how it went with Nigel and Sarah. That's my—"

"Brother and sister," Susan interrupted. "I wish I'd had a brother or a sister. What about you, Chaz?"

"Can't say I ever thought about it, but I think it's time we left. Emma will need her tea and it's her bath night tonight."

"Roy will be home before us and wonder where we are. I don't want him making a million phone calls trying to find me."

"He knows we're meeting Maggie. We told him, remember?"

"Oh, right, yes. No panic, then." She put Emma in her pushchair and fastened the harness. Tears pricked her eyes, because she didn't remember telling Roy about meeting Maggie. Her memory was, at best, patchy.

The waitress cleared the table, checking under every plate. Mrs Jessop always used to put the bill on her account and leave a generous tip, but the tall woman had paid in cash.

* * * *

Susan's smiling face stared at Roy from the photograph hanging in the hall. She had had two copies made. The other was on his desk at the office. It had been taken by Jimmy the day he and Jill had called around. A tiny baby Emma lay in her arms. He was sitting on the arm of the chair, his hair combed forward to hide the stitches in his forehead. So much had happened since then. The car accident—such a drama at the time—had faded into insignificance. His scar was fading too, which was just as well since he had a short haircut. Susan's mental scars were a different thing altogether. They bled at the slightest touch.

He waited for the operator to connect his call. "Anton. Roy here. I need a favour."

"What can I do? How is she?"

"Better for being home and, on the whole, I think she's better for being off the drugs."

"So how can I help?"

"I would like you to find a therapist in Provence."

"She would stay with us, of course."

"I'll bring her, but I won't be able to stay long. The business, you know."

"Leave it with me. I'll call you as soon as I have something to report."

"Thanks, Anton."

"We will speak soon. I am delighted to hear Susan is improving. I will pass on the news to Jeanette."

"Au revoir, Anton, et merci beaucoup."

He replaced the receiver, telling himself he hadn't really made a decision. Speaking with Anton didn't mean everything was cast in stone. There were still more questions than answers. A line had been drawn in the sand. No more. Something held him back.

Susan was so eager to tell him about her day he shied away from changing the subject. Delighted by her smiling face, he barely listened to her. They had met up with Maggie and had afternoon tea. That was good. And then he caught the words 'Threlfalls', and 'grave', and his ears pricked up. She had retraced her steps of that dreadful day and had even asked Chaz to drive round to Vine Street on their way home. She was facing her demons without the need of therapy. Maybe she just needed time.

Knowing she would be delighted at the prospect of returning to Provence, his head teemed with the possible consequences of such a step. Once crossed, that line in the sand could become an impenetrable wall. The big question was whether she would agree to see a therapist. Anton's friend had said he agreed with the use of drugs alongside therapy. There was no guarantee that Susan would agree to any of it. She wouldn't take the drugs, though. That much he did know. She would say she was fine, and he wanted to believe her, but knew she wasn't fine at all. He was fooling himself if he thought anything different.

Sitting next to him on the sofa, she chatted on like a child who had been on a school trip. Chaz had changed Emma's nappy and put her in her highchair. He could hear her in the kitchen as she prepared her food. Later, as he bathed Emma and put her to bed, Chaz would cook their meal. Susan might set the table and help clear away, or she might say she was too tired. And then there was his mother's suggestion. That really had come out of the blue. Sell the business and move to Provence? Whatever would Dad have said to that one? Thomas Barraclough's question echoed around his head. *What is your dream?* The question was both easy and impossible to answer. He dreamed of a happy, fully-recovered Susan. But, how to achieve it? That was the real question.

"Are you listening to me, Roy?"

"Yes, of course."

"So when are we going?"

"Where?"

"When can we go to Kilmain? To see Gran?"

"Sorry, I was miles away, thinking about Provence." There. He had said it. The cat was peeping out of the bag. "We could go to Ireland another time, when you're a bit stronger. Why don't you write to your Gran? Tell her we'll go in the spring. Chaz will want to go home to see Jérôme. She has her wedding to organise. You could help her."

CHAPTER NINETEEN

Her delight at the prospect of a visit to Provence was quickly followed by impatience. Roy's insistence that Emma should go with them meant a lot more organisation would be required. Diana could have looked after Emma, but Roy said his mother was too busy to look after her full time, and that it wasn't fair.

She and Chaz could have just bought tickets for the next flight and gone. How could she help Chaz organise her wedding if there was Emma to look after? The trouble was, Chaz agreed with Roy.

He was on the phone, speaking with Anton.

"Sounds good to me. Thank-you, Anton. We can discuss things further when we arrive. No, not yet, I thought she should get settled in first. I don't know. No. Au revoire."

"What will we discuss when we arrive? What don't you know?"

"Oh, nothing really. Jeanette has found Chaz's old cot in the attic. She wanted to know whether to put it in a spare bedroom, or in with you."

"In a spare room, of course. Why didn't you tell her Emma has her own room here?"

"Yes, of course. I wasn't thinking. You can organise it all when we get there."

* * * *

La Vieille Ferme spread before her, widening her eyes and catching her breath. What was it about this place? The drive from Marseille had been interminable. She flew from the car, scattering the squawking chickens and into the arms of Jeanette and Anton. Tears flooded down her cheeks. Chaz joined them as they walked over the threshold, followed by Roy, carrying Emma, and into the welcoming smell of fresh bread and coffee.

"So at last I meet your beautiful baby." Jeanette took a smiling Emma from Roy's arms.

Susan's stomach fell. In that moment, with those few words, an indescribable pulse ran through her body. All attention turned to Emma. Susan wiped her tears with the back of her hand and, with all the control she could muster, she walked outside. A palpable silence hung behind her, broken by Emma's cry.

Roy followed her and touched her shoulder. He took her hand, and they walked to the gate that bordered the fields.

"What's wrong with me, Roy?"

"Nothing that can't be fixed, love."

"How can I be fixed into being a mother?" She turned to him, unblinking, her tears all gone. "I'm frightened, Roy."

He put his arms around her and her rigid body began to relax. "You're safe here. Everything will be fine."

She buried her face in his chest, feeling the gentle touch of his hand as he stroked her hair.

He drew breath as if to speak.

"What is it?" she asked. "You were going to say something."

They walked to the fallen tree, and he lifted her to the exact place where she had been when he'd taken the little box from his pocket, and she'd agreed to marry him. "I wish I had a magic wand."

She felt a smile cross her lips. "Whatever are you talking about?"

"I wish I could make you better, right now." He paused. "I have a confession to make. Please know I've done this because I love you, and please don't be angry with me."

"Done what?" Her stomach clenched into a knot.

"I asked Anton to arrange for you to meet a doctor."

Her body stiffened. She pulled her hands away, her worst fears realised. "I will *not* take any drugs, and I don't want to see a doctor."

"I know, I know all that. This lady is a therapist. She just wants to talk with you, that's all. Anton's told her you won't take drugs."

"A lady doctor?"

He nodded.

"Will she want to lock me away?"

"No, Susan. No-one will lock you away."

"Just talking?"

"Yes, just talking."

"What about?"

"I don't know. About you, I suppose."

"When did you fix all this? Is this why we didn't come straight away? You wanted to get this shrink all lined up for poor, mad Susan?"

"You are not mad."

She turned her head away. The thought of everyone knowing, conspiring behind her back, and holding out La Vieille Ferme like a carrot to a stupid donkey, made the bile rise in her stomach. Did they honestly think that once they got her there she would just say, 'Oh, what a good idea'?

"Look at it this way, love. What have you to lose?"

He was right, of course. She had nothing to lose. But they shouldn't have talked behind her back. She jumped down from the tree and walked back along the path, stepping out briskly to avoid further conversation.

* * * *

Staring from the bedroom window, his bag packed on the bed behind him, Roy knew exactly what he had to do. The beauty of Provence stretched out before his eyes. He would never know whether he had been right or wrong about keeping secret his plans for Susan. For the past five days they'd had lots of wonderful food and many discussions. She'd been astounded when he'd told her it had been his mother who had suggested they move to Provence.

"You mean we could live here? Forever, and that was your mum's idea?"

"Well," he had said, "not here at La Vieille Ferme. We would buy our own place."

"You mean you would give up the business? Sell Jessops?"

And sell Orchard Cottage? All for me?"

"For us. You and me and Emma."

They had spent the day in Aix. He had bought a few canvasses and the artists had complimented him on his pretty wife and beautiful daughter. The place fascinated him. They had wandered through the fruit and vegetable market in Place Richelme, comparing the quality of the produce with that of Jeanette's kitchen garden. They had picnicked in Le Parc Jourdain, with Emma lying on a blanket between them in the shade of the great trees. But more importantly than all that, Susan had agreed to see Madame Allard, on the proviso that if she didn't like her she wouldn't have to go again. It was as much as he could hope for.

Chaz was waiting for him downstairs in the car. In the hallway Susan waited with Emma in her arms. Jeanette and Anton kept away. He had said his goodbyes to them and thanked them after breakfast.

"I'll be back as soon as I can."

Susan nodded, her lips trembling.

The car door slammed and the dust rose as they set off for the airport.

* * * *

"Come, Susan. Put Emma in 'er pushchair. We will walk in the ze garden, ze way the men do after dinner. I need some 'erbs for my cooking." Jeanette took her shallow basket from its shelf and donned her equally battered garden hat. Crisscrossed with paths, the sheltered kitchen garden had always been her pride and joy. Weeds were not permitted to grow and were uprooted as seedlings, preventing them from taking the goodness that was destined for her table.

"Do you know this Madame Allard, Jeanette?"

Jeanette tilted her head to one side, acknowledging that she had addressed her by her Christian name. "No. I 'ave never met 'er, but I know my Anton will 'ave made sure she is a good person."

"Anton says she might hypnotise me. I'm not sure I like

the idea of that. Have you ever been hypnotised?"

"No. Never, but I am told zat afterwards it feels like you 'av 'ad a good night's sleep."

Susan gave a little tinkling laugh. "That would be nice."

"Not everyone can be 'ypnotised, zat much I do know. Maybe Madame Allard will find another way zat is better for you. You 'ave to try."

"But not drugs."

"No, not drugs. I am sure she 'as been told you do not like to do zat."

They walked on, the wheels of the pushchair crunching the pebble path.

Jeanette stopped to pick some basil, holding it to her nose to take a deep breath of the sweet herb before placing it in her basket. She looked along the path ahead and then back towards the farmhouse.

"I t'ink it is like zis, Susan. Ze paz around my garden are ze paz of our lives. Zey cross where we meet friends, and continue on our way. Ze little pebbles are our everyday lives, and ze stones are t'ings we t'ink we 'ave forgotten, but zey can still trip us up."

Susan straightened Emma's sunhat and then, shading her eyes with her hand, blinked in the bright sunlight. "I don't understand. What do you mean?"

Jeanette pointed towards the farmhouse. "Zat way is your past, ma petite." Swinging her arm in the opposite direction, she continued, "Zat way is your future. I t'ink with Madame Allard you must first walk back to ze farm'ouse, and turn ze stones." Susan watched her walk away, and then call back, "You 'ave to live wiz ze past and not let it cloud your future. You 'ave to turn ze stones of life—take a look at what lies below and put zem back. Zen you can walk on to an 'appy future wiz your 'usband and daughter."

EPILOGUE

Emma's Story – August 1988

I once asked Mum why I never had any brothers or sisters. She looked at me all funny and walked away. I asked Dad and he said Mum would tell me if she wanted me to know. I think I was about twelve at the time. I asked Mémé Jeanette. She said Mum had been ill after having me and didn't want to risk being poorly again. It's my guess she had post-natal depression—big time.

Mum goes to see Cécile Allard once a month, because she says she keeps her head screwed on the right way round.

My mum is the most clued-up person I know. She does all the book-keeping for Dad and tells him off, in the nicest possible way, if she thinks he's paid too much for something. He always passes it off saying, "Send it to Ilkley. Someone will buy it."

Special paintings are always posted to Mr Barraclough. Dad says it was Mr Barraclough who got him going with the gallery, and that's why he likes to send him the specials. Dad's brilliant at spotting new talent. He gets really excited when there's a new exhibition on downstairs.

It's nice that they're still so in love. They're more French than some French people, the way they're always kissing and holding hands. I sometimes wonder what it would have been like if they hadn't moved here. I wouldn't be bilingual for a start. Mum says they had a nice cottage in the countryside, but that she was a towny, and that living over a gallery on Le Cours is as good as it can get, because she has the town and Provence all in one.

They took me to Ireland when I was fifteen months old. I don't remember anything about it. Great Gran is dead now. Mum was sad when she heard, and flew over for the funeral. Dad was really jittery when she was away.

Auntie Chaz called yesterday, asking if I would babysit when she and Uncle Jérôme go out for a meal on their wedding anniversary. It's not until October, but she likes to be organised. With four children under the age of ten I suppose she has to be.

Uncle Jimmy and Auntie Jill are coming at the weekend with the twins, Edward and Jayne. There's to be a party at La Vieille Ferme this weekend. Mèmè Jeanette is busy preparing stacks of food. Mum and Uncle Jimmy will be forty on Saturday. I didn't know until last week that their mums had first met on the maternity ward. The twins are twelve now, and spoilt rotten. Auntie Jill's mum and dad are always buying them stuff. I once overheard Auntie Jill telling Mum that they had a guilty conscience, and were trying to compensate, but I don't know why, or what it was all about. Edward and Jayne have passed an entrance exam to a posh school, so I suppose they were given a load more presents just for being brainy.

Dad has gone to the airport to meet Gran Diana. I like her. She gets on well with Mèmè. They always talk about gardening and cooking.

Mum got a bit upset when she heard Alf and Hettie couldn't come. Hettie has had a stroke. They're a sweet old couple Mum knew in Leeds. She told me he used to be a policeman and was very kind to her when she was little. I've never met them. Mum has written letters to them since forever, and now she says it's time to go back to Leeds for a visit. Dad didn't look too happy and said he would have to go with her. Weird. Mum said she wanted to go alone, and would stay with Maggie. I like Maggie. She's coming tomorrow with her boyfriend. Mum got all excited about it and told me Maggie had never had a boyfriend before. That seems crazy to me. I mean, it's weird enough an old person having a boyfriend, but you can tell Maggie was really good looking when she was young. I would have thought she'd have had loads of men after her. Mum says she's not old, but anyone over forty has to be old...

"Emma!" Susan's voice drifted up the stairs. "Gran Diana is here."

Emma ran down the stairs, two at a time.

About The Author

Barbara Phipps was born in Liverpool in 1950. Her earliest memory is of moving to the West Riding of Yorkshire in 1953. The family travelled by train, as few people had cars in those days. She attended Sandal Endowed Junior School and Wakefield Girls' High School, leaving in 1967 with a handful of 'O' levels, perhaps notably including English Language and Literature. Apart from a disastrous eight year marriage when she lived in Norfolk, Barbara has lived in Yorkshire ever since. She re-married in 1982 and has a son and a daughter.

She describes her career as that of a serial assistant to the medical profession, having assisted doctors, pathologists, vets, dentists and pharmacists. All of which have been very interesting and very badly paid. Now retired, she has been a Magistrate in West Yorkshire since 2000.

Her hobbies include reading, cooking, walking, and gardening. She shares an allotment, growing vegetables with limited success.

She has written several short stories. The Threlfalls was her first novel. This book, the third in The Threlfalls series, is her fourth novel.

Lightning Source UK Ltd.
Milton Keynes UK
UKOW04f2316100116

266138UK00001B/17/P

9 780908 325153